Last Man Standing

By

A P Bateman

Facebook: @authorapbateman

www.apbateman.com

Rockhopper Publishing

2020

The Alex King Series
The Contract Man
Lies and Retribution
Shadows of Good Friday
The Five
Reaper
Stormbound
Breakout
From the Shadows
Rogue
The Asset

The Rob Stone Series
The Ares Virus
The Town
The Island

Standalone Novels
Hell's Mouth
Unforgotten

Short Stories
A Single Nail
The Perfect Murder?
Atonement

For Clair and her unwavering support and
patience throughout.
Thank you.

For Summer and Lewis – you can achieve
anything.

"Beware that, when fighting monsters, you yourself do not become a monster... for when you gaze long into the abyss. The abyss gazes also into you."

Friedrich W. Nietzsche

1

Afghanistan

King adjusted the scope. There was a heat haze disrupting his view of the Taliban leader some seven-hundred metres away. The rocky terrain was white and beige and yellow, and the man wrapped in black robes with the distinctive pakol upon his head stood out, eerily so in the shimmering heat.

"Don't go getting trigger happy on me just yet," the Scotsman whispered. "Observe, evaluate and report until further orders."

"Not even got one in the breech."

"More fool you."

"Okay, I lied."

"Good. I thought I'd taught you better than that."

"Why are you here, old man?"

"Someone has to look after the kids."

"Nice," King replied, switching up the magnification. "He's looking pleased with himself."

"Got a new goat to fuck, I suspect." Stewart paused. "Or another wife."

"My money is on the goat."

Stewart adjusted his spotting scope. "Aye, aye, what have we got here then?"

Both men watched as a convoy of *Taliwagons* bumped and slewed into the village, dust plumes far behind them. The ubiquitous white Toyota pickups that had fought the might of the allied armies and been the workhorse of the Middle East throughout various campaigns and conflicts. The lead vehicle had a Soviet era 12.7mm heavy machine gun mounted in the flatbed on a bipod made from scaffold poles, while numerous fighters armed with Kalashnikovs and rocket propelled grenade launchers (RPGs) filled the beds of the other three vehicles.

"Mincer on the lead vehicle," King said of the heavy machine gun. "Locked and loaded."

"Check."

"Six RPGs, twelve longs," he said, counting the rifles.

"Everyone has a long out here," Stewart said quietly. "They give their babies a Kalashnikov as a christening present."

"Something very wrong with that sentence, boss."

Stewart shrugged. "Or whatever they do out here to wet the baby's head."

King smiled, wound the magnification back a touch to increase the wide-angle view. "Oh shit! They have prisoners. Allied soldiers!"

"Where?"

"Rear vehicle. Six men. Three IC1s, two IC2s and one IC3." King adjusted the scope to zoom in but consequently lost his wide angle. Wide angle kept you more informed. "Two French uniforms, two US Navy SEALs, one US marine and a US pilot."

"Fuck..."

King watched the scene as Stewart switched on the radio set. He scrambled around on his stomach, then rolled off the ledge behind them into the pine needles and almost into the bush they had been using to hide their kit. He knelt up to feed out the antenna. They had checked and the position was safe, with enough elevation and enough drop off to sit and get a brew on, stretch, take a dump into a plastic bag or eat some rations while the other kept their eye on the scope, their finger near the trigger of the Accuracy International .308 rifle.

"It's turning into a side show," said King. "There are some women coming out holding knives."

"Well, that's that then. They're done for."

King was reminded of the last two stanzas of the poem, The Young British Soldier by Rudyard Kipling.

If your officer's dead and the sergeants look white,
Remember it's ruin to run from a fight:
So, take open order, lie down, and sit tight,
And wait for supports like a soldier.
Wait, wait, wait like a soldier . . .

When you're wounded and left on Afghanistan's
plains,
And the women come out to cut up what remains,
Jest roll to your rifle and blow out your brains
An' go to your Gawd like a soldier.
Go, go, go like a soldier,
Go, go, go like a soldier,
Go, go, go like a soldier,
So-oldier of the Queen!

King got it now. He'd always thought it trite that a poem should advocate suicide, that the barrack room geniality of the British squaddie had influenced Kipling perhaps more than it should have. A little like reality television today, where the people become anything but real once they have garnered some attention and camera time. But since he'd been out here, he could see that those long-forgotten soldiers had a point. King had known that the Afghan women were cruel, but as he watched the men holding them back, the terrified soldiers on their knees in the dirt, their hands tethered behind their backs, he could see – almost *feel* – what those men must have been feeling. Pure unadulterated terror at the hands of women who wanted to start with their manhood and flail the skin clean off their bodies before they died. Before they *begged* to die.

A burst of gunfire erupted – King had seen this before and knew it was the Afghans' way to let the chatter of an assault rifle act like a loudhailer - and the women dispersed and regrouped a few metres further back as the man they had been sent to observe addressed the village, a large straight-bladed knife in his hand.

King knew it to be a *pesh-kabz* and it had probably seen time in the Khyber Pass against those same British soldiers Kipling had dedicated his poem to back in 1890.

Stewart was on the net. He raised his voice a little to reach King, but they had lain up for ten days and conversed in nothing more than whispers that it seemed difficult for him to break the habit. "There's an SAS patrol two hundred kilometres south of us with air support waiting in the next valley."

"Forget it!" King snapped. "The old fucker is sharpening his knife..." He paused, watching a cage being pushed through the dirt. The villagers gathered around the cage and the leader picked out a white soldier in a French uniform. He was set upon at once and dragged into the cage. King could see through the scope that the man was screaming, but from their distance the air remained eerily silent. "We have to move," he said.

Stewart shook his head. "French special forces are sixty klicks west, but they have gone dark..." He paused. "Sounds like they've got problems of their own."

"We need to move. Those men are as good as dead down there."

"We're going nowhere," snapped Stewart. "A chopper can pick up part of a SEAL team operating in the Hindu Kush and get them here inside forty minutes," Stewart added, ignoring King's observation.

"No good."

"If we give them a mercy shot a piece, then we're compromised…"

"Then if we're going to be compromised, we might as well try to do something," King replied.

"Or…"

"Or what?"

"Or we take five, have a brew and see what the lay of the land is afterwards," Stewart said with a shrug. "No break in the chain of intel, no compromised position and a hundred klick tab through hostile territory to get to a cold extraction. We just sit tight, do our job and go home."

"And leave six dead allied soldiers behind."

"But we're *not* soldiers, Son. We're a different bag altogether."

"What about our consciences?"

"I told you to ditch that years ago." The Scotsman paused. "You can't have a conscience in this game, Son."

"If that chopper can get here inside forty minutes having diverted to pick up a team of SEAL operators, then it can get here in less than twenty to extract six prisoners and a couple of agents compromised as a result of saving them…"

"Alex, wait…"

"Make the call…"

King snatched up his bandolier and his M4 assault rifle and took off down the slope.

"Alex… shit!" Stewart shook his head and called in for an extraction. He snatched up the map and called in the coordinates on the southern end of the village, then packed away the radio set and shouldered both King's and his own bergen. "That's right, let the old man do all the fucking work and carry your bloody bag…" He snatched up the rifle, ignored the spotting scope and set off after King, who was now two hundred metres further down the slope and sprinting hard over the rocky terrain.

King came to rest at the remains of a bombed-out mud hut. He had seen .50 calibre bullets bounce off these sun-baked constructions, so it was good cover and because of the commotion in the village, he remained unseen by the gathering crowd some one-hundred and fifty metres distant. He turned around and waited for Stewart to catch up, red faced and panting from the heat and exertion of the run, but the man did alright for someone in their mid-fifties who barely touched a vegetable and often had a measure of Scotch for breakfast.

"Get behind the rifle and nail that bastard!" King said sharply as Stewart dropped down behind the wall. "Then take out the guy on the mincer. Where's the chopper coming in?"

"Two klicks South. It'll be a bloody miracle if we make it. You really are a twat, Son." Stewart unslung his M4 and made it ready before propping it up against the wall. He rested the sniper rifle on top of the wall and dropped the two bergens on the ground. "We'll be needing those because our brief has changed. MI6 are not part of any extraction here, because *we're* not here, remember?"

"Figures."

"So, let's get these idiots out of here if we can, and hope we make it to tomorrow morning at least."

King nodded, taking out another magazine for his rifle. "We can always beg for a ride," he said. He was going in hot and would keep the first magazine for his ammo change tucked under his right armpit for a quick drop and swap. After that, well, that was far enough planning ahead. Nothing much worked to plan past the first gunshot anyway. "You smoke the Taliban warlord and get that mincer out of commission."

"Yes sir! Yer cheeky wee cock..." Stewart wrapped the sling around his left shoulder and elbow, pulled it tightly across his chest so that the tension would hold his aim firm, and sighted on the man in black, a foot taller than his men, the knife-come-sword in his right hand. "Shit, we're too late..."

King watched the knife come down and the soldier fell. The knife went up and came down, repeated the gory task again and again as a man split one of the men in two down the middle. A fountain of blood had sprayed the braying women who had got too close in their eagerness, but it subsided as quickly as it had erupted. King charged out from behind the wall, darted to his right to keep the crowd's backs to him and get out of Stewart's line of sight. He heard the savage report of the gunshot behind him and the Taliban leader fell out of sight. King was running hard, heard the second shot, and then a third. The man on the 12.7mm machine gun went down, and as King closed the gap by half, a fourth shot spun the weapon around on its mounting. A .308 bullet at this range was enough to twist the frame of the weapon and put it out of commission, especially if Stewart had managed to strike the action and working parts.

A flame ignited and burned fiercely, and to King's horror he realised that the soldier inside the cage had been set alight. The scream was gut-wrenching, and the form of the soldier shook the bars in vain. King shouldered the M4 and fired a double tap into the burning solider. It was all he could do, and he figured he'd have wanted the same in that position. He switched his aim to the villagers. Anybody with a gun in their hand. When he got into the mix, he shot anybody remotely near a weapon, the women included. He dropped the empty magazine, slotted in the spare and smacked the palm of his left hand on the bolt release button, chambering the first round. A woman had picked up the Taliban leader's knife and was setting about separating one of the prisoner's head from his neck. King shot her, but too late to save the soldier, who was lying on his side, bleeding out with his hands bound behind his back. By now,

Stewart was in the mix also, having ditched the sniper rifle, but he had slung his M4 over his shoulder on its sling, and was using his Sig P225 pistol in his left hand and slashing anyone in his way with his razor sharp *Kukri* in his right. King saw him leave the blade between a man's shoulder blades, calmly change his pistol's magazine, then retrieve the blade and set back to work.

King grabbed one of the prisoners and dragged him back behind the corner of a building. He took down a man firing his AK47 at him, then darted forwards again, dragged a second man back, then took a knee and used the building as cover as he laid down enough covering fire for Stewart to work his way back to him.

"Woo-hoo! We're in it now, Son! Fucking fantastic!" Stewart was high on adrenalin and lost in the moment. He was covered in blood and King doubted any of it was his own. He set about slicing the bindings off the men, then tossed one of them his pistol, sheathed his blade and shouldered his rifle. "Have some of this Taliwankers!" He sprayed the square with fully automatic gunfire with no regard to the injured or unarmed. Or age. He changed over magazines, selected semi-automatic and calmly put a bullet in anyone who hadn't made it to cover.

King pulled him back behind the corner of the building, but Stewart was like a dog that had got the scent. Primal, uncontrollable. "Boss!" King shouted, cuffing him around the head. "Exfil, South side!" King checked the compass he had fastened to the frame of his rifle with cable ties. He chopped his hand through the air decisively, indicating the direction with enough vigour that nobody could be in doubt of where they were heading. One of the men looked at him. He was black and his eyes were wide and white with fear. He wore the fatigues of a Navy SEAL and his insignia was that of warrant officer. His name tag read COLE. J.

"Thank you, brother..." Cole managed. He had tears in his eyes, and like the other two men had lost control of his bladder during the ordeal. Close enough to smell the blood and see how it ends.

King said nothing. He simply grabbed the man by his shoulder and pulled him to his feet and broke cover. King led the line. He fired at movement, bullets whizzing past his head or hitting the dirt at his feet. Stewart returned fire, but he was doing so from his hip, helping one of the men who had taken a bullet to his knee. The man with Stewart's pistol fired back at a group who had taken cover behind one of the pickups. King picked up the pace, just fifty metres to go until they reached the bombed-out building. One of the prisoners went down. King pulled him to his feet and threw him over his shoulder and pressed on, changing magazines and all the time finding too many targets to engage with.

Stewart was back in the game. The Latino soldier he had been helping was laying still on the ground. He'd retrieved his pistol and had engaged the enemy with both weapons, simultaneously. King had seen the man teach such things on the range, and he'd later discounted it himself, but it was working for him. He just needed a rocking soundtrack and perhaps a cigar to chomp on as he did it.

They reached the remains of the building and King hastily changed to a full magazine, then reloaded his pistol. He checked himself for gunshot wounds, his adrenalin level off the charts and likely, he would not feel pain until it was too late. Two prisoners had made it. Cole, who was a Navy SEAL and the US pilot slung over King's shoulder. The man was groaning and bleeding down King's back. Stewart was cursing that he was down to his last magazine. He picked up the sniper rifle and rummaged through his bergen for the box of Swedish match grade .308 ammunition. He tipped the ten rounds into his hand and pocketed five of them before reloading the rifle.

"Let's do some damage limitation," Stewart said calmly and eased out to the side of the wall. He fired, worked the bolt, and fired again. Ducking down, he edged past them and peered out from the other side of the wall. He aimed at the third pickup truck and fired again. Fuel was leaking from the tank, but away from the burning cage. "That's the fuel tanks hit. Now, get a flare in there and light 'em up!" King dug through his bergen. He pulled out the plastic bags of excrement they had been planning to take back with them and tossed them aside, no point worrying about leaving a trace now, and retrieved the flare. "Take your time, Son. Let the fuel get among them, give them a good soaking..." Stewart eased himself out and fired another shot, taking down a Taliban fighter who was trying to flank them.

"That ought to do it…"

King took a breath and rolled onto his side. He unwound the tape and struck the base of the tube. The orange flare fizzed across the square and smacked into the grille of the third vehicle in line. It bounced off and spun around on the ground like a Catherine wheel that had come off its mounting. King watched, transfixed, but suddenly remembering that he now was exposed. He shuffled back behind the cover of the wall as a bullet pinged off the rocks next to him. The fuel ignited and burned fiercely. King could tell it had been diesel by the less extreme ignition, but the flare burned at a high enough temperature to get the job done quickly and the men lying under the vehicles for cover were soon ablaze. There were screams and as they broke cover and headed for the wadi for safety, King caught sight of people burning and struggling to escape the fire which had consumed the vehicles and was spreading towards huts crammed full of hay and straw. From his experience in Afghanistan he suspected the huts would have weapons and ammunition caches secreted within and did not want to be within a thousand metres of the place if they went up.

There was a whump-whump-whump overhead and while a chinook made for a clearing in the fields of melons ahead of them, an Apache Longbow flying in support opened its gatling gun for a few seconds and rained empty brass cases on the roofs of the outer-most buildings, the point blank burst of fire changing the lives of the villagers forever. More firepower than King and Stewart could have brought if they had stayed there shooting at them for a week.

The loading crew of the chinook fanned out with their assault rifles to cover them while a gunner manned an M60 machine gun at the top of the ramp and fired short bursts towards the village until they drew near enough for the crew to take over. He kept the weapon ready, both he and the M60 held in place by bungee straps.

A medic shepherded the two prisoners up the ramp and a warrant officer held out his hand to stop King and Stewart from boarding. "Sorry, buddy. Orders." As if to reinforce his position, his M4 was pointing at their midriffs.

"Chuck us some spare magazines at least," said Stewart.

"Sorry, buddy." The warrant officer shook his head and waited until the crew were aboard, then walked backwards up the ramp. He shrugged his shoulders by way of apology and the ramp started to close.

King watched the last of the prisoners up the ramp. The SEAL named Cole turned and looked at him. He was black, the highlighted whites of his eyes burning fiercely with a look of intensity and rage as he realised that his rescuers were getting the shaft. He hesitated, but the warrant officer pulled him inside and the ramp levelled out.

"For fuck's sake," said King above the noise of the rotors but the warrant officer couldn't hear him, the ramp was lifting higher and was soon no more than a slit as the engine pitch changed and the helicopter prepared to leave them behind. He made a motion, a gesture towards the village, hoping they would turn their guns on them while they made their escape, but the leviathan started to lift and King and Stewart were consumed in dust. King grabbed Stewart by the arm, so they did not lose each other in the sandstorm, and they both ran for cover.

King watched the chinook fly away, its dual rotors seeming to spin impossibly slowly. The longbow banked without firing upon the village and took up position slightly above, to the right and behind the craft, like a flying bodyguard escorting a VIP. In the village behind them, ammunition was cooking off in the fire and bullets were pinging off into the sky, small explosions detonating one after the other as the fire released the hidden secrets within.

"Shit, I'm buggered," Stewart commented. He reloaded his pistol and holstered it while he got the sniper rifle reloaded and slung onto his shoulder. He dropped the M4 on the ground, took out a hip flask and drank deeply. "Scotch?"

King shrugged, taking the hip flask. "What the hell…" He sipped some down, handed it back to him. "Bloody Yanks," King said, reloading his own pistol. He was down to a dozen rounds in his M4. "Couldn't even give us some ammo…"

"Don't blame them. We don't exist," said Stewart. "There's no playbook for us. And it was British control who dispatched them and gave them their orders."

King nodded. He looked at the village where figures were moving about, congregating and regrouping. "We need to tab out," he said. "Drink the water, ditch the kit." He opened his bottle and downed the lot. He tucked it back into its holder on his webbing and took out a bar of Kendal mint cake and started to devour it, the sugar hitting the spot almost instantly.

Stewart smirked, took out an antique silver snuff box and tipped some white powder onto the back of his hand. "Good luck with your sweeties, Son." He sniffed the powder up his nose, squinted, grimaced, and shuddered. "That's the fucking go juice right there!" He looked at King, his eyes dilated and a maniacal grin on his face.

King watched, took the last bite of the sugary bar, and tossed the wrapper on the ground. "Well, if you're quite finished..." he said tersely and set his eyes on the mountain some three miles in front of him. "We'll get to that mountain, get a good way up the slope and then we'll have the high ground and tactical advantage..."

Stewart laughed. "The high ground? And what will we do with that with popgun pistols and seven or eight rounds for the sniper rifle while all the villages in the area unite and come at us from all directions?"

"I've got a dozen or so rounds left for my weapon..."

Stewart smiled. "Nay laddie, yer thinking like a sheep when you need to be acting like a wolf."

King frowned. "You mean, go back in there?" he asked, incredulously.

"Yer could have had the simple life, yer could have got a brew on and let things play out," Stewart said dryly. "But yer had to be the hero. Now we're finishing it. Because if we run, we're dead. Because they'll catch up with us, outgun us and then we'll be left to the hands of those woman. And they've lost a good many loved ones today. Enough to get themselves all hot and moist at the thought of lopping off our cocks and feeding us our own balls. Or god forbid, each other's," he laughed. "So, I'll be saving a bullet for you, and one for me." Stewart held the rifle firmly and headed back the way they had come. "When you're ready, Son. When you're ready..."

King watched the Scotsman walk away.

The man had saved him. Saved him from himself and a lifetime behind bars. Shown him another way, another purpose. He had broken him down, made him beg for mercy and when that hadn't come, then he had begged to die. And then he had built him up. Stronger, fitter, wiser than he had ever been. Given him a purpose, allowed him to see the greater good, the bigger picture. And now as he watched the man walk back into the battle that they had made for themselves, vastly outnumbered and outgunned, he knew he'd follow him, too.

Stewart turned and smiled at King as he caught up. He said loudly, "Fate whispers to the warrior, 'You cannot withstand the storm…'

King shouldered his rifle and replied, "And the warrior whispers back, 'I am the storm…' "

2

**Twelve years later,
Tuscany, Italy**

Cole sipped the limoncello and marvelled at the view. The house sat in forty acres of grounds, mainly forest and meadow, and atop a hillside of terraced gardens. Below them children frolicked and played in a narrow swimming pool that had been cut into one of the terraces. Cole knew them to be too young to be Giuseppe's children, but perhaps they were grandchildren or nieces and nephews. Below the pool terrace, gardeners were working with a hoist and ropes to plant a large olive tree.

"You see my newest acquisition?" Giuseppe waved a hand towards the scene of activity. He sipped his limoncello, replaced the glass to the smoked-glass table. "That tree is from Greece. Or Crete, to be precise, and it is thought to be more than two thousand years old." He paused. "Think about that. When our saviour Jesus Christ our Lord walked the earth..." Cole nodded, but only from courtesy and therefore self-preservation. He hadn't been to church since he had left home to join the marines, although he had been a part of many services for fallen comrades during the conflict in Afghanistan. Even then, his faith had no longer been present. Eroded by exposure to the worst things you could see in life. It had deserted him when he probably needed it the most. Giuseppe continued, "Many experts said that it would not make the journey, but I have faith. Faith in my people, the shippers, the soil that has been prepared, the grade of organic soil and compost and fertilisers my head gardener has readied. And they only water the plants with water from a nearby creek. Not from the taps with all the fluoride and chlorine and god only knows what else they add." He chuckled. "The same is to be said for my daughter's limoncello. Only the best water, the best of our organic lemons that we grow on the estate."

Cole raised his glass to the Italian. The man was in his late seventies, but he looked like a movie star. Satin-white hair styled and meticulously cut. His skin was bronzed and smooth and free of lines. But Cole had not yet seen the man's eyes. A pair of dark, sixties-style Ray-Bans with tortoise shell frames had hidden them from view since they had first met, almost an hour before. "This lemonade sure is great," he agreed.

"*Limoncello*. Not lemonade."

"So, what's the difference?"

The Italian don sneered but seemed to have second thoughts and stopped himself and said, "Limoncello is alcoholic and a celebration of the best lemons on earth. And it must be drunk ice-cold. We have a saying here in Tuscan; when the bottle of limoncello is no longer frosted, then it is time to stop drinking the limoncello..." He sat back, looking past Cole as the gardeners seated the olive tree in the hole. "You see, it is in our heritage. We celebrate tradition. You tell an Italian all pasta tastes the same and there's no point in there being

hundreds of different shapes, and you'll have a debate on your hands that will last hours. More likely end in bloodshed. I have seen people come to blows about the fact that one village uses onions in a regional dish where the neighbouring village uses garlic. The next village uses onions *and* garlic, and I guarantee one of those villages is going to spill blood over the matter."

"That desire for tradition, for heritage and simply the way things *should* be, is why I am here," said Cole.

"You are here for financial gain," said Giuseppe sharply. "Let us not dance around paying compliments or copping a feel of each other. Let us get down to business."

Cole nodded. "I agree."

"My son."

"I didn't know him, but from what I understand, he is greatly missed."

Giuseppe scoffed. "My son was a dog." He paused. "He cheated on his beautiful young wife, spent little time with his children in pursuit of… how you Americans say… *pussy*, and lived a decadent lifestyle," he said bitterly. "I know, you look around and see my house and gardens, my half a million-euro olive tree and you think I am just as decadent." He shook his head emphatically. "What I do here, I do for future generations. My children, my grandchildren, and their cousins. I do not buy every new Ferrari or Lamborghini, when the classic Alfa Romeo Spyder I have owned for almost sixty years gives me so much enjoyment on these mountain roads. Yes, I spend, but Luca was no different to those Russian scum he tried dealing with at every opportunity." He paused, sipped some more of his drink, but turned up his nose at the temperature. It was true, the frosting had melted from the bottle on the table. The time for limoncello was over. "And his decadence caught up with him," he said sadly. "Assassinated by the Russians while trying to snuff out a turf war."

Cole nodded. "Your information is out of date."

"You dare to correct me in my own home?" The bodyguard who had remained in the shade until now stepped out and walked to his boss' shoulder. Cole could see a hefty lump under the man's linen jacket. "You are either a brave, or extremely foolish man," said Giuseppe.

Cole leaned back in his chair. The guards had been thorough in their search, but they had missed the single shot .12-gauge pistol made entirely of plastic and carbon fibre composite. There had been no metal parts for their detector wands, the plastic firing pin sprung with a heavy elastic band, and even the solid slug projectile was revolutionary – made entirely of glass and as large as the top section of the average adult's thumb. He looked up at the bodyguard, confident he could reach for the cross draw and hit the bodyguard before the man could get his fingers around whatever oversized pistol he was carrying. From there he would take the bodyguard's weapon and take it from there. "You agreed to an audience with me *Il Signor Fortez* and for that, I am grateful. However, I don't just have information. I have a proposition."

Giuseppe raised a hand and dismissed his bodyguard as if he were waving away and irritant fly. "Indulge me, then."

"As I outlined in my letter, I worked for the CIA and the NSA, and I have information concerning your son's death." He paused. "The information I have concerns British intelligence services. One of their agents was coerced into killing your son, and the Russians he was dealing with."

"Coerced?" Giuseppe frowned. "By whom?"

"That isn't important. That person is dead, their project died along with them. But the intelligence service in question stuck by their agent. He wasn't fired, in fact, they have stood by him on other occasions when he has crossed the line. And in my book, that is as good as sanctioning him."

"I see your point."

"And that's where I come in."

"And I'm supposed to trust you?"

"I don't imagine you got as far as you did in business without taking a risk." Cole paused. "Especially the *business* you are in."

Giuseppe shrugged. "Perhaps."

"I know the organisation, the department, the man in question and his boss."

"And I only have your word for it." Giuseppe shrugged. "What guarantees do I have?"

Cole nodded. "I have transcripts seized by the NSA. Communications between the people involved. His team helped him in the field. If that doesn't indicate official British involvement, then I don't know what does."

"I can see them?"

Cole shook his head. "Not yet."

"Not until you have my money," the Italian smirked.

"I said, I don't just have information to sell," replied Cole. "I have a proposition."

Giuseppe nodded. "And that is?"

"I know him. Our paths have crossed. I know his team and how they work."

"And this is the information you will sell me?" Giuseppe looked at him incredulously.

"No," Cole said looking at the man intently. "I will kill him for you." He paused. "For a price…"

3

One week later
Virginia, USA

The water was like glass and it reflected the reeds and trees on the banks in the light of the setting sun, in a hue of orange and red and gold. The mirrored surface rendered only to life by the occasional trout leaping to feed on dragonflies and creating concentric circles of wake across the water, gradually depleting, and becoming still and mirrored once more.

Newman had been here once before. A lifetime ago. Or a year. But in that time, he had seen more of life than anyone should have. Or rather, death. A constant spectre at his shoulder. It was here that he had agreed to cross the line for his country, but over that year he had wondered how much his contribution had truly benefited the American people, or whether it had merely been another move by another pawn on a metaphorical chessboard nobody cared about played by the CIA. He knew there was no going back for him. He was sullied, dirty. He had given terrorists the means to carry out an attack, to rid the agency of enemies, and in doing so he had crossed a line chalked in place by morality. He had taken the commendations, the internal glory within the agency and enjoyed the feeling of notoriety. He had arrived. Been noticed. Had agreed to similar missions, more specialist training, each time veering further from his perceived career path and closer to the edges of morality, already a long way past the law. Not yet thirty, he felt like a world-weary veteran.

Robert Lefkowitz sipped his glass of iced herbal tea, grimaced and placed it back on the table. "Disgusting stuff," he said quietly.

Newman nodded. He'd accepted the CIA director's offer of a bourbon but had been surprised at the man's choice, given that the man always had a bourbon at this time of day. He sipped his drink, watched a trout breach the water and splash back down. "Do you fish, sir?"

"Not any longer," he replied. "The lake was here when we bought the place thirty years ago," he said. "I restocked it a few years back. There were catfish in there, some perch, but not much else. Eels, maybe. I thought I'd get the time to do some fly fishing if I stocked it with trout, but it never really materialised. I prefer to sit and watch them leap from the water these days."

"You're not retiring anytime soon, are you?"

"A little above your paygrade, but I guess at sixty-two I would have been clearing my desk pretty soon," he said. "No, I've got a few health problems, you see..." He picked up the glass and held it as if he was toasting Newman's health. "Hence the herbal concoction Emily has got me on. That and a vegan diet full of bran and grains."

"I'm sorry," Newman replied awkwardly.

"So am I," Lefkowitz replied quickly. "I'd kill for a steak and baked potato with butter."

"I meant the illness, Sir. Nothing too serious, I hope?"

Lefkowitz smiled. "Now, that *really* is above your paygrade, son." He paused. "Reilly tells me you're shaping up, finally." He smiled watching Newman shrug. "Which is to say you're one of the finest wet operatives the CIA has seen for some time." He watched as the young man grimaced. "You don't like the term, or you don't like the role?"

"A bit of both, I suppose."

"Everybody starts off like that, but most get to live with it in time."

"That's what I'm afraid of."

"Smart boy," Lefkowitz said without malice. He stared out across the water for a moment, a leaping fish vying for his concentration. "There's a situation I want cleaned before I leave Langley. If you get it done swiftly and effectively, I'll lift you from your current line of work and see you directing field teams in a theatre of your choosing. You'll skip two paygrades but lose the danger money. You should come out ahead financially and on the right path for a man of your capabilities. Your experience training on the farm and the tasks you've done for your country will give you an edge over the brownstone university graduates coming through. You'll be a man for all seasons with a past many will respect, but fear crossing. Somewhat like myself, I imagine. Who knows, you could be sat at a table with a man who reminds you of yourself in twenty-five years having a similar conversation," he said, then added, "Without the goddam illness, I hope."

Newman nodded, finishing the bourbon. "I'm listening."

Lefkowitz smiled, then said, "We have a good President , would you agree?"

"I think so…"

"Trust me, he's as good as you're going to get," replied Lefkowitz. "The nation thinks his predecessor was a hero."

Newman frowned. "He was…"

The CIA director nodded. "On paper."

"Standing had some issues with the press concerning his war record. Blurred events, the fog of war, maybe."

"Willard Standing was a coward." Lefkowitz paused. "Sure, he was a tough guy, and he was a killer. He led an armoured unit in Kuwait and Iraq during Operation Desert Storm, but he committed war crimes. He stole Kuwaiti gold, and he called in a broken arrow air strike on his own men. He was the last man standing, pardon the pun…"

"Jesus…"

"Classified information. You repeat it, and you won't live to repeat it twice," Lefkowitz said coldly. "Your former alumni at the farm will hunt you down and do all the things that old goat Reilly teaches so well…"

"I won't repeat it, Sir."

Lefkowitz nodded. "Willard Standing used the gold to bolster his business in the metals industry. Handy thing for a man with gold mining concerns. Although he would have later engineered it that way. He also made a fortune from his shares, building his credit with smelted Kuwaiti gold. The man looked to have the Midas touch, and that kicked off his career in politics."

"And we knew all the while?"

"No." Lefkowitz replied emphatically. "But someone pulled at a loose thread and then it started to unravel. By the time Standing sought to snip the loose ends, it was too late. And he did it in the worst way. He used somebody who had beef with the people responsible for uncovering it. There was always some doubt with Standing. The press and media occasionally turned on him, but he employed good lawyers and sued successfully, so most editors simply dropped a story on him for fear of being ruined."

"So, things got messy."

"Exactly. The people Standing used made it personal. Our relationship with the Brits has not been the same since."

"The British?"

"Yes. You helped put this down last year. Your work with the Islamic terrorists not only saw them extinguished, but the security firm doing Standing's bidding was taken out of operation." He paused. "But there was a man behind the scenes, and he went too far. He killed a female agent of MI5. A non-combative officer. An analyst. That struck a chord with one of MI5's agents. He went Rogue."

"Right…"

"He assassinated our President ."

"But Standing was killed in a domestic terror incident. Anti-government militia gun nuts," Newman said incredulously. "They were taken down at their compound in Idaho."

"That's the picture we painted."

"A British agent killed him?"

"Yes."

"And the men outside Boise? The Idaho militia compound?"

"Taken out by two of your boys at the farm, then chalked up to the ATF."

"And the ATF went with it?"

"A funding increase and a token court hearing. It didn't do them any harm. Welcome to the CIA." He took a large manila envelope from the side of his chair and handed it to Newman. It was warm from his thigh. "Your instructions are in there."

Newman nodded. "I take it this MI5 agent is good?"

Lefkowitz smiled wryly. "Son, I have no doubt he's the best at what he does."

"Reilly would love to hear you say that."

"I suspect Reilly would have to agree." He paused. "You see, you can have the army, the SEALS, special forces turn a man into a killer. You can have men like Reilly, men who have trained for decades, pass on what they know. But sometimes, there's something within a man that supersedes all that. Sometimes it's all down to nature, and the weapons training, the classroom lectures and the field experience can only take someone so far. This agent is a natural. He's like water. You can't stop it, you can't break it, you can't change it. You boil it, and the steam turns back to water. You freeze it and it melts back to water. You drink it, and you piss it right back out. Water is water."

Newman nodded. He opened the envelope and started to study the file.

"The light's fading," said Lefkowitz. Newman tucked the file back into the envelope. The man had dismissed him in the same manner a year ago. "Take it with you. Burn after reading." He shifted in his seat and Newman noticed him grimace. "And good luck, son. I have faith in you."

Newman nodded, but as he walked across the grass, he felt nothing but trepidation. He had wanted an out, but to get it he needed to enter the lion's den once more. This time, he wondered whether he would live long enough to get close to the beast.

4

Thames House, London

King replaced the photograph onto the pile and looked at the director of the Security Service. "Nothing I haven't seen before," he said testily.

"I know. But the fact that these have been sent to us means that it could only have come from one person," said Amherst.

"Undoubtedly," King replied.

"So, what does it mean?" asked Simon Mereweather, MI5's number two.

King shrugged. "Obvious, isn't it?" He paused. "He wants to rattle me."

"You alone?" Mereweather asked.

"Of course. His problem is with me," King said, trying to get the image out of his mind. He reached for his cup of tea. The other two sipped their coffees, each man grateful for the distraction. King added, "I rattled him. He thinks I crossed the line. He killed Marnie to send a message." He paused. "Tell me, does Rashid know?"

"No. But it's only a matter of time," Mereweather replied.

King pictured Marnie hanging from her neck in the woods. Lifeless, her skin like wax. Her eyes like a doll's. Rashid had had an on/off thing going with her. King's misjudgement had cost Marnie her life, and his and Rashid's friendship. They had managed to get past it now, but King did not anticipate that would last long when his friend found out about the previously unseen pictures. Marnie's killer had goaded King with a picture sent to his phone. King had since seen the coroner's own photographs, but these were new. These brought up the whole horrible incident with a renewed macabre tone. A second viewing. A second mourning for a friend and colleague.

"He clearly has unfinished business," said Amherst.

"Clearly," King stretched.

"Still haven't found a decent tailor?"

"I was hoping Simon would give me the name of his," replied King. "Just as soon as I stop needing my salary for three months for trivial things like food and a mortgage."

"Oh, my dear man, surely just two months, unless you want a waistcoat and a few pairs of socks as well," Mereweather drawled. "I believe Ramsay knows a few high street chains that could rustle you up a suit, shirt and tie for a fraction of the cost."

King rolled his eyes. "Well, I don't do dry clean only in my line of work." He paused. "And these jeans are new. I only wore the shirt yesterday, and the leather jacket is only just broken in."

"To get back on track," Amherst said. "This man, Cole. What do you know about him?"

King shrugged. "He was enforcer and go-to-guy to the NSA agent who was instrumental in running the secret prison in South Dakota."

"The man you killed at his home in Virginia?"

King stared at Amherst. "I believe he was taking a drink on his dock. He slipped and fell."

"Was pushed into the water in his wheelchair…"

"Not by me," King lied. He never sought reason to admit to the things he had done, even when it was for queen and country.

"The man was crippled during the prison rioting."

"Shame."

"Indeed."

"Am I supposed to care?"

"He tried to kill you."

"No, he had men drive me out into the Great Plains to do it for him. Cole was one of those men."

"Well, it clearly didn't work," Amherst said flippantly, like he may have been happier if it had.

"Bad for him, good for me."

"And this man Cole, he held a grudge with you. Why, exactly?"

King shifted in his seat. "I shot him in the leg."

"That would do it," Mereweather commented flatly.

"It could have been his forehead," said King. "Better all round if I had…"

"So, why didn't you?"

"I don't enjoy killing," said King. "I never have. But I'm effective at it, and there are too many men sat at desks who shirk at what sometimes needs to be done." Both MI5 deskmen looked a little hot under the collar at the remark and King said, "He was a pro. An ex-SEAL, doing his job. The yanks are our friends, okay they screwed us with Zukovsky, and we did a sight more getting him back…"

"As did you on your bloody rogue vendetta!" Amherst snapped. "Things have not been the same with our American allies since!"

King tossed the pile of photographs onto the director's desk where they spilled towards him like a child's pocketbook sketch animation, Marnie in her dying struggle, her eyes bulging as she fought for breath, each photograph more appalling than the last. Amherst hurriedly scooped them up, placed them face down on the leather tabletop. "Well, at least she got some payback from her friends," King said quietly. "And you should remember something, director. When push came to shove, the team followed me. Careers on the line, risking criminal prosecution and their lives in combat. And for what? For MI5? For you? For queen and bloody country?" he scoffed. "No. For Marnie. Because she was part of the team and that meant something." He paused. "The team is your greatest asset. The Americans will get over it and we'll all be pigs in the trough together next time there's a war or sanctions for someone who won't sell us their oil."

"You assassinated the President of the United States," Amherst said matter-of-factly.

King shrugged. "That was anti-government militia types. I saw it on the news. The ATF killed them all in a shootout. Case closed."

"We know it was you."

"No, you suspect it was me. And you're both living in cloud cuckoo land."

"The Secret Service were tracking you as a person of interest."

"I handed them information on Willard Standing's past. He was about to be indicted."

"It's a mess."

"Was. Looks like the new guy is a stand-up bloke. Best President since Roosevelt, according to the polls."

"And they never found the rest of Standing's gold. Just a few bars with Kuwaiti hallmarks from the missing bullion during the Gulf War. Enough to incriminate him, tie him to the theft. The treasury department has seized it and the details of Standing's involvement have been hidden from the public. The investigation is a merry-go-round."

King said nothing, picturing Standing's ill-gotten gains sinking to the bottom of an Alaskan fjord. He planned on visiting Alaska again someday, that was for certain. Right after his early retirement.

"If I may…" Simon Mereweather ventured. "We have an unresolved situation here. This man Cole has made it his business to goad us. We can only guess at his motives, but it's certain he will have marked King out as his target."

"Is this going somewhere?" Amherst asked impatiently, not appreciating the interruption.

"Sir, we need to nip this thing in the bud." He paused, glancing at King. "Whatever has happened in the past, the United States have printed their crib sheet. Standing was killed by domestic terrorists. As King said, case closed. This chap, Cole, risks dredging up the past, or having somebody reinvestigate it. The Americans screwed us when they took Zukovsky for interrogation and failed to hand him back. They started this. But by god, did we ever finish it. To snatch him back was a win. But like most wins, the cost is usually too great. It unravelled and we lost. An agent was killed in the most terrible way. King's vendetta evened the score. Thankfully, the Americans have a nice, neat end to Standing. Thank goodness for that because we could be playing tit-for-tat forever on this." He looked at King and said, "This man Cole, do you have history with him prior to the prison?"

"No," King lied.

Mereweather nodded. "Then for the sake of US-UK relations, I suggest you find this man and end his vendetta against both you and this department. Get your retaliation in first..."

Amherst glared at his subordinate. He had always given Mereweather a free rein, but he did not extend it to his office. "I had better be the one to hand out a termination order," he said. "Even when it's unofficial."

"Of course."

Amherst looked at King. "Where will you start?" he asked.

King pictured the man he'd rescued in Afghanistan. Broken, beaten and grateful for his release. He pictured the look in his eyes as he made his way up the ramp of the chinook. And then he saw the man inside the secret prison. The way his eyes had faded. Of course, he was an agent of the NSA used for assassinations and dirty jobs. That tended to take the sheen of innocence and humour off a person's eyes, but even so, there had been a significant change. "At the beginning," King replied cryptically. "At the beginning…"

5

Washington DC

There was little more time-consuming these days than ordering a coffee from a coffee house in the United States. This establishment had twenty beans, sixty recognised blends and options to mix blends to order, with different degrees of roast. Caramel, honey, chocolate and butterscotch syrups, cream, sprinkles, and chopped nuts ensured the consumer left with a beverage that was higher in saturated fat and sugars than a supersized burger meal with fries and a full sugar cola. Rachel Beam rolled her eyes as the woman in front of her stepped aside with her order. It had taken ten minutes to get this far.

"Coffee, black, house blend. Grande."

"Cream, sugar, sprinkles?"

"If I wanted anything else, then I would have asked. Black. In a go-cup..." She said impatiently and looked back down at her phone screen, breaking contact with the cashier, who placed the chit with the barista. She left a five-dollar bill on the counter, didn't check whether the cashier picked it up, ignored the loose change and got her coffee a moment later. She walked to a booth despite having the go-cup. This place charged an extra ten percent for drinking in, but she didn't care and was in the mood for a fight today. Today and every day.

"Sucks, doesn't it?"

Beam looked around, catching the eye of the man in the booth behind her.

"Eh?"

"Choices. We seem to have so many choices, so many opportunities to make the wrong one."

"It's only coffee," she replied, turning back to her cup.

"May I join you?"

Rachel Beam turned and studied him for a moment. He was too young, she decided. It wouldn't make her a cougar, at thirty-six she'd need to be trawling college freshmen for that. But he was barely thirty, she knew that much, despite his eyes echoing the intensity that went hand in hand with trauma or having seen more than most twenty-somethings should have.

"It's okay to make the wrong choice sometimes, Rachel." He paused. "But not rectifying it when you have the chance is a mistake…"

"Do I know you?" she interrupted.

"No."

"Then how the hell do you know my name?" she asked, but her right hand had already reached under her suit jacket, down to her belt where the compact 9mm Glock 19 sat snugly in its holster, her fingers wrapping around the weapon's chunky grip.

Newman smiled. "I know you're with the Secret Service, but I also know you'll never protect another VIP for as long as you serve. Not unless you have a victory."

The Glock eased out of its holster, her finger inching nearer the trigger. "Who are you?"

"Can I join you?" he asked again. "And I can assure you I'm unarmed, you can put the Glock away."

Beam smiled. "How did you know it's a Glock?"

"The Secret Service ditched the .357 Sig Sauer. I hear the FBI got jealous that you were the only law enforcement agency with your own dedicated calibre and weapon. And no matter what all you, independent law enforcement agencies say, the FBI is king. "

"And what does the CIA use?"

"You think I'm CIA?"

"You have the look."

"Young and gifted?"

"No. But I don't want to insult you until I've listened to what you have to say." She paused. "That is, if you ever get on with it..."

Newman grinned. "We aren't issued with firearms on US soil. And we're not law enforcement, we're intelligence." He stood up and walked around his table and slid into her booth. He had a cappuccino with sprinkles. He glanced down at his cup and smiled at her. "Guess I held the line up with that."

"It's not really a manly coffee," she commented flatly. "So, talk. How do you know who I am, and who I work for?" She paused. "Or moreover, why?"

"Willard Standing, junior."

Beam's eyes flickered. "*President* Willard Standing."

"Deceased."

Beam regarded him for a moment. "What aspect?"

"What have you got?"

"Nothing for you, unless you start shooting straight."

Newman grinned. "Well, I'm not here to talk about tattooed, bearded gun nuts from Idaho who live by the second amendment and disregard taxes and US law." He paused. "You and I both know that freedom militia pile of shit had nothing to do with the assassination of the President of the United States."

"That's not what the ATF say. The FBI, either."

"No."

"So, what are you saying?" Beam slipped the Glock back into the holster and sipped her black coffee. "And what's more, why are you asking me?"

"Because you were tasked with finding a man who was threatening him, carried out several attacks on him and I am sure, eventually made good on his promises."

"You need to convince me you know more than that."

"I know it was the Brits. Maybe not officially, perhaps not even with their knowledge. But a British agent was involved, perhaps a rogue agent." He paused. "And you know who."

"So, what's your angle?"

"Am I right?"

"I'll tell you later. Confirm or deny. But like I asked, what's your angle?"

Newman leaned back in his seat, used the motion to scan the room and see if he was being watched. He leaned forward and said quietly, "I have been tasked with finding the agent."

"And you want some background intel," Beam said quietly.

"No, I was going to make you an offer."

Beam leaned forward, intrigued. Together they looked conspiratorial. Two colleagues with office gossip or dissecting an awkward fling that should never have happened. She wondered what the other coffee house customers would make of them talking about the assassination, the real story of the previous President . "What?"

"Your career is on hiatus. You're investigating petty monetary crime for the treasury and your mentor is dead. He aligned himself with Standing, the criminal aspect of the man and that shit stuck on your shoe. You had an affair with him, Agent Caves, right?"

"Fuck you..." Rachel Beam sat back, putting as much distance between them as she could.

"Caves was on Standing's payroll. Privately, of course."

Beam closed her eyes momentarily. She pictured Caves taken down by the man shadowing Alex King with a rifle. Way far out. Damn near in another zip code. She had loved him once, but now she was tainted. The agent that nobody trusted. The agent with the cloud hanging over her. She opened her eyes and wiped a tear from the corner of her right eye. "Get on and say what you've got to say."

"Take some vacation. Help me find the British agent and redeem yourself. You can bust the bullshit militia story wide open, present a dossier to your superiors, the press even. You'll shake off the shadow of defeat and get on with your career, your life."

"I can't do that."

"I have unlimited funds and an even less limited remit." Newman paused. "I'll pick up the tabs, the airfares, hotels, whatever. I'll stay in the shadows so when we've got what we want, you can have all the glory. I was never there..."

Beam sipped her coffee, but it had cooled enough for her to gulp most of it down. She put the cup back on the table and said, "Is this on the record?"

"As much as any deniable CIA operation on an ally's shores…"

"And where does deniable leave me? I can't see how that helps me at all."

"Well, you get to see justice done." Newman shrugged. "The CIA will never want it on their record, but for an individual wrapping up a case, putting things right, hell, you'll be a hero."

"I couldn't care less about getting justice for Standing," she said callously. "I care about wiping the stain off my record and getting back on track with my career. I want back into the White House."

"You're right. And we can do this together." Newman paused. "You have the background on this agent, plus you've hunted him before. You got close by all accounts. Did you actually meet him?"

Beam thought about the first time she'd met him. In a booth not dissimilar to where they were seated now. When she had turned around, he had gone. Like a spirit. Unearthly. And from there on, he had been ahead of her, urging her to investigate Standing, taunting her to come and find him. She wasn't sure if she could get close to him again, but the chance to clear her record, put him in the frame as Standing's killer and report what had really happened was difficult to resist. "I met him," she replied. "I know what he looks like, how he moves and what he's likely to do next."

"So, you're in?"

Beam stared at him. "I'm in," she said. "Now, you tell me. Are *you* up to this?"

"Meaning?"

"Can you go up against this man, I mean, really?"

Newman thought for a moment, then said, "I can kill any man in the world." He paused. "Just as long as a get to him first and make the first move."

Beam nodded. "Who are you, I mean, what's your name?"

"Smith," Newman lied. It was the name in his passport, on his driver's licence.

"Right..." Beam stood up. "If you can't level with me about your name, then I'm not sure I can believe a word you say."

"Sit down," he said amiably. "I get it." She looked down at him, then conceded and took her seat. "As a CIA officer, I use a service name. But as I have asked you to work with me, trust me and take everything I say on face value, then I will afford you the courtesy. However, you must never quote me, or quote my real name in any documentation or hearing or debriefing."

"Okay."

"It's David Newman."

She held out her hand and he clasped it in his own. "Rachel Beam." They shook hands and she retracted hers and said, "Where do we start?"

Newman smiled. "At the beginning," he said. "At the beginning."

6

St. Petersburg, Russia

"You are either a brave and resourceful man, or extremely foolish."

Cole regarded the man in front of him. Seventies, skin and bone, craggy features, and a grey goatee. The man had experienced starvation in a Siberian gulag, Cole had discovered this and much more about him, and the man still had the skeletal look that victims of famine lived with. The weight never truly came back once the belly had touched the spine. His head though, was blessed with the thickest, most wiry hair he had ever seen, greying at the sides, but mainly black. Like the man's eyes. There was something unnerving about them. Like the eyes of a predatory shark. "I'll take a little of all three," he said.

The man nodded sagely. "I hope it is not too much of the latter, for your sake."

"It's just a business arrangement."

"I can have the man responsible for the death of my nephews killed. I can order anybody to be killed."

"But will they see it through?"

"Who knows. The people I use haven't failed yet."

"With respect, your nephews both died at the hands of this man."

"So, you say…"

"I do my homework."

The old man smiled. "As do I." He paused. "So, you will see, it is disconcerting to find so little about you. Certainly, my people found a great deal right up until you joined the marines. It was trickier after that when you joined the navy SEALs. They eventually got hold of your war record. Impressive, to say the least. But a wasted cause. I was also in Afghanistan. Many years before, with the same result. More or less. A sweaty asshole of a place. The might of the USSR couldn't break those goat-fucking peasants." He paused, his eyes cold and dead as he no doubt thought of a distant and forgotten war. "No, my people searched for more information, but after you left the military, the trail went cold…"

Cole nodded. "Like I said, I worked for the NSA. The department I worked in doesn't keep much documentation." He paused. "And a whole lot fewer records of their missions."

"I see." The old man paused, drinking thick black coffee from a glass with a silver holder and handle fixed to the base. "I have heard of this man you speak of. I still have my ear to the ground in government. The FSB and SVR are aware of him, and that MI5 are exceeding their remit with a team they use for both foreign and domestic missions. I was not aware he was responsible for the death of both my nephews. Ivan was recently killed by Albanian criminals."

Cole shook his head. "I'm not sure what your men have told you, but King killed him while rescuing the captured team involved in an unofficial MI5 operation in Albania. The Albanian Brotherhood and your nephew's wing of your organisation were at war. This war was instigated by MI5. An agency whose official remit is to operate on UK shores, but is ever unofficially expanding its overseas operations."

"And how do you know this to be true? That it was really MI5 who killed my nephew, and not those Albanian Brotherhood pigs?"

"I have a backdoor asset with the NSA who monitors MI5 and doesn't know I no longer work for them. That's the trouble with the NSA, they're *too* secretive…"

"And what of Dimitri?"

"It wasn't official, but Dimitri was in deep with something, kidnapped a girl and held her at his place in Georgia. King got her out." He shrugged like it was enough said, that King's involvement would simply speak for itself. In truth, Cole did not know more than that. He doubted his contact did, either.

The old man shook his head despairingly. "When my brother died, Dimitri took over. But he grew too greedy, had a taste for the insidious. Had questionable habits with women…" He shrugged. "That you say he kidnapped a girl does not surprise me. Maybe this King fellow did the world a favour…" He sipped some more of his coffee, then said, "Ivan took over. Just as bad, just as depraved. I now have the unenviable task of taking up the reins in a business I had long left behind." He shrugged. "But business is business, and if I do not avenge these family killings, then my competitors, should they ever get word, will see it as a weakness and my throat will be as good as cut." He nodded. "So, yes. I will act upon this information accordingly."

"I am glad," said Cole.

"And now, you can see yourself out."

"What?"

"I am grateful for your information, but I did not agree to buy it. And I did not agree to hiring your services." He paused, clicking his fingers at the two bodyguards a few paces from them. "Mister Cole was just leaving..."

Cole stood up, unbuttoning the single button of his suit jacket. "I understand," he said quietly. "But this man is a professional."

"We are all professionals, that is why we have lived so long playing such dangerous games."

"He's on another level." Cole paused. "I can get to him, make him hurt, make him bleed."

"I have people who can do it just as well, perhaps better."

"What, like these two clowns?"

"They have experience," he replied, glancing at both men. "You would be both surprised and horrified at what they have done in the past."

"King would eat them before breakfast..."

"You underestimate them, and in turn, you both underestimate and insult me!"

Cole smiled. "They searched me when I came in," he said. "Professional. Metal detector wand. Very thorough."

"You are trying my patience. Perhaps you require a demonstration of their professionalism?"

"Perhaps you require a demonstration of mine…"

The Russian clicked his fingers again and both men went for their weapons. Cole straightened his arm and the fibreglass knife slipped out of his cuff and into his hand. He threw it and it plunged silently into the nearest man's neck. Cole did not hesitate and drew his pistol – a curious-looking white, plastic gun which looked like a small hair dryer – and fired at the second man's chest. The weapon had no metal parts, merely a plastic trigger and firing pin given tension by a rubber band. The entire construction contained no metal, and even the shotgun cartridge inside was rimless and used a solid glass projectile, which penetrated the man's chest and shattered inside. He dropped to the floor and Cole side stepped him on his way to the staggering bodyguard clawing at the knife in his neck. Cole caught hold of the handle with his left hand and hammered the palm of his right hand onto the haft. The knife plunged in up to the hilt, severing the man's spinal cord. Cole withdrew the blade as the man went down and picked up a Makarov pistol from the floor. The other bodyguard had already bled out when Cole turned the weapon on the old man.

"Mister Romanovitch," he said coldly. "I will kill any man you send after King. He's mine. Now, I have offered you my services, and I advise you not to turn them down and go after King on your own…" He paused, seeing fear in the old man's eyes. The only glimmer of emotion he had detected since his arrival. "After I kill him, I need to disappear, and there's only one way I can do that, and that's with money behind me. *Your* money, to be frank." He looked up as two men rushed into the room, weapons drawn. He aimed the Makarov and fired a double tap, but both men fell, each with a bullet hole in the centre of their foreheads. Acute muscle memory. In the SEALs he had fired five thousand rounds through handguns every week in training. "I will forward you my bank details. You will transfer five million US dollars. The job will get done and you will be able to claim the victory for yourself."

The old man studied Cole for a moment, looked at the four dead men. His best men. He relented and said, "Very well."

Cole smiled. "Just like that?"

The old man shrugged. "If it ends this ridiculous business once and for all, then it will be money well spent." He shrugged. "The beast that lives to lick its wounds, lives to hunt another day..." Mikhail Romanovitch watched the American leave, then picked up his phone. "Uri," he said as the phone was answered. "Gather the men together and come over at once... How many?" He paused watching Cole leave his driveway in the blue Ford hire car on the CCTV. "Just the best you can find. Tell them they're going hunting..."

7

Tuscany, Italy

"But father, you have got to be crazy…"

"Watch your tone with me, Gennaro."

"But we now know who killed Luca. And we *will* take our revenge, but we should do it ourselves, not use some hustler and pay him five million euros!" He paused, shaking his head, and knocking back the grappa his father had poured them both. "What's to stop this man simply taking our money and disappearing?"

"*My* money, Gennaro…" Giuseppe glared at him. "Until I am gone, you will do well to remember that."

"Father…" Gennaro Fortez sighed. "But it will be looked upon by the other families as weakness."

Giuseppe chuckled, sipped his grappa, and smiled. "The old ways are the old ways," he said. "My grandfather was a farmer. A peasant. His son, your beloved grandfather got into transportation and exports, but to do this after the war required a cunning mind and a firm hand. My father and his brothers and cousins ruled the region. First, they fought with the police, the carabinieri. Then they bribed and intimidated. That was far more effective than shootouts on mountain passes." He smiled. "All my life, I worked to maintain this way of life. Luca did so too, in his own way. But he diversified into drugs, and drugs are bad news. And then he dealt with the Russians, for their weapons. You cannot trust the Russians. They will always want a bigger slice of the pie, until they have all the pie and do not share even a single crumb…"

"But father, we now know it wasn't the Russians who killed Luca. And we need to settle the score ourselves, to save face."

The old man shook his head. "A clever man will set about solving a problem, but a truly wise man avoids the problem altogether." He paused. "Five million euros is small change. Luca will be avenged, and we can move on with our lives knowing the pig responsible for his death walks the earth no more. We do better now with investments in *legitimate* businesses than we ever did the old way. We are established, have money and assets behind us and by paying taxes, keeping certain business interests within the letter of the law, we no longer need to play cat and mouse with the police. This is the way forward, Gennaro." He poured more grappa into both glasses and toasted. "Salute!"

"And what are we drinking to? Car dealerships and ice cream parlours? You have cut off our balls and accepted my brother's death, taking the coward's way out. Like the scared old man that you truly are..." He picked up his glass and poured the contents on the terrace. "I know the name of the pig who killed my brother. I know who he works for. I will avenge him, even if you will not. And I will carry on in the direction Luca was taking us, because that is what we do. We build business on other peoples' blood and protect it with our own..." He turned the glass upside down on the table and walked down the steps of the terrace to where his new Maserati was parked, his fists clenched for a fight. He took out his phone and dialled as he stared up at his father looking down on him. "Antonio, get three of our best men together and meet me at my villa in an hour. Tell them to pack light and bring their passports. And you're coming, too. Where? To

England. The summer is over, I hear it's hunting season there…"

8

Cornwall

King perched on the granite rock and stared out across the cliff and the sea beyond. The water was blue and calm, a white froth of shore break framing the golden beaches in the distance further down the coast. "I can't think of any other way."

Caroline sat down beside him, nudging him to budge up. "I'm just saying you can't do this on your own." She paused. "Or shouldn't have to, at least."

"It's not the sort of job for an entourage."

"An entourage? Blimey, we're all grateful to be in the Alex King show, but entourage?" she scoffed.

"Okay," he conceded. "A team, then."

"You should have protection, a safe house. *We* should have protection…"

"And what? Hide? Hiding won't find Cole and put a bullet in his head."

"You don't have to do this alone, that's all."

"I've got you."

"Without a doubt."

"Until the wheels fall off, baby…" he said with a grin.

She laughed, patting his leg. "Until the wheels fall off…" she smiled. "It's been a hell of a ride so far."

"It's not ending yet," he said and stood up. He adjusted the bum bag that he was wearing and caught her smiling.

"That's a good look on you."

"Shut up," he smiled. Inside the less than fetching bum bag, which he wore at the front and slightly skewed to the left, was a .45 Colt 1911 and two spare magazines. Caroline carried a more discreet compact Ruger LCP 9mm in a square pouch designed for running with a large smartphone. The pouch was strapped to her left bicep. MI5 did not issue weapons to its agents and operatives on UK soil, except for agents operating in Northern Ireland, but King had contacts and had naturally taken precautions after his meeting with Amherst and Mereweather at Thames House. "Come on," he said. "I'll race you back."

"Then prepare to lose. Again," she replied with a smile, but was already striding off along the cliff path towards home.

They covered the last mile quickly, and as predicted, Caroline was first through the gate to the field that bordered their property. She turned triumphantly to King and smiled. "My race, again! You're a Cleveland Bay, to my Arabian." She laughed. "Horses!"

"I'll take whatever horse you say I am, just as long as it's not fit for the knacker's yard. Anyway, I just let you win so that I could see that smile of yours..."

"Wow, you're either getting soft or hopeful."

"I'm always hopeful," he grinned.

"Well, you'll have to shower first..."

"Or shower together."

"That'll be fun," she said sarcastically. "Sex in the shower is a case of either being cold or being waterboarded and fearing you'll drown. Either way you end up wishing it would hurry up." She smiled. "And we don't want that. Do we?"

King laughed, took out his mobile phone and logged into the secure server running the four cameras around their property. He flicked through the action log. A cat who had been skulking around lately activated the camera in the garden and made a great show of sitting on its backside, sticking one of its hind legs in the air and going to town cleaning itself. King wound on, watched as the cat walked dejectedly through the hedge when it realised Caroline wouldn't be appearing with a treat. Apart from the self-felating moggy, nothing else showed up. King pocketed the phone, but unzipped the less than fetching bum-bag, the Colt .45 within easy reach.

They went inside and Caroline poured two large glasses of orange juice, handed one to King and drank from her own thirstily. King's mobile phone rang, and he pulled a face and sipped some juice before answering. He listened and nodded, and Caroline put down the glass and headed for the shower. She could tell it was the firm and wasn't in the mood for it. They had so very nearly been out of it, but King had been sucked back in with the promise of a new approach, a new offensive that would put British intelligence back on top. Maybe if the Russians may never fear them, then they could at least respect them once more.

King ended the call and climbed the stairs. The bathroom was already steaming up from the hot water. He entered, pausing to watch Caroline as she soaped herself, a stirring within that already made him want to forget the call and join her.

"Who was that?" she asked, her tone harsher than he had imagined in this scenario back on their run.

"Simon."

"What did he want?"

King sighed, the shower scenario wasn't going to happen anytime soon. "There's been some chatter," he answered, still wondering whether he should strip off, or wait his turn. Caroline sighed and he took his cue. He perched on the edge of the sink, keeping his tattered joggers and T-shirt in place. "A Russian informant say's he heard that there is a price on my head."

"You specifically?"

"Yes."

"But you already knew that. Hence the cameras and security measures."

"That was in response to Cole sending those pictures of Marnie..." He trailed off, the memory still raw. "Cole wants to let us know he hasn't forgotten to even the score. He may or may not have followed up on that, he may have just enjoyed unsettling me."

"But...?"

"The Russian informant says that the Romanovitch family, or at least an old man brought back into the fold has agreed to pay a man to kill me." He paused. "I think it looks like Cole is seeking some financial backing. Like he'll do the job, attribute the hit to the Russians, but get a pay day for his troubles. Interpol have picked up on the movement of Italian mafia personnel they had under surveillance and have recordings of them organising a hit on UK soil." He looked at her as she stepped naked out of the bath and nodded towards the towel on the rail behind him. He reached for it, cursing inwardly that the intimate mood had been shattered so conclusively. When he handed it to her, she covered herself and walked past him to the bedroom. "Interpol are digging, but these men are from the Fortez family, and as you know, I crossed swords with them when I was searching for you…"

"It's never going to be over, is it…" she stared flatly. She was staring out of the window, the sea beyond the fields blue and mirroring the scudding white clouds in the azure sky. "What do we do?" she asked.

"You were right about the safehouse scenario. Mereweather has a suitable place for us. There's no suggestion they know where we live, but it won't take a competent operative long to track us down here. We were so nearly out and clean, there will be a trail. Utilities, bank details..."

"We were sloppy," she said angrily. "Like we could *ever* be out of the game and live happily ever after!" she scoffed. "And now what? Say we deflect this, defeat all comers, what then? We'll lose this place... we'll have to start over again someplace new... I wanted to make proper plans here..."

"I'm sorry..."

She smoothed a hand over her stomach absentmindedly. "This place would have been perfect for a family..."

King sighed. "I know," he said. "Look, I'll go up to London and make a few enquiries, see what I can get from this Russian source's handler and contact Interpol. You pack some things and I'll meet you at the safehouse." He took out his phone and forwarded the address. "Simon sent it through. It's a holiday let in Dorset. Right on the coast. It'll be like a sort of holiday..."

Caroline scoffed. "A holiday! For Christ's sake! A foreign agent wants to kill you, and now possibly has the backing of two groups that want you dead! Members of one of those organisations are planning to come here themselves! What for? A competition? To avoid paying Cole his death fee? This is as bad as anything we've been up against, but it's on our home turf and we are not the hunters, but the hunted! It's personal, and we are not in control…"

King stared at her and nodded. "Where's your weapon?" She nodded to the pile of dirty gym clothes on the floor. King took off the ridiculous bum-bag and took out the 1911 and the spare magazine. "Stay alert, and pack quickly. The key to the safehouse is in a key safe attached to the wall."

"Let me guess, Neil Ramsay set it up and it's one-two-three-four…"

King smiled. "Atta girl, we can change the code when we get there." He paused, taking his duffle bag out of the wardrobe, and tossing in some clothes. "We'll get this sorted," he said. "Once I've gained some intel and we put a few countermeasures in place, we'll be back on top." He stripped off and headed into the bathroom.

Caroline remained where she was. Staring at the view and rubbing her hand subconsciously over her stomach. "This place would have been perfect," she said sadly. "Absolutely perfect."

9

Thames House, London

Neil Ramsay hadn't been down into the catacombs for a while. The network of offices underneath MI5's headquarters where sensitive and highly secretive departments did their day to day work. They had been converted from bunkers where Churchill's war planners had done some of their work, using a series of these bunkers all over London. Never in the same place long enough for espionage or sabotage to catch up with them. Many of these bunkers had been connected by a network of rail links, meaning cabinet members and intelligence officers could travel freely and safely while bombs rained down from above. Now updated to offices, this was also the location of the Russia Desk, dealing with sensitive Russian events of an espionage nature. It was where the service's best computer and communication techs worked to counter Russian state-funded hacking. Two men ran the Russia Desk, and although Ramsay had previously worked separately with both men, he wouldn't call them friends. He had never truly cultivated or invested in friendships, but he remembered somewhat taking a liking to Richard Beckinsdale, but not caring one bit for Stuart 'call me Stu' Baker.

"Don't get to see much of you these days, Neil," said Beckinsdale. He poured a coffee from a filtered jug sat atop a warmer and offered him a bowl filled with UHT milk portions and sugar sachets. "We don't get fresh milk sent down here," he explained. "I'm surprised they remembered we even exist."

"Russia still poses the largest threat to The West, make no mistake," Baker commented rather aggressively. "Well, you already know that what with all the fun and games your little *team* have had with them, one way or another, over the past couple of years." He paused. "We still require substantial funds just to keep that asset you laid your hands on. Vladimir Zukovsky's safehouse and the security team holding him under house arrest eat into our budget every month. Better when the bloody Yanks had him. Should have let them pick up the tab…"

Ramsay nodded. "Well, I'll see what I can do about the milk."

Stuart Baker smirked. "Funny. But seriously, Zukovsky is a parasite on our budget."

Ramsay took his coffee black and sipped some before replying. "That's debatable. He seems to release a little nugget of information from time to time. And the Americans aren't sharing so much intel these days."

"Your team haven't used him to sound effect, in my opinion. Hardly worth the bother of recapturing him," Baker replied. "Nobody has popped up there to have a friendly little chat in quite some time. It's almost as if you've forgotten about him."

"We've been busy."

"Evidently. Busier than he has, that's for sure. Like I say, the Americans should have been allowed to keep him. Either that, or simply let him go. He's an old man, what can he do?"

"The man tried to detonate a nuclear weapon," Ramsay said curtly. "His name then turned up on a dossier with Russia attempting to cultivate, develop and release a virus on The West, while they held the only antidote. No, I think he's safer where he is."

"I'm surprised that butcher you use hasn't put a bullet in his head yet," Baker continued, unperturbed.

"There's still time," Ramsay responded, sipping some more of his coffee. "And what do you know of the team?"

Beckinsdale smiled. "Come now, gents. Neil is obviously here for something important, not idle office gossip…"

"I know your methods are being questioned," said Baker. "There are a great many people within the Security Service who think you are trying to be the new MI6. We should let the toffs play the silly games and allow MI5 to concentrate on proper intelligence work that results in convictions. Just my own two-penneth…"

"I'd tend to agree with my colleague, here," said Beckinsdale. "These missions and the subsequent fallout from them get in the way of successful criminal convictions. Sometimes, we need to be more like police officers and less like Bond or Bourne."

Ramsay shrugged. "I've seen it from both sides. You can't make an omelette without breaking eggs. You get to learn that if you ever make it out into the field…"

Beckinsdale asked, "So, how can we help?" He was clearly attempting to ease the tension.

"Well, it involves the *butcher* you talked about," he said, staring at Baker. "There has been chatter of a hit. A Russian asset brought it to our attention."

"That's right," said Baker. "It came to the top tier through our desk, obviously."

"Just a rumour, I'm sure." Ramsay paused. "I'd like a file on everything you have."

Beckinsdale paced around the desk and opened a filing cabinet. The office was low-tech by design. Russian hacking and influence in politics in recent years had resulted in MI5 taking a redirection. Many computer terminals did not have network, internet or wireless capability and many reports were being produced in paper copy only. The files were then being uploaded digitally, inside the firewalls of the mainframe computer server. It was more time consuming and required more personnel and security protocols, but the result was a more secure system. Richard Beckinsdale took the file and handed it to Ramsay. "I'll have to log it out," he explained.

"Naturally."

"Got your man rattled, has it?" Stuart Baker asked, scarcely hiding his amusement. "He can hand it out, but can't live with the threat bouncing back his way…"

Ramsay shook his head. "At the end of this summer, it was decided that we would take a firmer approach on Russian aggression and belligerence. We'll most likely be keeping you two busy over the coming months and years. So, you can get on board with it now, or you can put in for a transfer." He paused, looking at both men in turn. "You're both in your late-forties, balding and overweight. You're both white, heterosexual, have considerable pensions accrued, and frankly, not ticking the demographic boxes that recruitment is looking at today. My suggestion is that you get on board, get in your place, and start to wave our flag a little harder." Ramsay paused. "And that's just *my* own two-penneth…"

10

United Airlines flight UA198
Dulles (Washington DC) to London-Heathrow
Mid-Atlantic

The cabin crew member brought the second round of drinks. Newman was drinking orange juice and lemonade and Beam had a double Scotch on the rocks. They were flying business class and Newman had secured the third seat in their row to give them privacy. As agreed, he paid the funds and Beam made the booking. Newman watched Rachel Beam drink the Scotch most of the way down with her first mouthful. He did not know a great deal about her, but he knew her career with the Secret Service was in the toilet and she was riding a desk with little chance of ever working in the field again. She was the woman who lost the man who did the thing that nobody would admit to but were not so willing to let go. President Standing was killed by white extremist militia. That was the story and that was all that America, and the rest of the world would know. However, had Rachel Beam not been played, had she used her instincts better, then it could have been a different story. For Beam, there was the status quo. She could not be fired for losing a man who did not exist, but her actions couldn't very well be overlooked. She would get the assignments nobody wanted, the leads that were impossible to trace. And she would do it all from a boxroom office on an unimportant floor, surrounded by people who at least stood a chance of getting further ahead. One day. But for Beam, she was done. Twenty more years, never to draw her weapon or carry out a threat assessment again. Just ink on paper and documents saved to servers, nobody to fetch her a coffee or meet with for a sandwich at lunchtime. Her office door would close and open again when her shift ended. She had the stench of defeat upon her and nobody wanted that near them. Career taint. Newman watched her finish her drink and knew that she was suffering.

"What?"

Newman shrugged. "Nothing."

"Good," she said stiffly and pressed the button overhead. The flight attendant walked down the aisle, reset the button, and smiled. "Another double, please," she said, giving the ice a shake in the plastic cup. "And a non-fat, macrobiotic kelp and protein shake for my colleague here…"

Newman smiled and shook his head. "No, I'm good, thanks." He watched the stewardess walk back down the aisle and said, "He's really gotten to you, hasn't he?"

"King?" she nodded. "Like you'll never know." She raised her glass and said, "Here's to collateral damage…"

"Collateral damage?"

"Yep. Here's to this mission and anyone we use to complete our objective." She paused. "Let fate and time be kind to them."

"Like they haven't been to you?"

She scoffed. "Alex King played me. Strung me out and played me like a fiddle. He knew what he told me would filter back and force Standing and his underlings to counter. But King can play a mean game of chess and he was several moves ahead, even when those moves involved him being, or at least *looking*, like he was on the back foot. He's a clever son-of-a-bitch, that's for sure…"

"Standing wouldn't have had to counter King's moves if he didn't have something to hide," Newman replied. He opened the file resting on the seat beside him and turned to a page he had used an adhesive tab to hold. "King chose Standing as a faux target. He wanted to be captured, and he knew that our hard line on terrorism, and with the right backstory, would see him taken out of the system. He was an agent with an allied nation, and they knew enough about our MO that they had a good chance of him being taken to the secret prison that was holding an asset of their own. Someone we stiffed the Brits with by taking for an interrogation and not giving back to them." He paused. "Now, I don't know the whys, the whens or the hows, but I do know that a mission like that takes some stones to plan and carry out. But, impossible as it sounds, he must have done it, because all I know is I was given a mission last year to help shut down and clear up after a private security contractor firm that Standing sent in retaliation."

"King said there was blowback from his actions," she said, sipping some more of her Scotch. "He was retaliating. So, I guess your mission was redundant." She paused. "What about after this? Tit for tat. Whatever we do, the Brits won't take it lying down."

Newman chuckled. "They'll probably get so annoyed, that they'll have a cup of extra strong tea and write a letter or something…"

"My bet would be on the *something*." She paused. "That's where the smart money would go. Riding that bet. So, we have to make sure this gets done and stays done."

Newman raised his glass and said, "I'll drink to that."

"And I'll drink to that." Rachel Beam clinked his glass with her own, drained hers in one mouthful and reached overhead for the button. "I'll drink to anything you want…"

11

Caroline dropped her suitcase on the kitchen table. She had been torn between travelling light and packing more than just the essentials. For the first time in years, she felt planted. Ready to grow roots and branch out in other directions, but always with King and from the home they were building together. The thought of moving, of fleeing their home because of a threat not only unsettled her but made her resent the life they had been living. She knew, without doubt, that if they could live through this, then she was done with intelligence work and done with the danger it brought to their door.

"Going somewhere?"

Caroline turned around, saw the man in the doorway. Five-ten, black, stocky. The whites of his eyes burning with intensity, white-hot like phosphorus. Caroline had never seen him before, but he was everything King had described. She glanced at the kitchen counter, the cooking knives in the wooden block. Cole moved to his left, placing himself a whole lot closer. She cursed herself, the Ruger 9mm still upstairs. There was a Walther PPK in the hall table drawer, but it would mean turning her back on him, and she knew she wouldn't make it, open the drawer and clasp the weapon before he caught up with her. Simple movement. She had more moves to make than Cole, who merely had to run. King kept a .38 revolver by the back door. Same deal, she'd never make it.

Cole solved the quandary for her. He surged forward, his guard up and his feet shoulder width apart, his left leg leading, and both knees bent. Caroline dropped into her stance, mirroring Cole's, her weight distribution at thirty-seventy, front to back. She could see Cole was heavy on his lead foot and as she edged closer, she switched lead legs, went toe to toe and swept his left foot with her right. Cole was taken off balance and she swung a backfist into his jaw and followed with a short, sharp front kick to the man's gut. Cole leapt back, the blow falling short. He came back in hard and fast. If he was surprised by Caroline landing the first few blows, he didn't show it. He jabbed and swung punches, but Caroline blocked and dodged them. Cole had the height and weight advantage, but Caroline was fast. She kept her eyes on his, saw the movement in her periphery and countered accordingly.

"Give up now," he said. "It'll be easier on you…"

Caroline didn't answer. Didn't take the bait. A fight required concentration and breathing. And breathing was almost everything. Air oxygenated the blood, fed the organs and muscles. Her heart was hammering against her chest and she breathed in through her nose and out through her mouth to steady her nerves. She knew Cole's training as a Navy SEAL had her at a distinct disadvantage. The man was a trained soldier and the SEALs had chipped away at him to make him an ultimate warrior. Caroline had served in army intelligence. She had done basic training, then specialised in intelligence work, only picking up a weapon when she accompanied a specific patrol that would take her for a meet with an asset, or to make a dead drop. Their military careers had been as different as apples and lemons.

Caroline had noted that he favoured his right leg. She knew the reason why and it gave her some comfort knowing that it had been King who had smashed his femur with a bullet and left him with the permanent limp that had cost the man his career. She snapped out another kick, catching him midway in the thigh. He grimaced and she couldn't help breaking into a thin smile.

Cole came in again, forcing Caroline backwards. She kicked out again, but this time he punched downwards and caught her knee. She gasped and backed up further, brushing against the table. Cole saw his chance and charged forwards, fists swinging and catching her in the face. Caroline dropped, but caught hold of his testicles and wrenched them towards the floor. Cole screamed, an agonising wail, but he hammered his fist down on the top of her head, compressing her neck, and she crumpled to the floor, releasing her grip. Cole stood up straight, both hands cupping his groin.

"Fucking bitch!" he managed between panting and blowing. "You'll pay now…"

Caroline tried to get up, but he kicked her in the face, and she sprawled into the table and chairs. Cole reached into his pocket and retrieved a stun-gun. It was the size of a smartphone with two prongs on the top edge. He switched it on, and an arc of blue-white electricity sparked between the two prongs like lightning. He smiled and pressed it against her left breast. Caroline arched and spasmed, thirty-thousand volts shooting through her body. When Cole took the device away, she fell limply to the side and stared motionless into his eyes.

"King took everything from me," he said. "He used my family for leverage. My wife and son are in the witness relocation program because of him. That's it for me. I'll never see them again. Two people among three-hundred and thirty million. Somewhere in one of fifty states. Trying to remain hidden, aided by an agency that will do everything in their power to keep it that way."

Caroline tried to talk, but her mouth wouldn't work. She tried to raise an arm, but it felt as though it was pinned to her side. She managed to splutter but couldn't even make out the words herself.

"My life ended the day he gave me this…" He rubbed his thigh soothingly, but he looked distracted, the memory painful and familiar.

Caroline slowly raised her hand and rubbed her mouth. The feeling was slowly coming back, like after a treatment at the dentist.

"Alex saved you," she slurred. "He rescued you in Afghanistan. And then at the prison in South Dakota, he wounded you when he could have killed you…"

"And cost me my career! My family!"

"But he rescued you. You came back from the war and started a family. He *gave* you that," she said slowly, as if fighting too much drink. The drunk talking to the sober, the added effort she was making in what should be a normal task. "You couldn't let go of the fact that he had bested you. You sought revenge."

"He contacted my family, used them to put pressure on me!"

"And you killed my friend!" she stammered. "Marnie was a non-combatant. A desk worker. You killed her parents, too. You're a sick man…"

"By whatever means necessary," Cole said quietly.

Caroline rubbed her mouth, then touched where the stun-gun had shocked her. The wound was burning, and her limbs tingled with pins and needles. "For what?" she asked indignantly. "For your honour? Jesus, you walked away. You were beaten. Accept it, put your energy into finding your family…"

"Well, that's not going to happen now, is it? It's gone too far. I have to rewrite my future."

He bent down and smiled as he arced the stun-gun, saw the fear in her eyes, then shocked her again.

12

She could hardly breathe. The fumes from the exhaust made her nauseous, and she feared she would vomit and the tape around her mouth would cause her to choke. She could see, but only from the faint ambient glow of the brake lights as the car slowed for junctions of other traffic. As the car accelerated, she was plunged into fearful darkness once more.

She couldn't remember being placed into the boot of the vehicle. She wasn't aware of anything between being shocked on her kitchen floor and waking up in the confines of the boot an hour or so ago. She tried to feel for her phone but realised that Cole must have taken it. Her hands were bound tightly behind her back with what felt like the same tape he had used on her mouth. She struggled against her bonds, but they were agonisingly tight and even the smallest of movements cut off her blood supply and rendered her with pins and needles in an instant.

The car slowed and took a bumpy track, and she was aware of puddles and rocks, the car either grating underneath, or splashing down into potholes. Then she heard a scraping sound and after a while, realised that it must have been brambles brushing down the bodywork of the vehicle. They were going seriously off road for the abilities of the saloon, and she wondered where they were going, but was already fearful of the outcome. She closed her eyes, thinking of her parting words with King. They had not been kind and she regretted having cross words with him. She had not felt the sensation before, but she felt like submitting to the situation, and with that, her entire body seemed to release tension and weight. Her muscles relaxed and her breathing became easier. And then, just as swiftly, the fight came back, and she kicked her feet and screamed muffled screams through the tape. She squirmed and twisted and kicked, but as the car drew to a stop, she realised she had left the fight too late and she neither had the time nor the ability to turn her struggle into a way to escape. The engine noise and hum from the exhaust died. Replaced with silence. Nothing. Emptiness. A whole minute passed, and she dared not breath for fear of missing a sound as she listened intently for a clue as to what was happening next. The door finally opened and closed with a solid thud that vibrated against her skull resting on the bulkhead. She finally breathed again, her heart pounding, blood coursing through her veins and already she could feel her legs were leaden, and her stomach was churning as she dreaded what was in store.

The boot lid made a clunking sound as it popped open and she squinted against the light. Cole bent down and she kicked out, catching him in the face. He recoiled and she swung her legs over the lip of the boot but was left with an impossibly difficult inverted sit-up to get out, and she lost her balance as her core gave out and she sprawled back inside. She tried again, this time making it as she rolled herself over the lip of the boot, but Cole was turning towards her, his hand clutching his jaw. Caroline kicked at the spot she knew him to favour – the middle part of his femur, which King had sent a bullet – and he grunted as she ran past.

She was running scared. Her hands bound behind her, and the tape around her mouth making it impossible to breathe with the exertion and fear. She simply could not get enough air in and out of her nostrils, and she could not scream for help.

She was running through forest. Uneven ground with fallen branches and mulching leaves. The smell of decaying and damp vegetation getting into her nose. There was little foliage, the wood almost bare in late Autumn, and the trees were stark, an uninviting woodland that could be a picture in a fairy tale warning about the dangers of straying into the woods. She had forgotten her training, pure fear overtaking her. Her primal instincts kicking in. She should have been weaving, she should have used the terrain to her advantage, but she had started to run uphill because the forest looked to clear in that direction. She was aiming for habitation, rather than using the gradient to aid her speed. To her horror she could hear Cole gaining on her.

It happened quickly. She felt her legs restrained and squeezed together tightly and she went down hard. Cole had tackled her, clamping her legs together and barging his shoulder into the back of her thighs, and without her hands in front of her to break her fall, she fell face-first onto the ground, twigs, mulched leaves, and earth grinding into her face. She had closed her eyes just in time, but still managed to get dirt in both eyes. Unable to wipe the dirt out, she had unwittingly surrendered, her focus now on trying to see, and blinking her watering eyes clean.

"It didn't have to be like this," he said, pulling her to her feet. He pushed her back in the direction of the car, keeping a firm grip on her shoulders. "That other woman accepted her fate. But you're one stubborn little bitch, that's for sure."

She mumbled behind the tape, her words muffled. Cole ripped the tape from her, and she gasped and panted frantically, eager for the rush of air to her lungs. When she had caught her breath, she glared at him and said, "You mean Marnie?" She already knew the answer, her stomach churning and her legs feeling as if she was walking in treacle. "Why are you doing this? You don't have to," she pleaded.

Cole said nothing as he pushed her back towards the vehicle. He pressed her down to the ground and stood on her left ankle as he opened the rear passenger door and took out a sports bag and a stool. He slung the sports bag over his shoulder, picked up the stool and pulled her up from the ground. She stood fast, refused to move when he pushed her. He tried again, this time forcing her forwards a foot or so.

"Move!" he shouted.

"You'll have to make me!" she screamed at him. "Because I'm not walking to my death like a lamb!"

"Your friend did..."

"Because you killed her parents! She wasn't trained in the military or as a field agent! She would have been terrified!" she screamed at him. "Which makes you just about the most cowardly piece of shit I've ever had the displeasure to meet!"

"Well, you've got some moxy, for sure..." He punched her left kidney and she gasped and fell onto her knees. He dragged her back to her feet and said, "I can make this clean, or I can make it last. It's your choice."

"Do your worst," she sobbed. "But I'm not making it easy for you..."

Cole shook his head. He looked around him, focusing on a bough above them. "Well, I guess here will have to do..." He took out the stun-gun and shocked her right over her heart. Caroline fell and shook on the ground, then went still. Cole took the length of rope out of the bag and coiled it, he played out the length with the pre-tied noose and swung it loosely, gaining in speed as he eyed the bough. He released his grip and played the coil out with his left hand and the noose arced over the thick branch and dropped down to the forest floor. He righted the stool and made sure it was sturdy on the uneven ground. Next, he taped on a small explosive charge to one of the stool legs. It was a shaped charge of C4 weighing just sixty grams, and the charge was both powered and controlled by a mobile phone. Caroline was coming round when Cole took out her phone and switched it back on. "I expect there will be many urgent calls in the next few seconds," he said. "You'll no doubt have missed calls and text messages, but MI5 will be calling the police, and the local police will be putting out an all points to home in on this signal. They'll track it right here. And they'll find you."

"The police will get you," she said defiantly. "Pray they do, because Alex will make you wish your grandfather had not been born…"

Cole dropped the phone on the ground. It pinged as the messages lit up on the screen, but he was ignoring it. He simply wanted it to act as a homing beacon. "I guess we don't have much time," he said and pulled her to her feet. He reached for the noose and pulled it closer. "Get on the stool," he ordered her. Caroline frowned at the stool, noticing the explosive charge, and looked at him earnestly. "You still have time. It won't be over for you until they come," he said. "They'll find you standing on the stool, the rope around your neck, but I will call in a bomb warning before they get here. I'll give King time enough to get here, to watch that charge blow off the leg of the stool and watch you swing." He paused, gripping her tightly and dragging her closer. "Now let's get the game started…"

13

Caroline waited. Waited for the chance that would spell disaster if she misjudged it. Cole adjusted the noose, beckoned her to bend forwards. Caroline thought of her friend Marnie, what must have been going on in her mind. She took a breath, readied herself and as she made to duck her head for the noose, she kicked out and caught Cole in his thigh again. However, this time as the man recoiled and gasped, she kicked again, catching him square in the groin. Cole let go of the rope and fell to the ground. Caroline leapt from the stool, landed awkwardly, but regained balance and kicked the man in his back again and again, then she stumbled and fell. She rolled and struggled back to her feet, her bound hands making it difficult, but as she got back up, regained her balance, she kicked him hard in the face, then turned and ran.

This time, she headed downhill, her pace gaining too quickly with the gradient. For a moment she thought she would lose her footing and fall, but she managed to get her balance and leapt over a barrier of brambles and briars. She did not look back, and this time she weaved and changed direction rather than bolting in a straight line.

Cole hollered after her. He was limping and cupping the side of his face with his right hand. He was angry, incensed. But he gained pace, the navy SEAL in him dealing with the situation. Like so many elite military units the SEALs had taught him to be fluid, and it was in his nature to improvise, adapt and overcome. Caroline was merely a problem that he would solve, a situation he would move past towards his goal.

The woods started to thin out, and Caroline could see a metal deer fence ahead. It was old and rusted, three rails high and with around eight feet between metal posts. It hadn't been designed to keep the deer in, but cattle out and allow the deer to move freely through the woods without getting caught or snagged on wire. It reminded her of fencing in country estates and parks she had visited, and the thought filled her with hope that she could be near habitation. And then a blur flashed by and she realised that a road lay ahead, a van speeding past at fifty or more miles per hour. Caroline focused on the fence. She couldn't hurdle it, but she could throw herself over and try to roll onto her shoulder, Ju Jitsu style, on the other side. As she gained on the fence, she could see that a wide grass verge would give her a favourable landing before the road.

She could sense that Cole was near. Like a spectre at her shoulder. She could hear his breath, his efforts, his pain. The sound of the forest debris being disturbed behind her, of leaves rustling and twigs snapping.

Cole was moving fast. He ignored his limp, the pain forgotten as he gained on his quarry. Caroline was thirty metres from the fence. She was running hard, which was no mean feat without her arms and hands to balance her. He had the stun-gun in his right hand, ready to shock her as she slowed for the fence. He watched, not letting up on his own pace, but she did not slow either. Three paces out from the five-foot-high fence, Caroline dived clean over the barrier. She twisted in mid-air, curled with her head tucked in and landed on her left shoulder. Cole stopped at the fence, fumbled to put away the stun-gun and caught hold of the top rail with both hands. He was breathing hard, and for a second, he looked directly in Caroline's eyes. She stared back, defiant. She knew she had won. She was now in the road. Help could pass at any moment. He turned and glanced back up the steep wooded hill. He had left her phone beside the stool and the ominously sinister rope hanging from the tree. He had wanted the timings to be tight, but now he risked the police arriving before he could get back to his vehicle. Cole looked back at Caroline. A flash of colour, a squeal of brakes and a gut-wrenching scream. Caroline was taken off her feet, spiralled twenty feet into the air and thrown twenty metres further down the road as the family estate car skidded and lurched across the centre white lines. The airbags had deployed, and its brake lights were flashing like strobes under emergency braking.

Still clutching the railing, Cole stared at Caroline's twisted form in the middle of the road, her legs twitching violently, before slowing and finally going eerily still.

14

King had been on his way to London. He was nearing Exeter on the A30 when he received the call. Simon Mereweather informed him that Caroline's phone had ceased emitting its passive pulse signal. Indicative with being switched off and SIM card removed. Mereweather had called Middlemoor, headquarters of Devon and Cornwall constabulary and explained that an operative could be in trouble, immediate threat to life. Armed officers had been dispatched before the end of the conversation. Although not routinely armed, the Devon and Cornwall police service could call upon armed response units constantly patrolling the A30. This was Cornwall's arterial route and in theory an armed response vehicle would only be twenty minutes away from any given point on the map.

"How the hell could he have found us so quickly?" King snapped, his phone synced to Bluetooth and his tone somewhere between brusque and desperate. Mereweather had certainly never heard such emotion in the man's voice before. "There has to be a leak…"

"We don't even know that Caroline is in trouble yet..."

"She is!"

"But there could be a reasonable explanation. Armed police are en route, let's leave talk of leaks in the department until we know something is wrong, and that she is in fact in danger."

King swore loudly and ended the call. He was driving at around ninety miles per hour but could go no faster. The old Land Rover was a wieldy beast, and both the knobbly off-road tyres and distinct lack of aerodynamics made the speed feel so much faster than it really was.

When King reached the turn-off for Bodmin, his phone rang again. It was Simon Mereweather. *"King, the police are at your property now. I'm sorry, there has been a struggle. Caroline is missing. And there's no sign of her phone..."*

"Right."

"Did you hear me?"

"I heard you," he replied with no emotion in his voice. "I'm en route, near Bodmin. ETA thirty minutes."

King ended the call and stared straight ahead. He had shut down his emotions. He could not function unless he focused, and he could not allow his emotions to cloud his judgement. Caroline was missing, but that didn't mean she was either dead or unable to handle her situation. He needed blind faith and steady judgement.

His phone rang again, this time it was Neil Ramsay's number.

"Neil..." King answered.

"Caroline's phone has reactivated."

King's heart pounded, his hopes lifted. "Where?"

"Carnanton Woods," Ramsay replied. *"It's pinging a signal in a wooded area between Newquay Airport and a village called St. Mawgan."*

King knew it. He had driven through it taking the scenic route to Padstow via cove called Mawgan Porth. "Jesus," he said. "I'm so close..." He hammered on the brakes and just made the slip road, the Land Rover rocking wildly as King corrected the steering and headed for St. Columb Major. "I know where the woods and the airport are, but give me the directions to her signal," he snapped.

"Wait," he said, and King could tell he had been muted. There was a delay of two minutes or so leaving him frustrated, then Ramsay unmuted and said, *"Alex, I'm sorry. There's been a terrible accident..."*

"An accident?"

"Head for the airport," he replied. *"The emergency services are there. I'll call and get put through to whomever is in charge and tell them to expect you."* He paused. *"I'm so sorry…"*

King heard the call end. His stomach was a twisted knot, and his fingers gripped the steering wheel so tightly, that his knuckles had turned white. He took a deep breath, attempting to calm his nerves, and it worked, right up until the moment he screamed and cursed and pounded the steering wheel so hard that he bent it out of shape.

15

King was seated in the corridor nursing a cup of tea. A kind-hearted and sympathetic nurse had brought him a mug from the staff room. He had not moved for the five hours Caroline had been in surgery. He had ignored the requests of the hospital staff to move to a family room, placing himself on the chair nearest to the operating theatre and staring blankly at the floor. When a security guard arrived, Simon Mereweather had shown his Security Service card and told the man to be on his way.

"She's one tough cookie," said Mereweather. "She's a fighter."

King nodded. "It doesn't make much difference," he said. "It's generally down to luck." He paused. "But I appreciate the sentiment."

"Christ, what the hell happened?" Mereweather asked, but King guessed the question was a rhetorical one. "The police found a car, and it was evident that Caroline was transported there in the boot. Obviously, DNA will confirm, but the colour and length of the strands of hair found gives a conclusive basis to work on. They found a rope with a noose in the trees, and a stool with a small explosive charge on one of the legs. Bomb disposal from RAF St. Mawgan made the device safe and swept the area." He paused, shaking his head. "Same modus operandi as poor Marnie, but with additional theatre using the explosive charge."

"Simon, do us a favour and piss off, will you?"

"Right…" Mereweather stopped pacing like an expectant father in the fifties and nodded. "Okay, I'll go find plod, see what they're doing. RAF St. Mawgan has a search and rescue helicopter flying with a thermal imaging camera to see if they can spot anybody in the area who isn't a legitimate walker or whatever. They're sending the police out to intercept. Nothing so far."

"Cole will be long gone," King said without looking up from a spot on the floor he'd been staring at for an imperceptible amount of time. "He knows the score. But you could get the police to check hotels and pubs in the area. There's one opposite the airport. He could be sipping a beer and watching the pub car parks for a ride. Sometimes, the closer you are to the start of a search, the safer you can be. Nobody thinks to look."

Mereweather nodded, took out his phone and started off down the corridor. "Good idea," he said. "I'll be back soon."

King looked up, saw a senior looking doctor heading his way down the adjacent corridor. He took his own face mask out of his pocket and strapped it on. It was still commonplace in public, and in a way, King felt relieved to wear it as it provided him with some protection from his own vulnerability, going some way to mask his emotions. As the doctor drew nearer, he could tell the man had news for him, and he tell that news wasn't good. Selfishly, he was pleased Mereweather was no longer here. Whatever news the man had for him, he didn't want to share it with anybody, and the only person he would want to share such intimate emotions with had been lying helpless at the other end of that corridor for over five hours. The thought stirred him inside, and he felt his eyes water. The first time since he had lost his wife, Jane.

"Mister King?" the man asked, quietly. The light played on his thick lenses and magnified his eyes underneath the glasses, giving him a look of extreme concentration. King stood up and nodded. "I am Mister Sinclair, consultant surgeon. Would you like to go somewhere more private?" King shook his head. They were the only two people in the corridor. "Caroline has had some, er, complications, but she is now stable."

King wobbled, his legs starting to buckle. Sinclair caught hold of him and guided him back down to his chair. He took the chair next to him and said, "She has multiple fractures, which we will set accordingly, some of them will need surgery."

"She's not fixed?" King asked. Realising how ridiculous he sounded he coughed and asked, "What is wrong with her? You said she had complications."

Sinclair nodded. "Mister King…"

"Call me Mark…" He shook his head, the name sounding foreign to him, not used for twenty years. "Sorry," he frowned. He put it down to the trauma and tried to move past it.

Sinclair looked at the clipboard in his hand. "You are Alex King, aren't you? That was what the nurses told me…"

"I am," he replied. "Just call me King, sorry."

"Right..." Sinclair checked his notes, then continued. "Caroline had extensive damage to her ribs, thorax and upper spine. This greatly affected her lungs and heart. We have worked to alleviate pressure from her internal organs, and I can report to you that it has been a success. However, due to the nature of the damage, she is on a ventilator to help her breathe and for this, she has been placed into an induced coma."

King shook his head, his eyes welling with tears. "Can I see her?"

"I'm afraid we need a little more time with her. She has suffered some swelling on the brain, my colleague Mister Henderson has worked tirelessly to bring it back under control, and she is showing signs of brain activity." He paused. "Superficially, she has fractured fingers, wrist, a fractured arm, most of her ribs, multiple leg fractures..." He checked his notes. "To her left leg..."

"Superficially?" King stared at him. A subconscious part of his mind wondering why doctors reverted to mister again once they'd become a specialist in their field. He shook his head, trying to open his mind up to the horror of what he was being told.

"Yes. They're not going anywhere, and we can look at those injuries in the hours, or days ahead. What is more important is to monitor her head injury, the swelling on her brain, and her breathing. We can look at trying her off the ventilator in twenty-four to thirty-six hours. If she breathes unaided and her brain injury is within safe parameters, then we can fix her limbs, bring her out of her coma and start talking about her rehabilitation."

"So, we're not out of the woods yet." King stopped himself, hating the analogy after what had gone on at Carnanton Woods, what she had endured, only to be struck down by a vehicle as she escaped.

"No. But there is light beyond the trees. Tonight, we will see if she can make it there."

16

London

Alexander Putin watched the vehicle pull into the deserted carpark. He sneered as the black Range Rover Vogue turned a wide circle and drew to a halt fifty metres from him, but kept its headlights on full beam, blinding him in the darkness. It was a powerplay meant to unnerve him, put him at a disadvantage. He simply flicked on his headlights in retaliation, and after a few seconds the Range Rover's lights dimmed, then went out entirely. He scoffed. It was meant to be a clandestine meeting, subtle. But the gangsters had hired the most expensive SUV available and had most likely already drawn attention to themselves. Putin had moved the section of security fencing enough for a vehicle to fit through. Another week and this site would be full of equipment, materials and have a pair of security guards patrolling through the night, while a team of construction workers and engineers would be building a multi-storey carpark during the day. Putin had used his SVR resources to find a suitable meeting point. But he had used those same resources at his disposal for a great deal more than that.

The SVR agent stepped out of the vehicle and looked around him cautiously as he closed the door. There was no need to check the silenced Makarov in the shoulder holster under his left armpit. He had already made the weapon ready back at his apartment. The weapon, and many like it, had been brought into the country in diplomatic bags which were exempt from customs searches.

Putin walked around to the rear of the car, popped the boot, and reached in for the sports bag. Again, he checked around him, then took a deep breath, retrieved the bag, and closed the boot lid. The walk towards the Range Rover seemed to take longer than it should; time slowing down with the adrenalin and fear of what may lie ahead. As he neared, the driver's window lowered and a man lit up a cigarette, briefly illuminating his craggy face.

No names. That had been the deal. And no comebacks.

"You have the money?" he asked, dropping the bag on the ground. He stood up straight, his jacket open and the pistol just a few inches from his grasp.

"We see the merchandise first."

"It is what it is. It's what was agreed with your boss. You don't get to try before you buy. Now, give me the fucking envelope and be on your way."

The man shrugged and opened the door. Putin took a step backwards, his hand moving towards the flap of his jacket. The man ignored him, handed him the thick envelope, and said, "No, don't bother checking it," he smiled thinly. "After all, it is what it is. It's what you agreed with my boss..."

Putin shrugged, snatched the envelope from him and walked back towards his car. The man picked up the bag, opened the rear door and tossed the bag inside. He got back in the Range Rover and drove slowly towards the gap in the fence. Putin looked up as he reached his vehicle, frowned when he saw the rear window lower, then went for his pistol, but was too late. Three silenced shots whispered in the still night air and the SVR agent fell forwards onto the bonnet of the car, then slid down slowly into the mud. One of the men in the Range Rover got out, paced over, and picked up the envelope.

The driver was ending his call to Mikhail Romanovitch to report it had been done. The

SVR officer had stipulated that there were to be no comebacks, and that was exactly what he had got.

17

His mouth was dry, his tongue furry. No amount of tea made him feel any more awake, and he was sick of the stuff. King needed a shower and to brush his teeth, get something to eat and to sleep, but he doubted he'd ever leave his chair while Caroline remained in surgery. He knew he needed all these things, not because he was hungry or uncomfortable, but because he knew the importance of maintaining function. Of being fuelled and rested and ready for action. You simply couldn't operate at capacity if you ignored the body's warning signs.

There had been complications and Caroline had been rushed into surgery to drain more fluid from her lungs and to stem an internal bleed. While there, it had been decided to pin the fractures to her legs and arms while she was under general anaesthetic, and a member of the nursing staff had informed King that upwards of forty people were involved in the theatre procedure. She had given King's leg a sympathetic squeeze and fetched him a cup of tea, but King knew people. He knew how to read faces and eyes and mouths. He knew what hands did when people were lying, where they touched – usually they fingered the lips (for that was where the lie was emitted) – and where the eyes would look when faced with a difficult or uncertain answer. So, he knew Caroline's condition was about as critical as it could be and that she would be lucky to get through this, despite the positive nature of the nurse, but her non-committal answers and poker-losing body language had hinted differently.

"You look shit, mate…"

King looked up, saw Rashid walking towards him down the deserted corridor. He frowned, "I thought you were heading off to Syria?"

"Something came up."

"This?" King asked, standing up and stretching.

"It's enough, isn't it?" Rashid patted him on the shoulder. "How is she doing?"

King sighed. "Not good."

Rashid nodded. "Well, she's doing a lot better than that bastard will be when I catch up with him…"

King said nothing. Rashid wanted Cole's blood, too. But King had dropped the ball and the man would never have gotten to Marnie had he not taken a risk. Strangely, King hadn't given much thought to retribution, his focus entirely on Caroline and willing her to pull through.

King glanced at his watch and Rashid said, "Why don't you go and freshen up? I'll come and get you if there's any news."

King shook his head. "No, I'm fine. I don't want to..."

"To not be here if there's news?" Rashid paused. "She's in a bad way, you're in this for the long haul. Twenty minutes for you to take a piss and splash some water on your face, grab a cup of tea and get some air isn't going to matter one bit." He opened his jacket to reveal a pistol in a shoulder holster. "Nobody is getting past me to finish the job, either. And there are two armed police officers at the other end of the corridor with hospital shift rosters and orders to check anybody going to and from this ward." He looked around him and said, "What's with this place anyway? It's deserted."

"This hospital ward and theatre is being kept isolated for an anticipated resurgence in coronavirus cases, or for extreme circumstances like a major RTC or terrorism attack. Caroline's injuries were so severe, they..." King trailed off, shaking his head. "Christ..."

"It's alright, mate," Rashid reassured him quietly.

King nodded and shrugged. "Well, they opened this ward back up and in light of the attempt made on her life, Simon Mereweather requested Caroline be kept on the ward here for security logistics. Last I heard, he was seeking permission for armed police to act as static guards."

Rashid nodded. "As I said, they're in place. Two at the end of the corridor, two more in an armed response vehicle outside." He paused. "And nobody is getting past me..."

King punched him gently on the shoulder. He wasn't one for man hugs. "Thanks," he said. Rashid knew that was about as emotional as the man would get, and took it as a compliment and validation of their friendship. "But I can't leave her."

"Ten minutes. Go freshen up. She's not even conscious." He pulled a face. "Sorry, but you'll be worth more to her if you get your head straight."

"Okay," King conceded. "Just ten minutes."

18

He had lost the car, but that had been the least of his worries. It had not gone to plan. He had wanted to hurt King. He had wanted him to feel as much pain as it was possible to experience. Not physical pain, that was nothing compared to the pain of loss and the vulnerability he would feel, the helplessness of knowing he had been too late. The device fitted to the stool would have meant he could have dropped Caroline Darby on the noose in front of King's eyes. The police would have to have cordoned off the area, sought the bomb disposal squad, in this case because of the close vicinity, the bomb disposal team would have been sent from the RAF base at St. Mawgan. Practically bordering the woods. In the same postcode. But procedure would have dictated caution. And whether King made it to the scene, or whether he remained teasingly close, Cole could have been the puppet master and pulled the strings, letting Caroline drop on the rope. But that wasn't to be. Caroline had stumbled into the road and into the path of the vehicle. Cole had stared for what had seemed like minutes but had been a mere moment. He had nothing against her. She was just a pawn. Bait. An unwitting commodity he had wanted to use. Now she was gone. Dead or still alive, he did not care which for her own wellbeing, but if she was still alive then she may still be of some use.

Cole had taken to his heels and run along the edge of the woods for close to a mile until it opened out into agricultural land. The going had been slow. His leg ached daily after King had shot him, sometimes the pain was too much to tolerate and he had turned to both drink and drugs over the past year or so and he knew he had changed because of it. Prescription painkillers turned to morphine and then opiates and now he extensively used drugs to get through the day. And now his leg throbbed from the pain inflicted upon it from Caroline. There had been bullet fragments left in place, and now he suspected they had been dislodged. Perhaps into his bloodstream. Perhaps they had snagged, a ticking time bomb waiting to kill him when they finally broke free and headed for his heart. He had shrugged off the thought, he could only afford to think about the present.

He had heard the sirens behind him, but by the time the police had put a helicopter in the air, Cole had reached the small regional airport and was on his way to Newquay in a taxi. After he had arrived at the Headland Hotel, he walked into the lounge and ordered a coffee, then using his burner phone he ordered a taxi to take him to the train station. From there he hobbled back through the town using many side streets and doubled back on himself several times. After he had reached the Sea Life Centre, he ordered another taxi after browsing the internet on his mobile phone for a different taxi company. The taxi took him back to the train station and from there he took another taxi from the rank to take him to the small coastal town of Perranporth. From there he ordered another taxi from a different firm based in nearby St. Agnes to take him to Truro. It was a circuitous route, using multiple taxi companies, but it created a wider search circle of travel and therefore, far greater parameters of search. He had ditched the burner phone and hired a car from Hertz at the train station, and then purchased another pay as you go phone from a Tesco supermarket in the rural market town. It was now dark, and he had taken several hours to cover a journey achievable in less than an hour, but he had put a great deal of variables between Carnanton Woods and Truro.

He had then checked into a Premier Inn just outside of the town and laid down heavily on the bed, gathering his thoughts and how he should regroup.

He had lost most of his equipment but had taken precautions and had stowed a spare passport, another undetectable weapon and a handful of adapted paper shotgun shells, along with a few thousand pounds and a change of clothes in a small rucksack. He just needed to retrieve them. It was time to end this.

19

Rashid waited until King had left through the doors at the end of the corridor, then got up and walked through the adjacent door. The corridor was deserted and silent. At the end, he reached a nurses' station where Caroline's details were written up on a white board. She was showing as second surgery. Her room post-surgery was indicated as #7. Rashid checked the signs, turned left, and counted down the rooms as he walked. Number seven had clearly been chosen because of its proximity to the operating theatre suite. A simple push across post-surgery, or if she needed to be rushed back inside for further treatment.

The room was a single, which made sense. Drip stand, monitors and oxygen were already in place. There was no bed, but he assumed she would be moved onto one and wheeled straight across. He walked to the window and studied the view. Below him, a garden and paths led to two buildings and it looked like they were joined by a covered walkway. Opposite, another building rose to nine levels, which was a whole two storeys above him. He estimated a distance of two-hundred metres. The building's top three storeys were clearly not in use, and he figured it had been left that way after the predicted admissions through another Covid-19 surge hadn't materialised. He remembered hearing how under pressure Cornwall's NHS would be if they suffered due to an influx in population through tourism. This was Cornwall's main hospital and it had prepared itself for war. Thankfully, that war hadn't happened, but wisely, the people running the show had retained the hospital's capability for future scares.

Rashid pressed his hand against the window, gave it a push, then tapped the glass with his knuckle. He then checked his watch and headed back the way he had come. King would be back soon, and he did not want him knowing where he had been.

20

There was a glimmer of sunlight edging over the horizon. A false dawn. The high-rise buildings shielding the sun from view an hour after it would have been seen outside the city. The early hour still felt ungodly, though. The air was crisp, indicating that autumn was starting to take hold.

DI Thorpe sipped her coffee in the go cup and grimaced. "You forgot the sugar."

"Give it a stir."

"Where's the stirrer?"

DS Rogers shrugged. "You might have to give it a shake, then."

"Christ..." Thorpe swirled the cup around, got bored with the seemingly ineffective process and did indeed shake the cup, cursing as a super-heated mix of coffee, syrup and cream spewed out of the tiny mouth piece in a thin plume, some of it ending up on her white, silk blouse. "For fuck's sake..."

Rogers suppressed a smile, but not very well. He offered her a paper napkin and shrugged. "I won't forget the stirrer next time," he grinned.

"You've seen the victim?" she asked.

"Briefly. SOCO are with him now."

"Thoughts?"

"Two bullets in the centre of his chest, one in his shoulder. One or both of the centre mass hits must have struck the aorta because he bled like a stuck pig."

"You said he had a weapon."

"Still in its shoulder holster. Don't know what it is yet, but one of the techs said it was fitted with a silencer."

"Suppressor."

"What?"

"It's actually called a suppressor because it *suppresses* sound. It doesn't technically *silence* the weapon."

"Oh."

"So," Thorpe pondered. "We have a man with a weapon in a holster. That screams of a professional to me."

"Or maybe not." DS Rogers ventured. "He was hit before he could clear the holster."

"Which might indicate he knew the killer," she said. "Or killers..." She looked up as the forensic officer approached.

"DI Thorpe?"

"Yes," she replied.

"I'm Victoria Mills, senior Scenes of Crimes Officer. I'll walk you through the crime scene if you'll follow me." She led them to a workstation of trestle tables under an open-sided tent which looked like a gazebo at a garden fete. "Overalls, masks, gloves and footwear covers. Make sure you put your hoods up, and don't touch anything."

Thorpe shared a glance with her assisting officer. This wasn't their first murder scene. Wouldn't be their last, either. There would be another one within two weeks on their patch. She covered up and stood to one side as Rogers covered his shoes with the oversized socks that looked like shower caps. The forensic officer walked to the scene without asking them to follow, but they caught up and when they reached the body DI Thorpe said, "Right, stop there and remain quiet while I take it in." The forensic officer was about to speak when Thorpe said, "This is where police work takes over. Allow me to do my job, and I will allow you to do yours..." She turned to the detective sergeant and said, "What do you see?"

DS Rogers looked at the ground, the body, the blood that had mixed with the mud and puddles making a large area a viscous reddish brown that looked like melted ruby chocolate. "Well, like I said earlier, he looks like a professional. Suit and tie, leather shoulder holster..." He turned to the forensic officer and asked, "What sort of weapon was it?"

"A nine-millimetre Makarov," she paused, walking to a trestle table, and picking up a clear plastic bag with a small pistol inside. Attached to the end of the muzzle was a thick suppressor approximately eight inches long. "That's not regular nine-millimetre like most Western firearms. It's a Russian design and actually nine-point-two-three millimetres. And the casing is a full millimetre shorter than a parabellum round, resulting in approximately two-thirds of the power."

"Has the weapon recently been fired?" asked Thorpe.

"That will need further testing, but the weapon is fully loaded, and he was carrying a spare magazine in his pocket. I wouldn't have thought he'd fired it last night if that's what you're asking."

Thorpe nodded. "Be sure to test his hands and clothing for gunshot residue."

"Naturally," the forensic officer replied curtly.

"He wasn't killed by your typical gangland thugs," DS Rogers continued. "They would most likely have been piss-poor shots. They usually prove to be, which is why so many innocents get shot in gangland crossfires. Besides, they would have taken his weapon for certain. Those two centre rounds are well placed. Just an inch apart. That takes practice and muscle memory."

"You know that for sure? The shooter could have just got lucky," the forensic officer interjected.

Rogers shook his head. "I was an armed response officer for three years. I don't hold a ticket now, so haven't used a weapon in five years. If I picked up a pistol now, it would take me twenty rounds before I started scoring bullseyes. It would take days and hundreds of rounds to pick up at the level where I left off." She nodded, as did DI Thorpe. "I'm thinking it was three, well-aimed, rapid shots and the third went wide as the man fell. It would have been quick, and I doubt your average Yardie would hit twice with fifteen rounds, shooting with the gun on the side, telling him he was going to cook the fool..."

"Not sure if that's a racist generalisation or not," Thorpe nodded. "But I'd concur." She looked at the forensic officer and said, "How long do you think it would have taken for him to die?"

The forensic officer stared at the body, the blood, the red-coloured mud. "At least a minute, possibly two. I can't yet see where the bullets ended up inside him, but on face value, they didn't catch the heart or lungs. Aorta would be my conclusion."

"Would he have been *compos mentis*?" Thorpe asked.

"That would depend on the individual. Shock is the biggest factor. Realising what has happened, how quickly he's bleeding out. And then there's the blood loss. If he lasted two minutes, the last minute would have him in and out. Like being inebriated. The last thirty seconds he would simply have started to shut down."

"Where was the man's phone?" asked Rogers.

Mills walked over to the table and picked up another plastic bag. She held it up for them to see and said, "Let me guess. You want me to get the prints and DNA off this as soon as?" she asked. "It was in his lap. There's blood on it, naturally."

"Has anything else been moved?" asked Thorpe.

"No."

"But you took preliminary photos?"

"Of course."

Thorpe nodded. "I do things a little differently, but we can't have everything." She handed Mills a card. "Email them to me ASAP, please."

Victoria Mills reddened, but she did not respond. Unlike the two officers she was reporting to, this was her first time supervising a murder scene and DI Thorpe didn't seem to take any prisoners. Mills reasoned that she may well meet her again now that she was supervising SOCO in the area. "Of course," she replied. "I'll call you and let you know what we find on the phone if you want. We have a good techie at the institute."

"Very well," Thorpe replied, but her eyes remained on the body. "This guy was hit by his own," she said. "He either knew his killer, or he trusted them." She looked around her, the one and a half acres or so of waste ground soon to be built upon. The fencing, the gap made by cutting the chain and pulling one of the sections out. "This was a meet. An exchange of some sort."

"You think?" Rogers said, looking at the same things she was. "Quiet, secluded, dark. Yeah, I get that."

"So, if this bloke was shot down by somebody that he either knew or trusted, then what the hell were they dealing in?" She paused. "This guy isn't a drug dealer, that's for sure." She looked back at Mills and said, "Prioritise the phone. I want to know who he had been talking to, and who was his last call to."

21

They're looking into the Russian threat

That was inevitable

They'll make contact with the asset

We'll have it taken care of

You'll have to be careful – make it look like an accident

We'll make it look like a warning…

Too obvious

My people won't care – we don't hide from anyone

They've changed tactics

They will still lose!

Don't be so sure. That asset will be a link in the chain. Get it sorted

We shall. And they will get our message. Do what you are being paid to do and wait for me to contact you.

Uri Andropov sent the text and shook his head as he put the phone back in his pocket. They had a line of information, a source that would prove invaluable, but now they were fighting on two fronts. He remembered his grandfather telling him how they beat Germany and the great war machine. All because Hitler sought a war on two fronts. His grandfather had lived his life by this. He never sought to over-complicate things, never have two conflicts, two lovers, two enemies, tell a secret to two people – and what Uri saw here was the start of a slippery slope. The British Security Service's asset needed to be neutralised. But the British also needed to be sent a message. They may well be taking a more direct, aggressive approach but they were fools and they had underestimated the sleeping giant. The Romanovitch organisation owned the FSB and the SVR. They paid high-ranking intelligence officers and gained much in return for their investment. The SVR had an insider within MI5's ranks, and now that asset was working for Mikhail Romanovitch, the once notorious enforcer for his brother, and now head of the Romanovitch concern. Out from his comfortable retirement and up against British intelligence who had done the brotherhood so much damage when they became mixed up in their operations. Uri was sure Mikhail would prevail. He was old school and a former soldier and survivor of a Siberian gulag, who had turned paid informer for the KGB, then used what he had learned, stolen funds, bribery and influence when the Iron Curtain of Communism fell to help his brother become one of four founding mafia families. He was the man to see this through and the man who knew what needed to be done to win a war he knew the British neither had the stomach for, nor the political remit to continue. But first, he needed to sever one of many links. The man who had betrayed them. The man who had told the British about the American who was going to kill their top agent.

22

Gennaro watched Antonio from the passenger seat of the BMW X5. Trepidation had turned to dread. They were out on a limb. Five Italians in a foreign land, dealing with a Croatian gang selling weapons at a premium. They had the money and there was nothing stopping the Croatians from pulling their weapons and taking the money for themselves. Which was why Gennaro had insisted on doing the trade in a motorway service station car park. Only now, as the early morning rush hour traffic filed in for fuel, coffee, and breakfast, it seemed too obvious. He had checked thoroughly and there was no immediate CCTV, but there would undoubtedly be cameras at the entrance and exit, as well as on the fuel pumps of the service station. It was a double-edged sword, and right now, as he watched his right-hand man inspect the weapons in the open boot of the old, battered Ford saloon in front of them, he would take the cameras every time.

The Croatians looked the part. They were basically skinheads who would not have looked out of place at a right-wing rally. Close-cropped hair, tattoos, skin-tight jeans, and cheap olive coloured bomber jackets made from polyester. All three men wore military boots. For men carrying illegal guns in the back of their car, they weren't exactly cultivating a convincing cover. One man at the rear of the vehicle, which Gennaro took to be the leader, and the other two leaned against the nearside of the car, smoking, glancing around and generally shooting the breeze while the deal went down. They had their backs towards the traffic, and occasionally spat into the grass verge.

Antonio walked back to the car. Gennaro turned to the driver and said, "Be ready to drive away, Gino. Ram them if you need to, it will slow them down. But watch the radiator." He paused, lowering his window. "And wait for my signal."

"Yes, boss," Gino replied dutifully. He had the large SUV in park, but the engine had switched off automatically to assist fuel consumption. If he slipped the car into gear, he wouldn't even need to start the engine himself, the car would do it automatically.

"What's wrong?" Gennaro asked.

"He wants to talk to you," replied Antonio. "He wants to put business our way, back home. He has wanted to deal with you for some time. I guess he wants an introduction."

"Fucking horse's ass." Gennaro paused. "What has he got for us in there?"

Antonio shrugged. "Two sawn-off shotguns, a revolver, an old Browning pistol, a pump-action shotgun and an old Kalashnikov assault rifle. Plenty of rounds for everything. It's all crap, but we can clean them up as we drive."

"And for that he wants ten thousand pounds?"

"It's the United Kingdom. The shotguns will have been stolen, the pistols will have been passed around the underworld since the government banned them more than twenty years ago and the Kalashnikov was probably bought back in pieces by soldiers after one of the desert wars."

Gennaro nodded. He opened the door and said, "Well, if this son of a fucking whore wants to deal with me, he can halve his horse shit price!" He got out of the car and walked up to the man Antonio had been talking with. "You wanna deal?"

The Croatian took a long drag on his cigarette and blew the smoke out in a thick plume, nodding as if he was being casually asked if he wanted another drink whilst chatting at a bar. "Sure."

"What is it, drugs?"

The Croatian nodded. "Sure, we could always use some drugs. Cocaine?" He paused. "Viktor introduced us to you, he must trust us, and you clearly trust Viktor. We can do much business together," he said thickly, his English somewhere between East European and Hollywood movie American.

Gennaro shrugged. "Okay. But we're on a tight schedule and I can't negotiate a deal here. And I'm not paying ten thousand pounds for a pile of junk, either."

The Croatian stared at him for a moment, then reached out and closed the boot lid. "The price is the price. You pay mine, and if we do a deal for drugs, then I will pay yours. I would not insult you with haggling like a tourist buying fake perfume at a bazaar."

Gennaro stared at him and smiled. "Viktor introduced us. He will have told you we are not to be crossed…"

"That's not what I hear," the Croatian shrugged. "I hear your brother was played for a fool. I hear the Russians killed him because he got greedy. We are not greedy, we just want fair price for our merchandise..." He eased back the flap of his jacket to reveal the butt of a pistol tucked into the waistband of his jeans. "You are the one buying weapons you clearly need. But do I need to remind you that we already have weapons of our own?"

Antonio shook his head and said, "You want to measure dicks over a lousy trunk full of guns, when you really want to reach into the big leagues and buy drugs from us? You are a crazy little runt."

The Croatian gripped the butt of the pistol and glared at him. "Better we know the score from the beginning. Better we all know how the other stands."

Gennaro raised a hand and snapped, "Enough! Antonio, pay the man his price and let's put an end to this." He looked at the Croatian and said, "My brother was killed. We will have our vengeance. And you are right, my brother was duped before he was killed. It wounded us. But remember this, a wounded beast is often the most dangerous beast of all..." He walked back to the BMW and clicked his fingers for the two men in the back seat to go to Antonio's aid. He sat down heavily in the seat and sighed.

"Is everything okay, boss?" Gino asked.

"Everything is fine, my friend." He watched the two men retrieve the bags and Antonio hand the man the envelope. To his consternation, the Croatian counted the notes thoroughly shielding himself with the boot lid, keeping his back to them. Not even extending the courtesy of taking the payment at face value. The man had shown no respect, insulted his brother's memory and still expected to be handed a drug deal of his own. The Italian mafia boss grit his teeth together and shook his head. "Fuck this fool and his bitches!" Gennaro snapped suddenly, taking a slim penknife from his pocket. He whipped open the stiletto blade, which was around four inches in length, and said, "Get ready to move!"

Gennaro got out and walked past the two men with the bags. He walked purposefully towards the car, Antonio frowning. Gennaro simply stabbed the man in the back, the blade gliding in and out half a dozen times, the man doubled over his mouth wide open in a silent scream. Antonio wasted no time snatching up the money and taking the CZ75 9mm pistol out of the man's waistband. He looked around him, but the steady stream of vehicles leaving the service station for the slip road to the motorway paid no attention. He aimed the pistol at the two men, who were oblivious and still smoking and spitting and nonchalantly chatting, but Gennaro was already upon the nearest man, and by the time the other man realised what was happening and started fumbling for his pistol, the blade had whipped several times into his neck. Gennaro pulled the man down onto the ground, on top of his comrade and sunk the knife in a few more times. Neither man was dead yet, but they wouldn't be going far. Gennaro took their guns and tucked them into his jacket pocket as he cleaned the blade on one of the men's leg and wiped his bloody hands on their jackets. Both men were groaning and Gennaro smirked at them as he backed away.

Gino had the BMW right up to the Ford, and its bulk was shielding the scene from view. Gennaro got back into the front seat and said, "Get us out of here. And take the first exit. We'll go the rest of the way using the back roads."

23

Hotel Café Royal, Mayfair
London

"We couldn't meet at the embassy?"

"Far too obvious."

"Well, excuse me…"

"Too many cameras, too many people watching."

"Who's watching?"

Newman chuckled. "Just about every foreign intelligence service with eyes on the US embassy. Whether it's electronic surveillance, or people in the street. Sometimes it will be people waiting in the line for a visa. But if we want to talk with the CIA in this town, the last place we want to do it is in Nine Elms." He paused. "Anyway, what's your problem? This place not fancy enough for you?" He smiled, taking in the luxurious surroundings.

"No, it'll do," she replied, sipping her cappuccino. "But perhaps we should have had the quintessential British tea. With the cakes and stuff."

"You mean afternoon tea."

"I guess. What's with that anyway? Tiny sandwiches and miniature cakes, barely enough for a meal."

"It's about *English* indulgence. Ladies would go to a tea shop and gossip over cake and tea, I suppose. I imagine the upper classes turned it into something even more special."

"I don't get the English class system. Either you have money, or you don't," Beam said emphatically.

Newman smiled, looked up as the waiter walked over carrying a silver salver. He coughed discreetly, bent down, and held the tray out for him. There was a folded sheet of paper on top of a folded square of cloth.

"Thank you," Newman said, taking the sheet of paper and unfolding it. He wondered briefly whether he should tip the man but got his answer when he saw him walking back towards the bar.

"What is it?" Rachel Beam asked.

Newman read the note and smiled. "Our contact," he said. "Wanted someplace more neutral."

"But he suggested this place."

"That was last night," replied Newman, finishing his espresso. "The guy's not taking chances. We could have set up a listening device, have people on the ground in situ. He's just playing the game, staying a move ahead. This is his turf, I guess he's entitled."

"Where does he want to meet?"

Newman smiled. "Lambeth Bridge." He paused. "Right in the middle..."

24

Royal Cornwall Hospital, Truro
Cornwall

"She's a fighter," said Mr Sinclair. "Her body was pretty much broken, but we've worked solidly, and she has responded well. Orthopaedics have set her fractures and her internal bleed has been staunched. There is still some swelling on her brain, but it's the right side of the scale and dissipating as time goes on."

King nodded. The consultant looked exhausted and he could only imagine how hard they had worked. Three teams working on her through the night. He had seen tired bodies shuffling between rooms at the end of the corridor. The new shift coming in and being briefed. "Thank you," he said quietly.

The consultant shook his head. "We've done all we can. It's up to Caroline now. But she's fit and young and that's the best hope for her."

"Can I see her?"

Sinclair hesitated, then said, "I'll get someone to make her ready and then come for you." He shrugged. "She's gone through a great deal, and of course, she's still on a ventilator and in an induced coma. My colleagues and I feel she should remain so for the next twenty-four hours at least, perhaps thirty-six. Just to settle the fractures and swelling and keep her still regarding the internal bleed. I'd like to see the swelling in her brain go down further before we bring her round."

King nodded and Rashid, who had remained by his side all night, patted him on the shoulder and said, "She's tough, mate."

King waited for Sinclair to go back through the doors and said, "Does it make a difference? We've seen the toughest men imaginable go down. I've seen hard men die quickly and the weaker ones fight the odds and pull through."

"Bullets are one thing…"

"It's no different!" King snapped. "People die of illness every day. They're no less tough or stubborn than a cancer survivor. Luck plays its part."

"And we've all had a bit of that!"

"Maybe more than our fair share."

"You're tired. Go in there, kiss her on the forehead and go home and get some sleep.

There's a police officer on duty at your cottage. Get a few hours rest and come back here refreshed."

"Cole won't stop," King replied ominously. "He's lit the fuse, and it'll keep burning until he's either dead, or I am."

"Well get some bloody rest, then. You can't take the man on if your tank is on empty. Highly trained armed police officers are guarding the ward and Mereweather told me that there's an officer outside your own front door." He paused. "The armed police train with the SAS these days."

"What, *Saturdays and Sundays*?"

Rashid patted him on the shoulder. "That's it, keep laughing." He paused, looking at his watch. "I have to go and run an errand. Kiss her, go home, get some sleep and I'll meet you back here later."

25

Uri Andropov read the file as the fields either side of the A303 rushed past. They were heading west and the traffic was light. Mikhail Romanovitch had kept Alexander Putin on his pay role and the SVR officer had proved to be a most valuable asset, arming them inside the UK was no mean feat. However, once Mikhail had asked Putin to funnel intelligence and provide weapons for the hit, he had naturally created a trail. But it was a circle which could be closed by Alexander Putin's death. Take out Putin and the trail would go cold.

The weapons were Makarov pistols fitted with suppressors. There were two magazines for each pistol and two, fifty-round boxes of ammunition. The weapons were new, without serial numbers and wrapped in waxed paper. They had been manufactured in the early eighties at the height of the Cold War and never been used.

The SVR agent had a contact in British intelligence and that contact had collated the information now in front of him. Uri doubted the British contact could close the circle now that

Alexander Putin was out of the equation. He would just have to hope that the information that the man had given him was correct, because there was no going back now.

London

Beam took one side of the bridge and Newman took the other. Newman had never met the CIA officer before, so neither of them had the advantage. The bridge was busy with pedestrians on their daily commute, and sightseers alike. Newman stared out across the slick, brown water downstream towards Westminster Bridge and the London Eye. Upstream was Vauxhall Bridge and Newman could see Rachel Beam looking towards Vauxhall Cross, the home of MI6 and sometimes referred to as The River House. The iconic building was distinct, looking like a *Lego* construction against the skyline of post-modern high-rise and four-hundred-year-old architecture alike.

"Smaller than you imagine, isn't it?"

Newman turned and looked at the man sharing his view. "The bridge?"

"The Thames, the bridges, Big Ben." The man paused. "It's all on a far smaller scale over here. When I was first posted here some six years ago, I couldn't believe how small the river was. This great serpent, snaking its way through one of the oldest capital cities in the world, is just one hundred and fifty yards from muddy bank to muddy bank."

"I guess."

"None of the buildings are amongst the tallest in the world, they're not the largest, either. The city isn't all that big, or at least it doesn't feel so. But it's the beating heart of the world, in my opinion. It is home to some of the poorest people and some of the very wealthiest. I doubt there's a place on earth where its government or monarchy has waged more war from, conquered more land, governed more provinces, destroyed more lives, gained more wealth or been at the pinnacle of power for so long. The Brits have been front and centre in world affairs for over a thousand years. They abolished slavery over three decades before us, but they got the whole slave triangle started, so I guess that cancels out the early finish to it." He paused, not taking his eyes off the river. "People own houses and the furniture and portraits within are centuries older than our country," he said, shaking his head at the concept of such an established history. "I suppose that's why I like working here. If there is something in the world that is going to affect the global economy, destroy relationships with other countries, threaten mankind or make the wrong kind of people richer, then it's going to happen here. Right here in a two-mile radius of where we stand." He pointed in the direction of Westminster. "But, in their funny little way, with their strange traditions and all the pomp and ceremony, inside this same two-mile radius lies our greatest ally, and possibly the greatest saviours to humanity, justice and freedom."

Newman nodded. "Well, I guess they have to try extra hard for all those wars, slavery, imperialism and general gutting and plundering of the world's resources."

"They didn't get to rule the world by being nice."

"But we rule it now, eh?"

"Exactly. But we can't do it alone."

"Those pesky Brits again, right?"

"Indeed." He paused and nodded. "I'm Callum."

"Really?" Newman chided. "And I'm Newman."

"Names don't matter, do they?" The man asked pointedly. "I don't shake hands anymore."

"Show me someone who does."

Callum nodded. "The woman is from the Secret Service. She doesn't rank highly."

"Career *seppuku*. She's just not been finished off yet."

"Where's a merciful blow to the head when you need one?"

Newman watched her cross over the road, waiting for the traffic. He turned back to Callum and said, "She'll be of use." He paused. "Do you have something for me?"

Callum took two envelopes out from his inside raincoat pocket. One was a folded A5 letter sized, the other was padded and heavy, but still no larger than a folded A4. He handed both to him. "Do what's needed to be done."

Newman tucked the envelopes into his overcoat pocket and looked at Rachel Beam as she crossed the second lane. He looked back to Callum, but the man was already twenty-five metres from him and crossing over the road. By the time Beam reached him, the CIA officer had disappeared behind traffic and pedestrians.

"I missed what he had to say," she said dejectedly.

"You didn't miss anything. A short geography and history lesson, that's all." He tapped the bulge of the envelope under his jacket and said, "Let's find somewhere to have a look at this."

27

St. Petersburg
Russia

The air was chill, the wind coming off the Baltic Sea from the north. It had the ability to slice through poor stitching and thin fabric, searing at the skin and chilling the bone. And it was not yet winter.

Sacha Goncharov buttoned up his collar and crossed the street. The Mercedes behind him kept at its crawl. Sacha increased his pace. Ahead of him, an identical Mercedes was parked on the opposite side of the road. Two men in the front. Waiting. He looked for an opening, a side street, but there were only dead ends, and he would not risk going down one of them, however fearful he was of being gunned down on the street. Besides, gunning down an informer wasn't their style. He couldn't hope to get off that easily. But then again, how would they know? He had used the same methods, the same protocols as before. This wasn't a sixties spy movie at Checkpoint Charlie with dead drops and micro-dots. This was the new Russia.

He used a pay as you go phone - a burner - and he always paid in cash. He would text the number from memory and dispose of the phone accordingly. He always had the phone switched off, the SIM card removed and only ever assembled and switched on for the time it took to get a signal and send the text. He would wait five minutes for a reply. If none came, he would switch the phone off and remove the card and try again at periods of ten-minute intervals. If a reply came, he would converse by text until there was a conclusion and again, he would dismantle the phone and dispose of it either down a storm drain or in the Baltic Sea at the port. They couldn't possibly be onto him. He also reported only fifty percent of what he discovered or had been told. And he made sure *never* to report something told to him purely in confidence or with nobody else in the vicinity. He knew he could be tested by the family at any time, and he would not fall into the trap of being the perfect double agent, even if the British paid him handsomely. That would be the beginning of the end, and he was convinced that he had been nothing but careful.

He glanced behind him again, but he was getting close to the other car. He suddenly veered out across the road, narrowly avoiding a works van, which swerved and hit its brakes. Sacha regained his footing and trotted past the van, intending to use it as a shield from the creeping Mercedes, but as he reached the side of the van, the door flew backwards on its runners and three men leapt out and rushed him. The crawling Mercedes sped forwards, closing any escape route and the parked Mercedes accelerated quickly, boxing Sacha in. He spun around and started to fight off his attackers with his feet and fists, but he was soon overcome and taken to the ground where he was kicked and beaten, hooded with a foul-smelling money sack and his wrists bound tightly behind his back with duct tape. Four sets of hands went on him, grabbed his limbs and he was unceremoniously tossed into the van, the door slamming shut a second later. He was beaten around his kidneys and struck several times with something hard on his collar bones. They were softening him up, and he knew what would happen, the horrors that awaited him when they got him someplace quiet and secure. They would not touch his face and head, as he needed to talk and needed to think. But nowhere else would be off limits, and he had seen how it ended for the unfortunate souls who had crossed the brotherhood.

The drive was thankfully short. They couldn't beat him as they moved him out of the van, and he was pushed and pulled and saved from falling when he stumbled on the uneven ground. The sounds echoed around him, and he tried to place where he might be. An alleyway. Tall buildings adding to the acoustics of the echo. A smell of damp and the bite of cold. Somewhere that did not see sunshine, buildings so close together that mould grew up the walls and became encrusted with ice for five months of the year. The communist-era tenements. Now home to the city's poorest – no change there – but now also the home of drug dealers, addicts, whores and a place where the homeless found somewhere to lay down for the night and shiver until dawn – the product of capitalism and the seismic gulf between incomes since the USSR fell and the dot com billionaires changed everything.

They pushed him up several flights of stairs, falling and getting dragged back to his feet, his knees searing somewhere between fire and ice as they broke his fall. When they reached a landing, they pushed him along for a dozen paces, then threw him down a short flight of four stairs. For all he knew it was the edge of a building and he tried to scream as the weightlessness rose in his stomach, and he gasped as he sprawled onto his front, his face breaking the fall, and his hands tethered uselessly behind his back.

They pulled him to his feet, pushed him down into a chair, and he was aware of tape being wound around his stomach and then his ankles. He could not move, could barely breathe, and had to fight against screaming, the fear welling up and rising through him like an oil strike. And then the room went quiet and he heard the men walking away and the door closing. And then silence. Absolute and foreboding.

28

Cole had parked behind the retail park across the road from the Royal Cornwall Hospital. The retail park employed a security camera and a parking attendant monitoring vehicle number plates on a hand-held device. The hospital would be a CCTV hotspot, but he had worked out that all parts of the hospital could be reached via a covered walkway that connected the buildings and this could be accessed at the main entrance. He did not risk parking in the hospital car parks, as they too used CCTV and both an automated payment machine and barrier arms on the exits.

He had watched King leave. Frozen for a moment, his quarry so tantalisingly close and unaware, but he would not make the mistake of underestimating the man again. Using the parked vehicles as cover, he watched him climb into a battered Land Rover Defender and drive out through the barrier onto the road. His heart was thumping inside his chest. It would be more satisfying this way. He wanted the man to suffer. To lose someone, just as he had lost his own family. When the man was on his knees in the agony of bereavement, then he would offer him a quick release.

Inside the entrance there was an information desk on the left. Two security guards and several volunteers looked at him and he said, "I have an appointment with ENT..." and kept walking. He had earlier researched the layout of the hospital and knew he had to go to the end of the corridor and down two flights of stairs to ENT, but that would also put him on the right level for the walkway and from there he could access the entire hospital.

Cole took a right halfway down the corridor and entered the men's toilets. He went into a cubicle and locked the door, then pulled up his shirt and took out the neatly folded white technician's coat, shook it out and slipped it on. He had earlier searched the internet and designed a generic NHS card using logos and font from the NHS website and thumbnail head and shoulders image of himself and printed it off using a small, wireless photo printer. He had bought a blue lanyard which had been displayed along with keyrings and wallet chains at a service station on the way into Truro and attached it to the card which he now wore around his neck. He fished it out from under his shirt and collar, then checked his image in his phone. He looked the part and smiled at the fact that since the Black Lives Matter protests and the heightened awareness in race and race relations, it would be doubtful that anybody would ask a black man in his forties if he was a doctor, or if he should even be there in the first place. He had read online that the hospital relied upon many agency staff and was confident that nobody would give him a second glance.

Instead of heading downstairs to the ENT department, where he would be able to access the covered walkway, he headed up the stairwell for five floors, and made his way out into the corridor and turned left, pausing at a large window where he could survey the other two tower blocks and the road and pathways below. He could see a police car below. To him it was just a cruiser and not recognisable as a specialist armed support vehicle, but even from here, he could see that the man in the passenger seat was cradling a Heckler & Koch MP5 9mm machine carbine, secured to his chest with a webbing strap and clips. He couldn't make out the driver from the angle, but he could take it for granted that he would be heavily armed as well. He wasn't bothered about the opposition. But he could tell from the way the vehicle had parked that it had been strategically placed to both observe arrivals and be ready for pursuit. Caroline would have been admitted here, and the fact that there was a vehicle posted outside not only told him that she was still alive and he would be able to use her, but that she was nearby. He studied the other two blocks. Like all hospitals the lights were on regardless of the time of day, but the floor directly opposite him looked deserted. It was the top floor, but the building wasn't as tall as the one parallel to it, or the one Cole was observing from. He had read online that the trust had kept several wards and floors closed in anticipation of a resurgence in the coronavirus, or in the event of a disaster. It would make sense to use this facility for somebody with an armed guard. Somebody whose life had been threatened. Someone like Caroline. He thought back to seeing King walk across the carpark. The man didn't look to be grieving, merely exhausted. Broken, even. But not distraught with grief. Cole smiled. *But give him time…* he thought.

Cole headed back down the flights of stairs and down onto the ground floor minus one. The hospital had been built on a split level and he was now a level under the entrance floor. He headed in a clockwise direction, and as he passed through the adjacent building, he could see the two, armed officers in the BMW X5. He passed hospital porters and cleaners, nursing staff and doctors and nobody gave him a second glance. He took the stairs in the next building and headed up to the fifth floor where he could see two armed police officers standing guard at the end of a ward. He continued up the stairwell another flight and saw that this floor appeared to be empty as well. Only emergency lighting remained, and it was virtually silent.

Cole closed his eyes and took a breath. He doubted this would be easy, but he was a former US Navy SEAL – Sea, Air & Land special operations soldier – and he had learned more about unarmed combat in his training with the NSA's special assignment group than these two police officers could even imagine. He took out his mobile phone and looked at the screen as he opened the door and walked towards the door that the two, armed officers were standing guard in front of. He pretended to scroll through his messages, apparently oblivious to the presence of the two police officers. As he reached them, he looked up, feigning surprise. His expression was one of shock, fear and concern and he said, "What's going on?" He dropped his phone and one of the officers bent down to retrieve it for him wholly by instinct. Years of serving the public had nulled his primal instincts and despite all the specialist weapons training he had received, his overriding instinct through what Cole would imagine to be more than fifteen years' service, was to help. Cole snapped his knee up into the man's face and dropped a knife-edged hand onto the nape of his neck, turning and taking on the other armed officer, who had only just started to react. Cole gripped the end of the MP5 machine carbine's barrel and held it away from him as he hammered the palm of his right hand upwards into the man's nose, then as his head snapped back, Cole finished him off with an identical strike to the point of the man's chin. Both men sprawled onto the floor, but Cole knew the first man would simply be suffering a pulse of blood to the brain and he would regain consciousness soon. He stamped down onto the man's head and there was a second crack as his head hit the solid floor.

Cole went for the pistols, but they were both secured to their holsters by a ring in the butt and a coiled lanyard of plastic-coated wire. He cursed loudly and looked around him to see if he'd been compromised. He opened the door of the ward and dragged one of the men through and holding open the nearest door with his foot. It was a ward of four cubicles each housing an empty bed. He dragged the man around the first bed, then dropped his leg heavily on the floor. He was breathless from the exertion and his leg was aching, but he pressed on and dragged the second man inside. He quickly removed both pistols, ejected the magazines and kicked them across the floor, before removing the chambered round in both weapons. Next, he used their handcuffs to secure them to the beds, then stamped on both men's heads. He could see they weren't going anywhere anytime soon, if at all. He then unstrapped both MP5 carbines and took one of them and the magazine from the other and stashed it under the pillow on the first bed. Cole straightened his collar, took a deep breath to steady his nerves and quell the adrenalin, then pulled the door open and stepped back out into the corridor.

At the end of the corridor there were four plastic chairs and a vending machine which had been emptied and switched off. Opposite the chairs was another corridor and Cole could see a nurses' station at the other end and a series of doors on either side. He opened the door and walked confidently down the corridor. He was aware of people nearby, and there was nobody in the small wards off to each side of the corridor. Directly opposite the nurses' station, and the nearest door to the operating theatre, a room was in use. Cole stared through the tiny window in the top third of the door and felt a wave of euphoria wash through him. He opened the door and stepped inside. Caroline was lying in the bed, her eyes closed and a tube in her mouth. Cannulas were fitted in both hands and a series of drips were hanging from drip stands both side of the bed. Her eye sockets were bruised, and she had cuts to her face and arms, which had been cleaned and the ones requiring more attention had been dressed. He stepped forwards and was caught momentarily off guard by the nurse seated in a chair beside her patient. She looked up and frowned. Cole smiled, but she wasn't buying it and she stood up and reached for the alarm. Cole grabbed her and threw her to the floor. She screamed and he kicked her in the face, knocking her backwards into the sink. He bent down and jabbed her in the side of the neck with his fist and she was out cold.

Cole cursed and headed back for the bed. There was no time to savour the pain he was about to inflict upon King, so he threw off the bedsheet, exposing Caroline in just a hospital gown. It rested on top of her, as they had not been able to put her arms through the short sleeves. Her left leg was in plaster to the knee, but her right leg had been pinned and there was a metal contraption keeping the leg braced, with screws going into the skin and bone. Underneath her leg was a padded dressing with blood stains on it. The screws looked painful, but he knew she was feeling nothing. He would make this quick anyway.

He felt the force of the bullet and the sound of breaking glass at the same moment and was thrown into the door, before sprawling on the floor. He was winded, dazed. He looked up at the neat golf ball-sized hole in the pane of glass, then his instincts took over and he rolled onto his side as the next bullet shattered the entire window, which had now been considerably weakened, and a neat little hole about the diameter of a pencil punched into the wooden door where his head had been. He remained prone, but shuffled around Caroline's bed, using her as cover. He cursed loudly and could hear people's voices outside the room. It was now or never, and he whipped out the knife. He would have to plunge it wildly into her, not the effect he had planned, but it wouldn't look pretty, and he could at least know that butchering her would also hack away at King's soul. He had wanted to bare her insides to the world, to give King an image he'd struggle to live with. So that his death would come as a relief. But now, he would just have to stab what he could reach. Cole plunged the knife but misjudged and stabbed the mattress. He got up onto his knees, keeping his head down, and raised the knife above Caroline's stomach. He snatched his hand back as if he had been scalded with hot oil. The bullet had not only gone through his hand but through the handle of the knife and into the wall. Three more bullets struck the wall and Cole scrabbled to his feet and charged to the door, two bullets punching through the glass panel near his head as he struggled to pull it open. He dived out through the doorway to the sound of shouts and screams from the hospital staff, who had now convened at the nurse's station.

Cole clutched his bleeding hand, not yet looking at the damage that had been done. He remembered the MP5 he had stowed, and he staggered into the room and threw the pillow aside. He saw some basic medical supplies in the glass-fronted cupboard, and he grabbed out gauze and dressings and a bottle of antiseptic and stashed the items into his pockets, blood painting everything he touched.

He took the stairs two at a time. He was in trouble. His hire car was four-hundred metres away parked behind the retail park and he was covered in blood, carrying a machine gun. He needed a quick exfil, and he needed it now. The gunman had troubled him. It had been the last thing he would have suspected. Had it been a trap? Surely King would not have used his own fiancée as bait? He knew the man was ruthless, but even *he* would have his limits.

Cole stumbled into the men's lavatory and into a cubicle. He tore off the technician's coat and pulled up his shirt. The bullet had struck him in the ribcage, embedding itself in the level III Kevlar vest he wore underneath. He had been lucky. The bullet would have gone through his lung for sure. He looked at his hand. The bullet had gone right through, but he suspected the knife handle had aided a clean exit. Like a buffer plate on a leather punch. He could not move his fingers, but that wasn't surprising. He couldn't think about long term damage yet. He needed to stop it bleeding and get out of the hospital. He ripped at the packages and doused the wound in antiseptic before binding his hand tightly. When he finished, he unbuttoned his shirt and wedged the MP5 under his armpit, pulling the shirt together and keeping his hand there to conceal the weapon. He tucked the spare magazine into his pocket, his hands shaking with pain and adrenalin. He knew he had to move. Losing momentum meant failure, and failure would only end in capture or death. And he was damned if he was going to wind up with either one of those outcomes.

29

Rashid had been torn between holding the zero over Caroline's bed, being her protector, and going after Cole. He could only assume that Cole would run. But it had been a roll of the dice. The man could double back and finish what he had started, but Rashid knew he had hit him twice, and at such short range, for his particular skills at least, he had seen the blood on his hand, but not on his coat. He had seen colour behind the white coat in the torso shot but no bleeding, indicating that Cole had been wearing body armour. He was sure he had well and truly rattled him, seeing the expression of fear on his face as he had made for the door, but he had resisted a further shot. He had taken enough risks from over-penetration, not having a suitable backstop and being unable to see who was behind the wall and door. He simply couldn't take any more chances.

Holding his aim for close to a minute, he was confident that Cole wasn't coming back. Medical staff were now flooding into Caroline's room, and he had watched them start to move her and the masses of equipment needed to keep her alive. Rashid got up from his position two-hundred metres across from the main building and sprinted for the exit, leaving his gun slip and jacket at his lying up place, or what he would call his LUP. He bolted down the stairwell and sparked shrieks and shouts and chaos as he bolted through, M4 rifle in hand and people clearing from his path like the biblical parting of the ocean. As he tore out of the nearest exit, he caught sight of Cole walking quickly on a path with grass either side. Rashid stood in the road, shouldered the rifle, and took aim.

"Armed police officers! Put down the weapon!"

"Armed police!"

Two calls, both close. Rashid didn't move, tried using his peripheral vision to see if he could make out their position.

"Armed police!"

There was separation in the shouts. They had flanked him in a pincer movement. Cole wasn't in his crosshairs yet, there were people in the line of fire and a busy carpark beyond him. He swore and dropped the rifle, placing both hands on top of his head. He took a knee, and then another.

"British security forces!" he shouted in return.

"Remain still! Do not move!"

Rashid wasn't going to tickle an itchy trigger finger. His colour was already several shades the wrong side of racial profiling.

"I am an officer with the Security Service!"

"Don't fucking move!"

Rashid recognised fear and panic in a voice, and he knew he was close to being double tapped right there and then. He decided to wait it out and live to fight another day. But as he watched Cole reach the carpark and disappear behind the vehicles, he vowed the man would not walk the earth much longer.

30

The door opened and the men returned. Sasha froze at the sound of them walking down the stairs, heavy heels on the floorboards. The footsteps grew closer. He knew something was coming, and he had expected to be beaten again before they removed the hood, but it was ripped from him and he blinked in the dim light from a gap in the boarded-up window. He flinched as the man patted his cheek, grinned down at him menacingly.

Sacha recognised the man but did not know him. He knew the large Ukrainian behind him, a man called Davidoff. He recognised the shorter man to his right, knew him to be a Georgian called Vaz. These were men who had turned their backs on their homelands for what they could earn working for the Russian mafia family. They were the worst kind of men. Contract killers motivated only by money.

"Please…" he stammered, regretting his lack of courage, embarrassed by it. But then again, he had never been tested in such a way. "What is this about?"

The man shrugged. "Mikhail knows you are a traitor. A stool pigeon. That is what the Hollywood gangster movies call a man like you, no?"

"I am not…"

The man turned around, bent down, and unzipped a large canvas hold-all. He took out an electric extension reel and passed it to the Ukrainian. The big man dutifully walked up the steps and out of the room. "No electricity here," he explained to Sasha, taking a domestic iron and a hair dryer out of the bag, and placing them on the floor. He looked up as the Ukrainian came back in, reeling out the flex and walking back towards them. He pulled out some slack and placed the reel on the floor. The man plugged in the iron, studied the settings, and turned a dial around until he was satisfied. Next, he plugged in the hair dryer and stood back up. "I'm going to hurt you a bit," he said casually. "And then, when you know that the pain is real and that I do not care how far I go, I will stop and ask you some questions…"

Sasha's eyes widened as the man switched on the hair dryer and walked towards him. He struggled, but the tape restrained him and all he could realistically do was move his head and shoulders around erratically as the man brought the hair dryer towards him. The heat was pleasant at first, for a fleeting moment in the chill of the derelict room, and then it became savage. The man placed it over Sasha's right nipple and pressed it hard against his shirt. The fabric was hot within seconds and he screamed as the heat tore at his skin, the fabric of the shirt starting to singe. Sasha screamed and the man continued unperturbed, neither visibly enjoying nor deploring the action. It was merely a process in the procedure, and he carried out his work objectively and without emotion.

When he finally took the hair dryer away, the air smelled of burned fabric, singed hair and of burning electrical wiring. A heady mix of acridity in the room. Sasha was sobbing and groaning.

"Whoever would have thought a woman's beauty appliance could create so much pain," the man commented. He licked his finger and brushed it against the iron, where it hissed, and his saliva bubbled on the hot metal plate. "We will save this for a time when you are not useful. If you fail to tell us what we wish to know." He paused. "Held against the left side of your chest, it will eventually boil your heart. Cook it like a stew as you die…" He held up a hand and said, "But it will not come to that, will it?"

Sasha shook his head. "No!" He trembled. "Just ask me a damned question!"

The man smiled. "All in good time," he said, reaching into the bag. "My girlfriend, she is a good-looking woman. She has Tik-Tok and Instagram and is always posting stupid crap on it for the world to see. Like she's a fucking celebrity nobody has ever heard of. But she can't leave the fucking house without her makeup and her hair looking like she has spent a fortune at a salon. Women, eh?" He plugged in another device and held it up for Sasha to see. "She left this fucking thing in the windowsill to cool. It's called a hair straightener…" He held it up for Sasha to see. It was approximately twelve inches in length and two inches in diameter and when the man pressed the handle, a flap opened. "Hair goes in there," he said. "Fuck knows what they do with it, but you see the shape, get the idea by now, I'm sure…"

Sasha looked at it, stared at the man and whimpered, "No…"

"You do see!" The man turned to the other two men and laughed. They all shared the joke, but when the man looked back at Sasha, he was quite serious again. "I don't have to explain to you where I will insert this for you to cook from the inside out, do I?" He paused. "Trust me, it will certainly get hot enough. That stupid Instagramming bitch of mine nearly burned our fucking apartment down last year…"

"Please, no…" Sasha pleaded, his eyes not leaving the appliance in the man's hand. "You still haven't asked me a question!"

The man shrugged. "Mister Romanovitch has had confirmation of your treachery. "You are working for MI5. The British recruited you after you handed Interpol information. You have been working for them for some time."

"I am not!" He screamed. "Bring Mikhail here! I will tell him myself!"

"You think the old man, the big boss will come down to this stinking cesspit?" He looked at the other two men and shrugged. "Either of you want to go and ask him?" The two men chuckled, shaking their heads. Both men displayed toothless grins, and those teeth remaining were yellow and chipped. "No, he wants to teach you a lesson. But right now, is there anything you can tell me that you think will spare you? Some wonderful golden nugget of information?"

Sasha knew this was a trick. If he admitted spying for the British, then it would be certain death. The thought of the iron boiling his heart, or the sadistic treatment with the hot hair straightener filled him with terror. But if he said nothing, then he may well meet his end the same way. The die was cast.

The man turned to the two men and said, "Hold the rat still. It's time to bring the pain…" He bent down and picked up the iron. Again, he licked his fingers and dabbed the plate. The saliva bubbled and dried an instant later. "There's a nice point on the front of this iron," he said. "Let's see if I can write something fitting on your cheek…"

The two heavies grabbed Sasha by his shoulders and one of them clawed at his face, heaving backwards on his cheek, which in turn, tightened the other cheek. Like a blank canvas ready for the artist. His face was so contorted that he could not let out the scream which welled inside him and it sounded as if he was humming a morbid tune. The heat was significant a few inches from him, and when it touched, it seared the skin and the air filled with the acrid aroma of burned flesh. Sasha struggled, but thirty or more stone of muscle held him clamped in place, as the man brought the tip of the iron down in a straight line to make the first part of the letter K for крыса, pronounced *krysa*, the Russian word for rat.

Sasha saw past the man, saw the door opening. The image seemed to take the pain away, as the three men concentrated on their torture. The man in the doorway stood almost as tall as the frame and filled the opening with his shoulders. A man-mountain. He wore olive combat trousers and a tight navy sweatshirt which showed off dinner plate pecs underneath. His face was as black as coal, highlighting the brightness of the white in his eyes. In his massive hands he cradled a machine pistol, which looked like a child's toy, such was the scale.

The man started on the uptick of the K, but Sasha barely felt it as he watched the man in the doorway raise the weapon. He could see that the entire barrel looked like a bulky silencer and there was a sight on top of the weapon that looked like a small, yellow pane of glass in a black plastic frame, the man's eye now lining up with it. There were three muffled shots and all three men fell. The man sprang lightly down the steps, surprising for someone of his massive build, and he seemed to fire at the men's heads without aiming, but all three bodies rocked on the floor and the bullets exited, splitting the heads like melons.

Big Dave slung the weapon over his shoulder on the webbing sling and took out a knife. He worked quickly at the bindings, then stood back. "It's your lucky day, sunshine," he said, his accent part Fijian, but mostly London. "We look after our own."

31

London

Detective Inspector Thorpe pressed the intercom beside the smoked glass door of the *Inventa Institute* and stood back to wait while DS Rogers did his best to finish off a cigarette. The institute was a freelance forensic science laboratory that did all the Metropolitan Police Service's scenes of crime work in nine of the London Boroughs. The institute pulled in some of the brightest minds in criminal forensic science and were well-funded, but benefited from a healthy financial stream of private work, which in turn, gave the police access to the best forensic personnel and resources in the country.

They were buzzed in and greeted midway by a young female technician and shown to Mills' office. The technician offered them coffee, which Thorpe declined on their behalf and left them alone.

"A coffee would have been nice..." Rogers commented dejectedly.

"You don't want to drink in places like this," she said seriously. "They cut up bodies and handle dangerous substances all day long." She paused. "Christ knows what they've got that apprentice working on…"

Rogers looked around the sparse office, thought about the clinically clean and minimalist surroundings he'd seen so far. He had been warned that DI Thorpe had her idiosyncrasies when he had joined the team. Downright bonkers, had been an experienced detective constable's assessment and veiled warning. But she got things done and had the highest murder solve rate in the borough. Perhaps even in the entire Met, which was why he had asked and pushed for the transfer. He'd called in a few favours and paid some forward, too.

"Cause of death is simple," said Mills walking in behind them. She made her way around the desk and sat down. "No need to chat across the body from one another like in some TV crime drama. I have a complete recording of both the procedure and my findings. Two bullets did the deed, each one would have done it sooner or later, but together they set things in place for a swift demise. Soft-nosed hollow points, rather messy inside. A minute, probably not much more." She paused. "Coffee?"

"No. Thanks," DI Thorpe said quickly.

"The third shot wouldn't have killed him if it hadn't been for the other two. Well, not unless it went untreated. In a warzone he would have been classed as walking injured and sent back in a truck instead of a helicopter." She paused. "The bullet was a nine-millimetre Makarov. That's the name of the calibre, and likely the make of the weapon which killed him."

"So, a Russian connection?" DS Rogers asked.

"The victim's clothing was largely purchased in the UK, but his jacket was Russian, as were his socks, of all things." She paused. "His dentistry was undoubtedly Russian, or former Soviet Union. As was a pin in his right, upper femur. Quite a severe fracture, by the looks of it. And his weapon was undoubtedly manufactured in Russia, or more accurately, the former Soviet Union. The ammunition was Czech. Former Czechoslovakia from Sellier and Bellot, now owned by a Brazilian company, called CBC," she said, looking at a piece of notepaper in her hand for confirmation. "*Companhia Brasileira de Cartuchos*. But in this case, I would conclude that it was ammunition manufactured in the mid to late eighties."

"How do you know that?" asked DI Thorpe.

"They cleaned up their act, changed the formula. A little less smoke, a little more whizz. Most manufacturers have tweaked things in the past ten years as well. Rather like vehicle emissions."

"A Russian mafia killing?" DS Rogers ventured.

DI Thorpe turned to him and said, "That would be for us to find out. Ms Mills here gives us the forensic evidence and we make the connections."

"Ma'am…"

Victoria Mills shrugged. "You'll want to know about his phone, then?"

DI Thorpe stared at her intently and said, "You've opened it?"

Mills nodded, picking up an envelope and handing it to her. "That's what I pulled off it. We run a whisper programme that coverts it to a Word document, so all the files are threads of texts and missed calls, made calls, and received calls. There's not much, to be fair. He had a limited address book, but most of the numbers are from Russian accounts. I've taken off the pin codes and account numbers for you to approach his service provider." She looked at her notes, then said, "MegaFon. Some Russian outfit, so good luck getting the info you need."

"Great work," said Thorpe, still looking at the file.

"Thanks," Mills replied, wishing she hadn't. She made a note to be more aloof in her new role. Her predecessor had told her to watch out for senior detectives. To be the link they needed between discovering the evidence and solving the case. "His weapon troubles me. I haven't seen the like of it before…"

"The silencer?" Thorpe ventured.

"Suppressor. And no." Mills paused. "There were no serial numbers on it, so I went on the internet to see where the standard stamps are for a Makarov pistol. There should be one on the frame, one on the slide, one on the butt plate under the left grip and one on the base of the barrel where it is fixed to the frame."

"And?" Thorpe asked, somewhat tersely.

"Nothing. Now, it is common practice for criminals to file off the serial numbers, so I treated the areas to a thorough clean and degreasing, used acid and chemical reagents compatible with the two different metal compositions and went under the microscope," she said, looking at both of them. "Nothing. Not a trace. This weapon left the Baikal plant in Russia, a company contracted to make the weapon by the former Soviet Union, having never been stamped."

"Stolen?" Rogers asked. "Wouldn't be the first time a factory worker took his work home with him."

"Possibly. But for my money, I'd say it was a special requisition. Not only are there no serial numbers, but there is no maker's stamp, either. I'd say the KGB had a hand in it."

"So, he was possibly a spook…" Thorpe said quietly. She looked at Mills and asked, "Is that all in the report?"

"All of it. My findings in their entirety."

"And photographs post-mortem of the victim?"

"Yes. And a mpeg of the autopsy, along with the link to view it." Mills paused. "There is one thing. I'll tell you now to avoid sitting on it until you discover it in the file. One of the numbers called on the phone was to a line in the Russian embassy. It was the last number the man dialled."

Thorpe smiled. "Thank you." She turned to Rogers and said, "Come on, Dave. Fancy a trip to Kensington Palace Gardens?"

32

Russia

Big Dave pulled the Toyota Landcruiser into the forest track, bounced the vehicle over the rutted track and turned around in a small clearing, bringing the 4x4 back facing the way he'd driven in. He switched off the engine and opened his window. The forest was silent. Well-spaced birch and pine trees, a flat forest floor of mulched leaves and pine needles, the occasional break in symmetry made by fallen trees at forty-five-degree angles, held in place by its neighbour.

"Why are we here?" Sasha looked worried, he was clutching a wet cloth and had been alternating it between his burned cheek and nipple. He had the look of a man who had been worn down and feared he would never recover. He stared at Big Dave and said, "You're going to kill me, aren't you?"

"I saved you, dickhead. If I wanted you dead, I'd have just left you there."

"Yes, but you could just have wanted to stop me talking, to stop me from revealing my contact..."

Big Dave opened the glovebox, Sasha's eyes transfixed on it as the lid dropped. He took out two wrapped subs and handed one to Sasha. "Ham and cheese, but you Russians don't make either taste good..." He unwrapped his sandwich and took a bite. "There's a shift change at fourteen hundred. The border guards coming on duty are alert and the ones leaving for the day can't wait to be done. They're the ones we want."

"What about the Finnish side?"

"We'll worry about that later."

"Right..."

"Shut up and eat your sandwich."

Sasha nodded, took the smallest bite to humour him, but chewed unenthusiastically. "Where are you taking me?"

"I have a passport for you under an assumed name. It won't cut the mustard on this side, but in Finland it shouldn't be a problem. Another couple of hours and we'll be at the airport. Five or six more and we'll be in London."

"What then?" Sasha finished chewing but wasn't in a hurry to take another mouthful. "What will happen to me then?"

Big Dave shrugged. "That's above my paygrade. But brace yourself for a month or so of interviews."

"Interrogations?" Sasha shook his head. "No!"

"Chill out..." Big Dave took another mouthful and chewed a few times before swallowing. "Interviews. With coffee, in a nice, comfy safehouse. After that, you'll get a place, a small bounty and a new identity." He paused. "Relax, you're on easy street now."

"Oh..."

"Are you eating that?"

Sasha looked down at the sandwich, then up at the man-mountain beside him. "No, you can have it."

Big Dave nodded, took it out of his hand and started on it like he hadn't eaten in days. He glanced at his watch and said, "Right, let's get on with it." He paused, opening his door. "Come on..." Big Dave closed the door behind him and opened the rear door. "Open yours as well." Sasha did so, and Big Dave pointed at the rear footwell. "Get yourself in there. Lie down and tuck your limbs in."

Sasha did as he was told, but he did so slowly, as if it was the last thing he would do. A prisoner to the gallows. Big Dave waited for him to get comfortable, then he pulled the base of the seats forwards and tipped the seatbacks until they rested flat. He closed the door and walked around the vehicle. Sasha was barely visible, and when he closed the offside rear door and peered inside, he couldn't see him at all. He opened the rear hatch and spread the contents of the boot and his own sports bag forwards, then turned and walked into the woods thirty paces or so and lifted the edge of some camouflaged netting to reveal five crates of vodka. He carried them one at a time back to the vehicle and placed them down in the boot, reassuring Sasha to remain calm and still each time. Next, he took the silenced Uzi machine pistol, ejected the magazine, and cleared the chambered 9mm round. He placed the weapon, spare magazine, and loose round into a plastic bag, double tied it and walked back to the camouflaged netting and tucked it underneath. He had made a record of the coordinates on his mobile phone and would tell Ramsay to notify the Russia Desk when he returned. A weapon cache like this could prove invaluable in future UK intelligence operations.

Back inside the Landcruiser, Big Dave checked behind him. He could make out Sasha's form from this angle, so reached behind him and pulled his coat down over him. He tucked it into the gap, then started the engine and eased the vehicle out of the clearing and back onto the track. As they re-joined the road, Big Dave checked his watch and said, "Right on time." He paused. "If you need a cough, sneeze or a fart, now's the time, sunshine."

The border crossing town of Vaalimaa was intersected by the European Route E18, which cut through Finland, Sweden, Norway, England, Scotland and Northern Ireland – although there was no longer the promise of a direct link as Norway to England no longer had a direct car ferry route. But the idea had been nice. Big Dave checked his watch again as he joined the end of the queue of traffic. The line pulled forward a car length every thirty or forty seconds, which was an encouraging sign. As Big Dave neared the first guard, he lowered his window just a touch. He had found that the colour of his skin singled him out in Russia and Eastern Europe. There were one hundred and forty-five million people in Russia, and only fifty thousand black people. Not even half a percent. But perhaps today it would work in his favour. He checked his watch. Right on time. Ten minutes until the Russian Border Control shift change.

Big Dave took out his passport and visa. The guard was smoking, had a modern AK12 assault rifle slung over his shoulder and looked thoroughly bored. Big Dave smiled, big white teeth beaming. The guard stared at him, then waved him to the side where an oxbow layby was located to single out vehicles and keep the queue rolling. The guard tapped the window, then took a long drag on his cigarette. He said something, but Big Dave shrugged, handed him his passport and travel visa, and said, "I'm going back to Helsinki." He paused. "Just done a vodka run."

"Vodka?"

"Yeah, mate. It's so cheap here. No wonder everybody's pissed."

"Pissed?"

"Hammered."

"What is hammered?"

Big Dave grinned. "Drunk."

"You think we are all drunk?"

"You must be to sell it off this cheaply."

"You are carrying more than a litre?"

"I'd say."

The guard peered in through the window, saw the crates stacked in the back and shook his head. "No, you cannot take…"

"Would you like one?"

"What?"

"Well, I didn't know I couldn't take it through. I haven't exactly hidden them, have I?"

"And you are offering me a bribe?"

"Not a bribe. But I do need to get on a flight and Finland is in the EU, so when I fly back to Britain, I can take the lot back with me. I don't want to miss my flight, but I don't need everything I bought, either. I got carried away because of the price." Big Dave looked at his watch, noticed the guard looking at his own. "My flight is in two hours."

"I need to search your vehicle."

"Really? You must have friends who'd all like a bottle of vodka. Why don't you just help yourself to a case and allow me to get on my way and make my flight?"

"Your flight?"

"Yes."

"You are smuggling alcohol."

"Not on this side," Big Dave said amiably. "Looks like this is going to be a lot of paperwork for a few lousy crates of vodka. Do you have long left in your shift?" The guard stared at him for a moment before ordering him to open the rear door. Big Dave got out slowly, towering above the guard. He walked around the vehicle and opened the rear door hatch. He looked at the man and smiled, "I'm sure your friends would like a bottle each, take a case and I'll be on my way. Like I said, I got carried away when I saw the price."

"What was the purpose of your trip?"

"I've been working in Sweden and Finland. I work as a rigger in the oil business. I was so close, it seemed stupid not coming over and seeing St. Petersburg, even if it was just for a couple of days. I mean, I can say now that I have been to Russia..."

"You like my country?"

"Oh, hell yeah!" He paused. "I can't wait to come back, sometime." He looked at his watch. The shift change was in less than ten minutes. He pulled a case over and opened it. The bottles nestled in between a cardboard grid two by three. "It's good stuff," he said.

The guard stared at it and then looked around him before looking back at Big Dave. "The limit is one litre..."

Big Dave nodded. "So, you'll need to write up a report, give me a customs receipt and take possession, put it into storage." He shrugged. "My bad, I should have checked. Well, I guess I'm going to miss my flight now. Your shift just got longer as well. Unless…"

"Unless, what?"

Big Dave said, "I need to get going. I'm going to miss check in at this rate. I guess I don't need a receipt or anything, if that saves you writing a report, too."

The guard looked past Big Dave and signalled for his colleague. Big Dave tensed, his adrenalin pumping. He was all out of options, other than dropping the two men and running for the woods. He wouldn't get far if they got a chopper in the air, but he had a weapon nearby and if he could get to a car…

The two guards conversed quickly and conspiratorially, then the new arrival started unloading the crates. The first guard took a bottle out and handed it to Big Dave. "The Finnish guards will make it difficult for us if you are found on the other side of the border with illegal contraband," he said. "Now, go. We don't want you missing your flight…"

33

Cornwall

King crossed the police cordon and identified himself to the young, uniformed police constable standing guard at his house. He noted the man wasn't armed with anything more than a taser and a retractable baton known as an asp. He could see that the police had dusted for prints, but he doubted they'd get anything. Both he and Caroline had touched everything a thousand times, and Cole's fingerprints wouldn't show up on the PNC. He checked the kitchen drawer where they kept all the junk they'd probably never need. Batteries of indeterminable life, old mobile phones, and loose euros that they always forgot to take with them. The Walther PPK was in there, too. He picked it up and could see from the indicator pin in the hammer assembly, located above the firing pin was out. This let the user know a bullet was chambered. King often wondered why the feature did not appear on more weapons, but he dropped the magazine and checked it was fully loaded, before checking on the live round in the breech. He tucked it into his jacket pocket and walked out into the hallway where he checked inside the hall table drawer. His crudely customised snub-nosed .38 was still there. He had sawn off the fore sight, removed the rear sight, and welded a guttersnipe channel in place. A simple grove to line up on the target. He had also sawn off the thumb grip of the hammer so that it wouldn't snag when he drew it from his pocket. The sights, barrel length and trigger pull meant that the weapon was only good for twenty-five metres, but he doubted he'd ever use it from any further away than ten feet. He pocketed it, planning to leave it in his vehicle as a go-to piece.

Upstairs, King took a shower. He ran it as hot as it would go, soaped up and let the hot water sooth the aches and pains he found he lived with near constantly. He had pushed his body further than most, punished himself to get the job done and survive. When he had rinsed off the soap and shampoo, he dialled the shower down to the coldest setting and let the icy water play over his neck and shoulders, heightening his senses and driving thoughts of sleep out of him completely. He towelled off quickly then put on some clean clothes before heading downstairs. Caroline's bag was still on the kitchen table where she had left it, and he looked around the place, knowing he'd likely never come back. He had an enemy to face, but he had been compromised. He had started to live comfortably, just like normal working people, and there was no room for that luxury in the job he and Caroline did. It was time to face the fact that he needed to keep moving. He had tried to put down roots, but they had been uprooted by a storm. He closed his eyes and thought about Peter Stewart and their mantra as they faced overwhelming odds in some of the poorest, least hospitable, and deadliest places on earth.

Fate whispers to the warrior, "You cannot withstand the storm…"

And the warrior whispers back, "I am the storm…"

34

The Russian Embassy
London

"I said, I wish to talk to the Ambassador…" DI Thorpe held her warrant card out for the guard, but he remained wholly unimpressed.

"You will need an appointment," he replied. "But if you are here on police business, you will have to go through the proper channels." He smirked. "The Ambassador has diplomatic immunity, and I suspect the proper channels will not involve you. Why should he speak to a detective inspector? This is a lowly rank in this country, no?"

Thorpe gnawed at the inside of her cheek, something she did when she needed to resist saying or doing something that she would later regret. In this case it was punching the man square in the face, but she'd been around the block enough to know that would be the start to something she wouldn't necessarily finish. Taking a breath, she said, "It concerns the body of a man I suspect works here." She paused. "So, if the Ambassador isn't the right person to talk to, then it would be in your interest to point me to the appropriate person."

"Who?"

"Forgive me if I say you're probably a bit lowly for even the likes of me to talk to…"

The guard regarded her for a moment, then said, "Wait here."

Thorpe turned to DS Rogers and said, "Can you believe this place? It's like a palace."

Rogers nodded. He had been taking in the polished marble floor, the sculptures and statues, the exquisite paintings. But they had only gotten as far as the desk, and there appeared to be several more to wait at before they would speak to someone other than a security guard.

The guard returned and ushered them to an ornate teak door on their left. "Wait in there, someone will be with you shortly." He turned and looked at the next person in line, as if the presence of two detectives and the mention of a body was nothing to him.

DI Thorpe paced around the room, while DS Rogers checked his phone. After five minutes, Thorpe concentrated on the view outside the bay window and Rogers took a seat and quietly drummed his fingers on the table.

After another ten minutes Rogers took to pacing and Thorpe had caught up with her own phone messages. When the door abruptly opened, both looked up expectantly, but it was only the guard who told them they would not be kept waiting long. Another thirty minutes passed, messages were rechecked, the room was paced some more, and the view became familiar and uninteresting. When the door opened again, a dour-looking woman in her early forties entered and walked to the head of the polished mahogany table without looking at either of them.

"Natalia Orev," she said tiresomely. "How may I help you?"

Thorpe opened the envelope she had been carrying and tossed a ten by twelve glossy photograph in front of her. It was a facial shot, but anyone could clearly see that the man was dead and that he sat this photo session out on a gurney. The woman had barely started to look at it when Thorpe tossed her another. This one was of the victim lying in mud and blood with three bullet holes in him. The next photograph travelled across the polished table like a card dealt from a croupier. Naked on the autopsy table, the three bullet holes cleaned and staring back at them, black and deep and final.

"I'm DI Thorpe, this is DS Rogers, and we have reason to believe that this man is known to you."

Orev stared at the picture, then looked up at her and said, "Why?"

"We believe he is a Russian citizen."

"The Russian Federation is a big country."

"Do you know him?"

"No."

Thorpe nodded. "He was found with a pistol on him. A Russian-made pistol. A nine-millimetre Makarov."

Orev shrugged. "I believe the Makarov was made in several countries during the Soviet Union's rule. Bulgaria, for instance. And Hungary, to name but two. There must have been millions of them made." She paused. "I don't see…"

"This one was without the maker's serial numbers."

Natalia Orev looked at her impassively. "So?"

"Weapons are stamped with serial numbers. All over the world."

"I wouldn't know."

"But you know the name Makarov, and at least three countries where it is or *was* made." Thorpe paused. "An unstamped gun in a country with the Soviet Union's reputation would suggest it was made for clandestine purposes. Like the KGB."

"Well, fortunately, the Soviet Union, and the KGB for that matter, no longer exist." Orev paused. "As for reputation? Well, I find that particularly insulting."

"Just stating a fact."

"You are stating nothing, but a one-side perspective cultivated through Western hate and hypocrisy. An agenda that is as defunct as the Soviet Union. Russia is a peaceful, progressive country."

DI Thorpe shrugged. She wasn't going to push it. That wasn't how productive questioning worked. "But nevertheless, weapons such as these would have been manufactured without serial numbers for special purposes."

"I was only nine at the time the Soviet Union collapsed. So, I fail to see why you think I should know of such things…"

"Sorry, I thought that someone in your position…"

"And what position is that?"

DI Thorpe smiled mirthlessly. "Resident spook, of course. Now, are you FSB or SVR?"

"I am attaché to the British delegation for the Russian Ambassador of the Russian Federation."

"Then this man in the photograph, *he* was your resident spy?"

"We have no such position within the consulate. Russia has no *spies*, as you put it, in the United Kingdom." She slid the photographs across the table towards Thorpe. "This meeting is over. I am sorry that I could not be of any use to your investigation," she said as she stood up.

Thorpe tossed the envelope on top of the photographs and got to her feet. "No, hang on to them, they're your copies," she said amiably, but perhaps a little forced in her delivery. "Seeing as you could not be any help, I'll get some copies sent over to the press and put out an appeal." She walked ahead of Natalia Orev to the door, prompting DS Rogers to push out his chair and bound over to catch her up. "Thank you, Ms Orev, goodbye."

35

Cornwall

King was on the road heading back towards the hospital when Simon Mereweather called. He contemplated leaving it to ring but decided to pick it up, reasoning that Mereweather might have dropped by the hospital and could have news. Not having Bluetooth fitted, he shouldered the phone as best he could and kept an eye out for a layby.

"King?"

"Yes."

"Oh, thank god! I've been trying to get you for ages! Bloody Cornwall and its network signal!" He paused. "There's been an attempt on Caroline's life... don't panic... she's fine! But I needed to tell you, god forbid before you heard it on the news..."

King slammed on the brakes and ran the Land Rover up the considerable grass verge, scraping the side of the vehicle down an unforgiving Cornish stone hedge. "What happened?" he asked, trying to keep his composure and think on how the MI5 mandarin had delivered the news, telling himself to focus on *she's fine…*

"Cole came for her, tried to kill her with a knife."

"Who stopped him? She's not conscious, is she?"

"No. It was Rashid. When he left you, he positioned himself across from the building and waited. He had a hunch. If Cole got away cleanly from the site of Caroline's… er, accident… then he would assume she had been taken to Cornwall's only fully equipped trauma unit. It's the main hospital for injuries such as the ones she sustained. Rashid felt Cole may stake out the site. If he saw you leave, then he would seize his chance."

"The bastard…"

"Cole is a ruthless individual, indeed."

"No, Rashid. He used both Caroline and me as a stalking horse."

"And you wouldn't? Move on," Mereweather replied tersely.

"Where is Rashid now?"

"He bloody well got himself arrested. I'm heading into Truro now to get him out."

"Well, don't hurry…"

"Rashid said that Cole escaped, heading for the carpark. He feels that Cole will head straight to your place, see this thing done."

King glanced behind him in the wingmirror and swung the big off-roader out into the road and into a U-turn. The road was barely wide enough, and he glanced off the hedge, adding to the graze down the side of the vehicle. He didn't even register as he ended the call and dropped the phone onto the passenger seat beside him.

36

There were any number of roads he could have taken to get to the coast southwest of Falmouth on the edge of The Lizard, but Cole had not been comfortable driving on the narrower roads the county had to offer and had learned that the main route was not necessarily the quickest. As he rounded the headland, he could see the old coastguard cottages and two distant farmhouses. He pulled up on the edge of the road and used a pair of binoculars to study the lay of the land. King's Land Rover wasn't there. He could see Caroline's Mini Cooper S on the drive, and it hadn't moved since he was there yesterday morning. He dipped his head as a Range Rover blasted past him taking up most of the road, then continued to watch the area. The Range Rover headed past the entrance to the lane for the coastguard cottages and towards a distant farm. Cole got out of the car and scrambled over the hedge. He dropped down heavily on the other side and checked around him before keeping to the edge of the field and walking until he was adjacent with the cottages. On the hedge bordering the property, a large blackthorn, leaning heavily from a life battling the prevailing winds, provided him with cover. He could see the lone police officer leaning against the cottage. Bored and underprepared, but it was his lucky day. Cole reached up and retrieved the trail camera, then crouched down and replaced the SD card, swapping it for a new one before reattaching it to its clip-on housing, which he had earlier wired to the trunk.

Back inside his car, he took a handful of the ibuprofen he normally used in conjunction with paracetamol and Oramorph – a liquid morphine – to control the pain in his leg. He thought of ibuprofen as M&M's, and exceeded the hourly doses all too regularly, but the pain in his hand was acute and he couldn't wait to get the Oramorph out of his bag when he had more time, but right now, he couldn't imagine there being any time soon.

Cole put the SD card into his laptop and viewed the motion-activated images. Used by wildlife lovers, hunters and ornithologists the world over, the high definition trail camera allowed enthusiasts to capture images and build up knowledge of their chosen animal's movements, and thanks to a high-resolution night vision capability, could work through the night as well as the day.

Cole watched as the Range Rover came back towards him then pulled over and parked close to the grass verge. He looked back through the last actions and saw King leave in the Land Rover. He cursed loudly before winding back further. King had stayed for thirty minutes and left ten minutes before Cole had arrived. He cursed again, removed the SD card, and switched off the laptop. The Range Rover concerned him. If he had been on US soil, he would have thought they were Feds. Government agencies usually used black SUVs like the Chevrolet Suburban. Maybe in the UK they used Range Rovers. It was usually prudent for governments to use domestic makes, and he couldn't think of any apart from premium brands.

King was not here and there was no getting around that. If he remained static, he could become a target himself. He was the hunter and he needed to control his position to avoid becoming the prey. Everything King cared about was lying unconscious in the hospital and that would be the best place to find King again.

37

King took the country roads with abandon. The Land Rover wasn't the best vehicle at handling the bends, but in the right gear he could use the engine's torque to maintain speeds of forty to sixty miles per hour, scraping the hedges and ploughing through the gaps left by terrified oncoming drivers. Most of the time he used third gear and the high revs gave him good engine braking as well. By the time he reached the cliff road, the vehicle was smelling hot and the brakes were starting to fade.

King slammed the vehicle to a halt on the side of the road and studied the property. He could see a black SUV parked between the two cottages. The other cottage was under refurbishment, their plan was to let the place for an extra income, but he couldn't imagine a day when he would allow normality and the outside world to come so close to them again. He reached under his seat and retrieved a pair of binoculars and took a closer look. He could not see the police officer who had been standing guard. King continued to watch, and saw a man skirting the cottage carrying a weapon. He adjusted the magnification, losing the wide angle he preferred, and identified the weapon as a silenced pistol. There could be no mistaking the crime underworld or hostile intelligence services connotations of such a weapon. He took out his mobile phone and went through the camera footage. In the last action, he could see his own vehicle from the camera he had mounted to cover the entrance to the property. He used the scroll function, saw the vehicle – a black Range Rover – drive slowly up the lane. The young police officer approached the vehicle, then stood back with his hands raised above his head. A man stepped out of the Range Rover, a pistol in his hand aiming at the young officer. Another man got out and walked around the vehicle. Between them, they marched the police officer towards the cottage. King cursed, knowing he now had a hostage situation to contend with. He scrolled on through the film, changed the cameras and saw a blue saloon parked in the same place he was. He watched, saw Cole and his stomach tightened. He scrolled on, Cole went out of frame, returned ten minutes later. The timer showed him turning and driving away. He took a screenshot of the best image and sent it to Neil Ramsay with a short text. If anyone could get a clear image of the numberplate it was him.

King checked the .45. He had only just checked the Walther, which he slipped into his back pocket. The .38 revolver was in the door pocket, but he removed it and put it in his jacket's inside pocket, because he had plans for the Land Rover and leaving the weapon in it was pointless. Besides, you could never have enough weapons or ammunition in a gun battle. He drove slowly onwards, then stopped short of the entrance and got out. He used his knife to cut a thick piece of sycamore which was sprouting five-feet high from the hedge. He trimmed the thickest part, then tested it as he got back inside the vehicle. He trimmed some more until he was satisfied with the result, then folded and pocketed the knife, took a deep breath, and drove into the lane.

King thought of Peter Stewart, his mentor, the man who shaped him and made this life for him. For good or bad, for right or wrong. The man's mantra echoed in his mind as he tucked the .45 into his waistband. *Fate whispers to the warrior, 'You cannot withstand the storm…' And the warrior whispers back, 'I am the storm…'*

"And then some," King said out loud, flooring the accelerator. "And then some…"

The Land Rover lurched up the lane and King shifted into second and almost immediately into third. He floored the accelerator, shifted his left foot over as far as it would go and pressed the length of sycamore onto the accelerator and jammed the other end into the bolster of the seat. The vehicle was building speed slowly, the low rev-building diesel producing enough torque to refrain from stalling but climb steadily. King opened the door and leapt out onto the grass verge, rolling away with momentum and coming to rest in the hedge. The .45 had come loose, and he picked it up giving the muzzle a cursory glance to see if it had been plugged with mud. He watched the Land Rover gain in speed, heading directly for the cottage. The man with the silenced pistol ran out from behind the cottage and watched the oncoming vehicle. For a moment he looked unsure what to do next – head inside the house or run for cover – and while he was trying to decide, King aimed and fired once, and the man went down. A solid shot, centre mass from seventy metres away. King ran along the hedge, waiting to see what happened next. He got his answer almost immediately when two men bundled out of the house, weapons raised and started to fire at the Land Rover. King could see the pistols, and above the noise of the vehicle's tyres on gravel, he heard nothing, but could see the muzzle flashes and hear the bullets striking metal and glass. One of the men ducked to his left, right into King's path. King stopped running and fired. The man spun like a top and hit the ground. He was crawling away when King drew near. He fired into the back of the man's neck and ducked behind a wall as the Land Rover smashed into the house and kept going. The front of the vehicle rose high in the air and hammered back down, a section of wall falling inwards and the large bay window smashing with the force.

King aimed at the other man and fired but he missed, and the man turned and fired several shots in return. Chips of stone fragments and earth flew into King's face, the impacts making more noise than the silenced weapon. King fired a double tap and the man screamed out as he made it to the edge of the cottage and disappeared from his line of sight. King was down to just one round, so he tucked the weapon into his waistband and took out the .38. It had the power advantage over the Walther, and he was close enough to use it. He decided against entering the cottage, choosing to head off the wounded man by running down the side of the cottage into a belt of ash and oak trees that provided the house with protection from the wind off the sea. King had great cover, and he threaded through the trees and out into the rear garden, which was home to three large conifers that had grown too big. He hadn't had time to fell them and free up the land, but right now the cover they provided was invaluable. King used them to his advantage, edging cautiously closer to the building, crouching low with the pistol in front of him. As he reached the extremities of the cover the conifer provided, he saw the man hunched over holding his side, his weapon shaking in front of him. King crept forwards. There were only a few paces between them when he rushed out and smashed the butt of the revolver on the top of the man's head. The man fell forwards, poleaxed. King pulled him backwards by his ankles, back into the cover of the conifers. Working quickly and expertly, he unbuckled the man's belt and looped it back through the buckle. He pulled both ankles back towards the man's backside, looped the belt over them and tied the other end into a slip knot. He looped the man's wrists in the noose and when King stepped away, both loops pulled tightly together as the man's legs relaxed. He was completely incapacitated. Hog-tied. King just hoped the blow to the head, or the graze of the bullet wouldn't kill him before he had the chance to question him.

King could see the Range Rover parked between the buildings and he used the cover of the second cottage to come around on it from the other side. He checked cautiously, the rear tinted windows making the task difficult, but the vehicle was locked and unoccupied. He skirted the vehicle and picked up a silenced Makarov next to one of the bodies, checking it as he backed away into the lee of the building. He had no idea of the numbers he was facing, but the Range Rover could comfortably seat five and it was possible they could have had a couple more men in the loading bay. He checked the weapon over but decided to leave it be. He had no idea whether it was reliable and it only contained a few rounds – none of them compatible with his own weapons. He was way past needing silence now.

Naturally, King knew the property well. And that gave him the advantage. But clearing a building required logistics and time. Anybody taking up a defensive position – especially someone experienced – would choose to have a height advantage. Laying on their stomach with a weapon aimed through the spindles of the stair banisters, their sights aimed at the hallway, King would have little hope. But he had an advantage of his own. The Land Rover had grounded, and irresistible force had met an immovable object, but the engine was still howling at maximum revs and the wheels were still turning, all four wheels spinning for purchase. The overworked diesel engine was loud, and there was a huge amount of smoke coming from the exhaust pipe and from underneath the engine. King could smell oil and fuel and heat. He looked at the side of the building and tucked the revolver into his pocket. Sprinting forwards, he leapt and grabbed the drainpipe and started to climb, his desert boots gripping on the granite stonework, and the metal downpipe taking his weight. King trained daily and regularly performed pull-ups for upper body strength and endurance, making it easier for him to pull himself up onto the roof, but it was still difficult and he scrabbled his feet for grip before eventually getting up onto his knees and steadying himself on the roof. He knew the layout below him, so tentatively walked across the roof until he was above the spare bedroom. King had repaired the roof, so he knew exactly where the roof joists were, and he dug his fingers under a tile and pulled it upwards, working the tiny roofing nails out. Once he had the first tile removed, he was able to easily remove enough to create a hole large enough for him to get through. He tore the underfelt, and pushed the insulation into the attic space, before taking out the revolver and easing himself down into the darkness.

King could hear the hum of the Land Rover all around him. From outside, and through the house. He wondered whether whoever else was in here had heard the change in pitch when he removed the roof tiles, but it was too late to worry about things out of his control. King used the torch on his phone to get into the right position. The house had been fitted with what Caroline had described as ghastly doors, and instead of burning them, King had spread them out across the beams of the attic to make a cheap temporary flooring. He removed one of the doors and propped it up against a roof truss, then switched off the torch and pocketed his phone. He checked the Walther was secure in his pocket, then took a breath and readied himself.

At a shade under six-foot and fourteen stone, King was the build of a light-heavyweight boxer. Powerful and fit, he was used to putting his body through its paces. He knew the distance to drop would be just under seven feet, because he had installed the six-feet-six-inch doorframe. He stood on a beam and pressed his right foot on the plasterboard he could feel it give a little. King then stamped hard and the plasterboard spilt. He leapt in the air and put both feet together landing in the middle of the cracked plasterboard. The drop was over in a second, but even still, his stomach felt like it was in his throat. He landed heavily, but kept on his feet, darted for the door, and opened it, raising the revolver, and looking down the guttersnipe sight. As he'd predicted, the man was lying prone and as he looked behind him, clearly shocked at King's entrance, the silenced pistol came round with him. King fired twice and both .38 bullets struck him between the shoulder blades. King stepped forwards and kicked the weapon away. The man was dying, and King knew from the rattle that it would not take long. But he was no longer a threat, so King ignored him and cleared the other bedroom and the bathroom. He stepped over the dying man and headed tentatively downstairs, then checked the lounge. The police officer's body lay motionless on the floor. He had been shot in the back of the head. there was no point in checking for vital signs, the man was clearly dead. King checked the study, and the kitchen. There was nowhere else to search, and he tested the back door, which was still locked.

King headed outside and walked around the Land Rover. He reached in through the window and switched off the engine. The silence was absolute, the noise of the high-revving engine and struggling wheels cancelled out by the isolation of the property. King's adrenalin was subsiding, and he could feel a wave of exhaustion washing through him. The sky was blue and largely clear and what clouds there were, were white and scudding quickly at high altitude. The distant glimmer of the sea made the day seem fresh and new and fitting with how King felt, emerging from battle with that familiar feeling of emptiness he had learned to live with, and what should have been the euphoria of survival, quelled by what that victory had entailed. As usual, instead of elation, he merely felt numb.

Behind him, stepping cautiously, though transfixed on his target, a fifth man emerged from the undergrowth, his pistol raised and held steady between both hands.

"You are the man they call King," he said somewhat triumphantly. "No! Do not move!" He snapped as King had started to turn. "Drop the gun, you bastard!"

"Who are you?" King asked, tossing the revolver onto the ground. He had already weighed his options, and they weren't great. The Colt .45 was in his waistband and he only had the one shot. The Walther was in his jacket pocket, and there was no way he'd make the draw. "I'm guessing from the accent, you're a Romanovitch? You guys weren't professional enough for FSB or the SVR."

"My name is Uri Andropov, and I work for the brotherhood, yes. And as for professional? Well, I'd rather be me than you, right now."

"Fair enough…"

"And now I will show you how it ends for people who think they can cross us." He stepped closer, taking care not to lose his footing on the three slate steps down to the driveway. "It won't be quick," he said. "But you already knew that, right?"

"I figured I'd have to hear you drone on about all kinds of bullshit, that's all I'm worried about…"

King heard the whizz and impact of the bullet, the sound of the crack a split second later and the distant rumble a second after that. He turned around and looked at the man on the ground. The bullet had struck him dead centre. Where the ribs met the sternum. His eyes were open and staring up at King, and he blinked and tried to swallow as the blood flooded across his chest. He had dropped the pistol but wouldn't be capable of reaching for it. King looked down the lane and saw a figure with a rifle heading his way on foot. He smiled, then looked back at Uri dying on the ground, the tables turned, and new ending written for him. "And now you know how it ends for people who think they can cross *us*…" said King, the moment before the man died and his eyes glazed over.

"Saved your arse again," said Rashid as he reached the driveway, the M4 rifle cradled in his hands.

"I had it covered," he replied sardonically. "Thanks for what you did at the hospital," he added. "But I'm not sure whether you saved Caroline or used her for bait."

Rashid shrugged. "A bit of both, maybe."

King nodded. He wasn't enthralled, but there was no denying the man had just bailed him out. "We'd better take a good look around, check it's clear this time."

"No doubt." Rashid nodded towards the cottage and the wreckage of the land Rover. "I like what you've done to the place…"

"It's purely cosmetic…" King was cut short as a section of granite wall dropped and crushed the bonnet of the Land Rover. "Slap of plaster here and there…"

"You don't do good handiwork." Rashid took out his mobile and dialled, then said. "It's okay, bring the car up…"

"I think my days of DIY are done," he paused. "Who were you speaking to?"

"Mereweather. He bailed me out, so to speak, and drove me straight here."

"He's going to shit the bed when he sees all this," said King, watching the black Jaguar saloon coming towards them.

"Got any answers for him?" Rashid shrugged. "You know, when there's a shootout like this in the UK, it's kinda good to have an idea of what the hell was going on."

King grinned and said, "I took it easy on a guy. He's tied up out the back. I think we should go and have a chat with him."

Rashid nodded. "Definitely..."

38

London

Detective Inspector Thorpe looked up from her desk, a sea of papers in front of her and her computer logged onto the Police National Computer system. DS Rogers stood in the doorway, his face ashen and a new stain down the front of his shirt. He had a bacon roll in his hand, and HP Sauce had trickled out over his knuckles.

"The big guns are here," he said.

"Colby?"

"Chief Superintendent Colby is straightening his tie and checking his nose hair for this one," he said, saw her frown and decided there was nothing to be gained by being cryptic. He hadn't worked with DI Thorpe for long but had learned to his cost that she was bluntly direct and couldn't abide beating around the bush. "The Chief Constable is on his way over with someone from the Russian embassy. I think Colby is shitting bricks."

"That uptight lying FSB bitch. She knew more than she let on, and now she's got the top brass on it. Just wait until I see her…"

"No, she's not part of the posse. I think they're a bit higher up than her." He paused, shaking his head. "Well, he is. It's the Ambassador."

Thorpe frowned. "Okay…"

"Want me to come with you?"

"What, to hold my hand?" She snapped. "Actually, yeah, you can see how politics gets in the way of justice. Better you learn now, early on in your detective career."

"Cease and desist?"

"If the Chief Constable is coming over with the Russian Ambassador, then you can count on it." She logged out of the PNC and walked past DS Rogers and across the CID office suite with Rogers following somewhat begrudgingly. He clearly hadn't been planning on making waves so soon, just two months into the job. CID was an upwards career move for him, having come from beat policing to armed response, then working for four years in traffic. His heart had always been in investigations, and although he had worked on many during his career, being in dedicated detective work was where he wanted to be. He had targeted DI Thorpe for her reputation, but that tenacity clearly had its drawbacks. One of them being a political upset and a visit from the highest authority.

Chief Superintendent Colby was hovering outside the family suite and looking at them earnestly. DI Thorpe turned to Rogers and said, "Brace yourself."

"What for?" he whispered.

"Grabbing your ankles and taking it right up your arse. Best not to resist at this stage." She looked back at Colby and gave a little mock salute. "Hello boss…"

"Oh, you've really done it now, DI Thorpe."

"It was Sally-Anne not so long ago." She paused. "How's your wife?"

Colby flushed red, glanced at DS Rogers before looking back at Thorpe and shepherding her over to the desk and away from Rogers. "Do you have to be so indiscreet?" he whispered.

"I don't remember signing anything."

"Sally-Anne…"

"Well that's a little more like it. Back me up, Clive. Don't screw me in there. You don't do that anymore, remember?" She stared at him and said, "What am I facing?"

"Just apologise for your attitude," he whispered. "Apologise to the Russians and swear to God you're not going to go to the papers and most of all, accept whatever shit the Chief Constable gives you."

"I already briefed my partner on the dry buggery that's about to ensue."

Colby pulled a face. "You don't need to drag your subordinate into this," he said. "He's shadowing you for experience and fetching your coffee." He looked over Thorpe's shoulder at DS Rogers and said, "On your way, Sergeant." DS Rogers shook his head, looking at DI Thorpe. "I said, on your way! That's an order!" Colby raged.

"It's alright, Mark," she assured him. "Get on with checking the CCTV around the murder site."

"You will not, DS Rogers." Colby paused. "Check your backlog and leave this case alone, for now."

Thorpe watched Rogers go, shaking his head and punching the double doors open ahead of him. "So, how bad is it?" she asked, still watching Rogers at the end of the corridor.

"I'm going into bat for you," he replied. "But the Russians have this at Downing Street level, and they're not happy about you threatening to take the photographs to the papers."

"I'm just trying to do my job, Clive." She turned around and knocked twice on the door before entering. "And I'll never apologise for that."

39

"I'm going to use up a lot of favours on this," Simon Mereweather said as he surveyed the scene. "The bastards killed a police officer," he said quietly, the image of the young officer shot execution style and lying in King's lounge would be with him forever. "And Cole killed both the armed guards at the hospital. Do you know the last time a police officer was killed by someone down here? Other than on the roads. No? Nineteen-seventy-three. Shot trying to make an arrest. That's what the Chief Constable told me upon hearing two of his officers had been murdered. Beaten to death. Now there's another officer lying dead in your lounge. Christ only knows what I can do amongst the backdrop of this lot."

"Give the credit to the police and commend them for a job well-done," King replied. "I can see the headlines... Russian organised crime gang halted in their tracks by a team of crack anti-terrorism police... Months of surveillance and intelligence gathering... another blow to Russian Federation sponsored interference..." He paused. "Like I said at the end of summer, don't apologise, and show the world that MI5 won't be crossed."

"Easier said than done, politically."

"Screw them," Rashid said sharply. He waved a hand around the scene of carnage. "We show the world that if you bring it, we'll finish it."

Mereweather shook his head. "Like I said, easier said than done. The police will want specifics. Like why an MI5 agent was carrying a weapon on UK soil."

"So that I don't get shot..." King replied glibly. He shrugged. "Seal it. Silence the police and silence the press. Keep it ongoing, be evasive, give them something else they can get their teeth into. This time next year, it will all be forgotten, or they just won't care anymore." King walked on down the side of the building and stopped when he reached the hog-tied Russian. He bent down and removed the belt. The man groaned. King rolled him over. "Let's start with the simple stuff," he said. "Who do you work for?"

The man looked like he was drunk. He had trouble focusing and was trying to swallow, like his mouth was dry. "Get fucked..."

King nodded, looked at Mereweather and said, "Go and get a glass of water. A large one."

Simon Mereweather frowned and replied, "What are you going to do?"

"Just get a bloody glass of water!" he snapped. He watched the deputy director of the Security Service walk away briskly, then looked down at the man. "I know that the man heading the Romanovitch brotherhood sent you here." He paused. "He has come out of retirement, now that both Romanovitch sons have been killed."

"Then why ask me?" the man replied, wincing, and struggling for breath.

"It's a start," said King.

"I don't snitch."

"You're dying, pal," said King, looking at the blood on the ground and the amount on the man's shirt. "Got any family?"

"What's it to you?"

King shrugged as Mereweather returned with a large glass of water. King took it from him, placed it on the ground just out of reach of the man.

"What the hell are you going to do with that?" Mereweather asked. "Are you going to waterboard him? We can't torture him, I won't allow it."

King ignored him, looked at the man and said, "The blood is black. I got your liver. It was a forty-five hollow-point. So, basically, you're in the shit." He paused. "My boss here has already called an ambulance, when he fetched the water…" He glanced at Mereweather, who looked away uncomfortably. "He's not a field man, hasn't seen what we've seen, doesn't know what you're feeling. I've been shot a few times…" He pulled up his shirt and showed the man the scars. Mereweather stared at him, mouth agape. King had been shot in the stomach and had bled internally, and surgeons had to do a lot of work inside to staunch the bleed. It looked as if a shark had taken a bite of his entire torso and changed its mind. "You're feeling like you would kill your own mother for a drink, aren't you?" The man nodded reluctantly. "Tell me what you know, and you can have the drink and we'll let you die in peace."

Mereweather glanced at his watch and looked down the lane towards the coast road.

"The American said he'd kill you for us… for the honour of the brotherhood, but he wanted you dead anyway." The man clenched his teeth together. "Just a sip…" he said pleadingly.

King shook his head. "Keep going."

"Romanovitch paid, but only to keep the American off guard. The American killed four of his bodyguards when he and Romanovitch had some sort of disagreement. He ordered Uri to kill both you and the black American. Otherwise we would look weak to our rivals."

"Big boy's games..." King smiled. "Big boy's rules..." He paused, then asked, "Where is Cole... the *black* American?"

The man shook his head. "I don't know."

"So, how did you find me? How did you know where I live?"

The man said, "A drink, first. I don't think I have much time..."

King nodded. "Dry as sawdust, eh? How did you know?"

"Romanovitch has friends, spies in Russia. The FSB or the SVR, I don't know which."

"But they could only know things if they..." Mereweather trailed off, the colour draining from his cheeks.

"Had someone in MI5..." King finished for him. He bent down and handed the man the glass. The man gripped it weakly, but King did not release it. "A name," he demanded. "Give me a name."

The man released his grip, his hand slapping the concrete. "I don't know. Uri didn't even know." He paused, taking a shallow breath. "I'm not important enough."

King bent down and placed the water beside him. The man took it gratefully and drank thirstily. As he swallowed, the blood oozed out of the wound. The man didn't seem to notice, but King guessed his bullet had clipped the man's stomach, too. He stood up, hearing sirens in the distance.

"Will he make it?" asked Mereweather.

"No. He's done." King patted the man's pockets, again he barely noticed, then King turned around and checked the bodies in front of the house. He found the keys for the Range Rover and looked at Rashid. "I'm heading for the hospital. For all I know, Cole is already headed back there. Are you coming?"

Rashid shrugged. "Got nothing else on…"

"What about this place?" Simon Mereweather.

"Well, you called the ambulance, that's fair," said King. "But did you call the police?"

"Of course," Mereweather replied. "We're accountable."

King nodded. "Well, now I'll guess we'll see if you are prepared to stand firm, take the fight to our country's enemies and become a force to be reckoned with..."

"Or what?"

King tucked the revolver back into his pocket and headed for the Range Rover. As he opened the door, he stared back at the deputy director and said, "Well that depends on you."

40

King drove the Range Rover past the car park and headed towards the maternity wing of the hospital, where he had earlier noticed a row of spaces outside, as well as a crescent of spaces on a small roundabout. He figured expectant mothers and panicked fathers needed a short stay option and he felt some guilt parking the oversized vehicle in one of the spaces. There were police vehicles dotted around the area and two armed officers on the main door. He hoped they would be more than just for show, and that there were other armed officers inside. Rashid had told him that Cole had escaped with one of the officers' weapons, and the thought of what an experienced SEAL with the element of surprise could do with an MP5 and two, thirty-round magazines made him shudder at the thought. Caroline had been lucky that Rashid had been there. But with a determined and skilled assassin as an enemy, a run of luck would only last so long.

"I'll stay here," said Rashid. He had the M4 assault rifle in the footwell, the stock resting against the centre console. "I've had enough run-ins with plod for one day."

King nodded as he got out and closed the door. He knew Rashid would be watching out for Cole, but even he had to admit the likelihood of him trying something again so soon would be slim. King knew he had used Caroline to hurt him, but that element had played out. Surely the man would dispense with the theatricals and come for him now. He had already seen that Cole had returned to his cottage, but that would now be a hotbed of police presence. He wondered whether Simon Mereweather had pulled the national security card or not.

King showed his credentials to the police officers and made his way inside. There were more armed officers patrolling the corridor, but how effective their presence was would be debatable, as medical staff, orderlies and cleaning personnel were going about their work freely enough. Two more armed officers guarded the floor and one approached King immediately.

"Mister King? We were informed you were on your way up," the officer said. He asked to see King's card, and when he obliged the officer showed him through and returned to his post.

King didn't do small talk. He was assessing the security as he walked and decided he could have breezed through it with his bare hands. Which was exactly what Cole had done. These armed officers were trained in hard arrest tactics. They weren't soldiers and they lacked the mindset required to secure an area tactically. Simply having a firearm on display was enough to quell ninety-nine percent of British troublemakers, and that was what armed response officers relied upon.

Mr Sinclair was checking a medical record at the nurses' station and looked up when King drew near. He put the clipboard down and walked over to greet him. King presumed the record was Caroline's.

"Are you alright?"

King nodded. "Fine," he replied.

"You've got blood on you," said Sinclair. "And mud, and what looks like oil."

"It's been a rough morning."

"There's a man coming in with a gunshot wound," he said. "His chances aren't rated as survivable. If I were a betting man, I'd say that you were involved."

"And I'd say, you're a surgeon, not a priest."

"Fair enough," Sinclair shrugged. "I need to talk to you," he said, motioning him towards an empty ward. "It's… delicate."

King walked ahead of him, his heart racing. For some reason he thought of Jane and the finality of seeing her on the bed, the note, her stillness. The feeling that he was at the end again, only darkness ahead. "Spit it out," he said, not looking at the consultant, instead staring out the window. There was part of a golf course visible below, and as he watched two golfers pulling their clubs on trolleys, he thought how different peoples' lives were on any given day. The heartbreak in this room right now, the joy of new life in the maternity building across the way, and the pursuit of recreation on the golf course below. The large pine trees and green of the course seemed altogether more inviting to look out on, than to turn and let the man see the sorrow in his eyes. "Please…"

Sinclair sighed. "I don't know if you knew, but I wanted you to know before you risked reading it in her notes," he said quietly. "Caroline lost the baby…"

"The baby?" King turned and looked at him. "She was pregnant?"

"I assumed you knew, I'm sorry." The look on Sinclair's face said it all. The man felt for him, but he also looked like he realised he may have taken a step too far. Caroline's pregnancy, or the loss of it, was her business and hers alone. He had his reasons for telling King, but now he was feeling that perhaps he shouldn't have.

King thought back to yesterday morning in the cottage, the way she had rubbed her stomach. He'd been a fool not to realise, and that was why she had been so annoyed at having to move. No, he thought. Not so much annoyed, as heartbroken. "We were trying," he said distantly.

"I'm not sure if this helps, but it is far more accurate to say she miscarried at this stage. Into the second month."

"Not really. But I get it."

"Caroline is making good progress." Sinclair said, moving the subject on as best he could. "Her vital signs are strong and the swelling to her brain has dissipated dramatically."

"Can you bring her round yet?"

Sinclair shook his head. "My colleagues and I agree that it would be beneficial to leave her in the induced coma until the swelling is well within the safe parameters." He paused. "The internal bleed has been staunched, it would be far better practice to allow the injury to knit together. A day or two more," he said.

"Can I see her?"

"Of course," Sinclair replied. "Come with me."

41

London

"This guy Cole was black-ops, his files have been sealed."

"There it is again, black-ops," Big Dave paused. "Black equals bad. It's everywhere."

"What's everywhere?" Ramsay paused. "I'm describing the target's operational status."

"People like you using black as a negative label." Big Dave shook his head. "I'm fed up with it, society is passive racist. More than passive, ignorantly active. It's ingrained."

"What?" Ramsay shook his head. "Black-ops is an American term."

"And we use black bag to describe an illegal mission advocating extreme action and use of violent force."

"Because it's dark."

"And so is the slur." Big Dave shook his head angrily. "You have a relative who is undesirable and they're the black sheep. Depression is the black dog. A bad mood is a dark mood. Angel food cake is white, but devil's cake is dark. Dark, dark, dark..."

"Are you being serious?"

"Of course! Black sheep, black heart, dark mood. Hell, even when I was growing up and the Saturday morning telly was crap, the hero in the Western always wore a white hat, while the villain always wore a black hat. And there's another one; black hatted. That's work carried out by a black hat, or a computer hacker. And when you join a club if you don't get in, you're black-balled..." Big Dave punched the steering wheel and said, "Picture God in Heaven. White robe, white beard. Everything's white. He's surrounded by angels in white, white wings, a glorious white glow. Shit, they're even playing a white harp. Where the black angels at?"

Ramsay nodded. "I'd never thought about it before..."

"Nor had I. Not bad, eh?"

"What?"

"I just made that all up to mess with your head." He paused. "But the more I think about it, the more I think that I may have a point."

"You're an unwitting genius. Or generally unwitting, one or the other."

"You're easy to mess with."

"Rashid does the same thing."

"Yeah, we give each other notes."

"Really?"

"No. But maybe we should. It's a lot of fun. Christ, you're the poster boy of middle-aged, middle-class white bloke. The epitome."

"We're soon to be the only true minority. We're not cool enough for snowflakes, woke and millennials to get behind..."

Big Dave laughed. "Christ, that was humour! I'll have to tell the others." He paused, pulling the car into the side of the road and parking along the pavement. "This is it," he said. "Shall we both go in?"

"No, you might scare her away," Ramsay said as he opened the door.

"Is that meant to be humour again?"

"Take it any way you like..." He closed the door and took the steps up to the house. Like many in the street it had been turned into flats. Ramsay checked the name and pressed the bell.

After a few seconds it crackled and a woman's voice said, "Who is it?"

"DI Thorpe, my name is Neil Ramsay, I have a couple of questions for you."

"Press?"

"No."

"Well, just go away..." Ramsay pressed

the bell again and she asked, "Who the fuck are you?"

"DI Thorpe..."

"It's Ms Thorpe. There's no DI anymore."

"That's what I came to talk to you about."

"I'll ask once more, and then I'm going to bed for the rest of the day; who are you?"

"I'm from the Security Service," he replied quietly.

"MI5?"

"Well, yes..."

"Got any ID?"

Ramsay looked above him for a camera and saw a simple fisheye lens above and to the right. He looked into the lens and said, "Ms Thorpe, I'll show it to you, but I can't have it filmed. Sorry, but that's the deal."

"Well, get packing, then. I never invited you, so I don't have to hear what you came here to say."

"I want to talk about the SVR agent you found killed at a building site this morning." Ramsay waited for the intercom crackle and the distant voice. "Hello, Ms Thorpe?"

The door cracked open and Thorpe peered from behind. "Let's see that ID first."

Ramsay showed her. Designed by the late

Rodney Dennys, the Somerset Herald of Arms, the MI5 crest featured a golden winged sea-lion on a blue background. Not to be confused with the real sea lion, but a mythological beast, half-lion, and half-fish. It represented MI5's historical association with the three armed-services. The lion's head stands for the Army, the fish's body for the Royal Navy, and the wings for the Royal Air Force. Gold traditionally represents virtue. The colour blue in the background signifies the UK's overseas ties. Surrounding this central emblem are three further symbols: a green cinquefoil (a leaf with five petals), a portcullis and a red rose. The cinquefoil's five petals allude to the "5" in MI5. The colour green has been associated with intelligence since the First World War. The portcullis, traditionally a symbol of parliament, relates to MI5's key task of upholding parliamentary democracy. The crown at the top of the uppermost portcullis refers to the Crown, the legal embodiment of the State. The rose has historical associations with state intelligence work. Sir Francis Walsingham, Queen Elizabeth I's spymaster in the 16th century, used it on his seal. He is widely regarded as the first intelligence chief in British history. The rose's five-lobed petals are another allusion to the "5" in MI5.

"Have you ever seen a Security Service card before?" he asked

"No."

Ramsay shrugged and held it out for her. "A redundant exercise, then."

"I can get a feel for things when they're not right."

"Well, that's why I'm here…"

"Seems legit," she said and opened the door. Her eyes were puffy and red, and moist. She had been crying, for certain. "Come in."

Ramsay stepped over the threshold and said, "Thanks."

"Your driver not coming in?"

"No, he can sit there in the rain."

Thorpe closed the door and led him up the stairs to the first-floor landing and opened her door. Inside, the flat was spacious, and the lounge window looked down onto the street. Ramsay could see Big Dave in the driver's seat of the Jaguar eating a chocolate bar and patting the steering wheel along to something on the radio.

"You're here because of what I said to the spook at the embassy. So, he was with the SVR," she stated flatly. "Well it doesn't matter now. I've been suspended pending an enquiry."

Ramsay nodded. "Sensitive souls, aren't they?"

"I don't find it funny. I've got a mortgage to pay on this place, and it wasn't cheap." She paused. "My boss has sold me down the river to cover himself. Nothing's going to stick on his watch. The bastard…"

Ramsay nodded. "The least you could expect is a little loyalty," he agreed. "Especially since you two had been sleeping together."

"What the hell is this?" she fumed. "You know about that?"

"We know a lot of things."

"So, you're going to threaten me with that as well?" She strode to the door and snatched it open. "Get out!" she snapped.

"I'm not here to threaten you with anything. Quite the opposite, in fact." He paused. "Look, the Russians are playing quid-pro-quo. Whitehall have a line of common interest and don't want to upset the apple cart. Quite amazing, considering we've been at each other's throats these past years and months, but in a bid to level things out, the subject of gas and oil has come up again. Russian gas and oil to put it into context, and Britain PLC needs to think of her interests. But we do like to keep the war cold, and while Whitehall, Her Majesty's Government, various oil companies and part of the Russian machine are sidling up to one another, we at the Security Service, and our esteemed colleagues at SIS, or those shits across the river, as we prefer to call MI6, are keeping our war against Russia as cool as we can. Except for the past couple of days, when it looks like we have a Russian influence in our ranks, and some rather questionable activities going on right under our noses. That dead SVR agent for one, and the fact that there is a line of communication between our intelligence services and Moscow, not to mention the Russian mafia…"

Thorpe frowned. "So, what do you want from me?"

Ramsay smiled. " We'd like you to come and work for us."

"Really?" she asked somewhat dubiously.

"You're one of the best detectives on the force. A fact not gone unnoticed by us, even considering your mid-level rank…"

"Thanks."

"Don't mention it. You love what you do, which is why you have shied away from promotion. A detective inspector still gets out into the field. A DCI never leaves their desk and oversees a dozen investigations without taking a breath of fresh air. You also have an incredible case solve rate, especially in murder cases, and you aren't afraid to stick your neck on the line." He paused. "We could use someone like that."

"It's all young Oxbridge types with first class degrees these days, isn't it?"

"We have more than a few," he replied, thinking about the many analysts and case officers, and then he thought about the members of the team and their backgrounds. Far from it, he thought. "But we also have some people with specialist skill sets, and a good mind for investigation processes and an in-depth knowledge of police procedure would prove invaluable."

"But I'm on suspension."

"Walk away. We'll smooth it all over, transfer your pension and give you a salary commensurate with one rank higher than you were on."

Thorpe studied him for a moment, then said, "What would I be doing?"

"At the moment, the Security Service is full of graduates analysing data and running agents. These agents are civilians who do the spying for us. So, Muslims who suspect radicalisation. A couple decades or more ago and it was all about running informers within the parameters of the IRA. This is much like the work performed by the SIS, or MI6 as they prefer not to be called. We have surveillance experts whom we call watchers. In latter years we've used a team of operatives with various talents. In essence, sledgehammers. Great for smashing down walls of concrete blocks, not so good for cutting diamonds. We need to start boxing clever and this is where your influence would come in. For as much as we can occasionally look the other way and get the grittier tasks done, we need to finesse our way around the law and present cases for successful prosecution."

Thorpe nodded. "And these... sledgehammers... will they continue to operate outside the law?"

"Omelettes and eggs..." Ramsay shrugged. "I have always been one for protocol," he said. "But in recent years, we have gone head to head with enemies that have proved both ruthless and determined and we have taken the war to them. I see the value in these missions, but I also see the value in accountability and remaining within the law. Convictions work well to stem the tide, but only if they stick and the perpetrator is sentenced."

She shrugged. "That's police work in a nutshell."

"We need some balance," he said. "But we also need subtle investigations into delicate matters. That's where you would come in."

"Would I have a team?"

"That would depend on the case. And of course, the specific team you would be placed with."

"Huh, vague and mysterious, like a typical spook."

"It's fluid. If there's a case or an assignment that calls for a military style raid, then the most suitable operative is in charge, likewise, if we have a police style investigation, then I wouldn't hesitate giving you the lead. I liaise between the field operatives and the top tier." He paused. "Not that the public will ever know about raids of the type I've just mentioned."

"I thought you use the SAS?"

He shrugged. "I can neither confirm nor deny." He paused. "How about it?"

"I'm a detective. I'm not a secret agent, and I certainly wouldn't kill anyone. Orders or not."

Ramsay looked away. He had thought that, too. But when his life had depended upon it... He had trouble sleeping now, realised he probably always would. "You would never be ordered to do anything of the sort."

"What about the dead Russian agent?"

Ramsay smiled. "Let me tell you what I would like you to do..."

42

King stroked Caroline's hand before bending down and kissing her gently on the forehead. He would have loved for the heart rate on the medical monitor to quicken in rate, her eyes flicker and have the Hollywood moment of her awakening, but this was real life and nothing happened, but for the heaviness increasing in his heart. He reminded himself of the fact she was in an induced coma for her own safety, and likely would come round when the time was right. At least, that was what he hoped.

King looked at the four readings on the medical monitor. Her heart rate was low, hovering around the high fifties. He remembered she was usually mid-sixties at rest. Her blood pressure was low, too. He didn't understand brain pressure, but her oxygen saturation was hovering around ninety-eight. All fine. Except she was broken.

He pulled out the chair and sat down heavily, resting his head on her stomach as gently as he could. There was little area where he could touch, her legs broken and her arms either in bandages or cast. He remembered her ribs and sat back up, the fragility of her testing his emotions. But he could not weep for her. That would come later if she succumbed. But not until then, not now. He needed to be strong. But most of all, he needed his head in the game and he needed to find Cole. With Caroline comatose then being here would erode his strength and resolve. He stood up decisively, then turned around as the door opened. Sinclair framed the doorway, but King could see Simon Mereweather hovering behind him at the nursing station.

"Mister King, if I may?" he asked, waving King towards him. "I have been speaking with your, er..."

"My boss," King finished his sentence for him. He nodded at Mereweather and looked back at the consultant.

"We have been talking, and the matter of continued security, not to mention the incident earlier is making the staff, and myself, extremely uneasy." He paused. "And we think we have a solution."

King nodded, a little impatiently. "Go on."

"There is a Nightingale hospital facility at RAF St. Mawgan. Built in anticipation of the

NHS being put under too much strain with the initial coronavirus outbreak. It's an unusual location, but Covid patients don't exactly get visitors, and the security for such scenarios can't be bettered on a military base," he said. "Caroline can be taken there by air ambulance and receive medical attention which is second to none. All military surgeons, doctors and nursing staff work closely with the NHS, in many cases they use the military for free training. When they return from war zones, they bring their experience to the NHS by way of sabbaticals."

"Can you go with her?"

"Well, I..."

"That shouldn't be a problem," Mereweather intervened. He looked at Sinclair and said, "I can sort that out immediately, if you don't mind? Just until she is out of danger. It would be one less thing for King to fret about and we are in an incredibly sensitive and awkward situation of national importance and security."

Sinclair looked at them both, then shrugged. "Well, okay, what the hell... You'll have to speak to senior management, but I suppose they will be able to claim some funding back. That's usually how it works. Some grant or bursary of some kind. I'll email the medical administrator and tell them what we need. And I'll need the air ambulance to take me with her."

King looked at Mereweather. "And I want soldiers from the RAF Regiment to operate a security detail to the top VIP level. The sort they reserve for a visiting royal. Cole is just deranged enough to try something audacious. I want him met with a war if he tries to get near her."

Sinclair made a gesture like he was uncomfortable with the direction of the conversation and headed out through the door.

"Well played," said King. "Pulling the national security card when this is a simple vendetta."

"Well, after this morning, I'm getting well practised," Mereweather said sarcastically, then looked at King curiously. "How do you know Cole?"

King shrugged. "He was the NSA agent's go-to guy at that secret prison in South Dakota. An ex-SEAL turned assassin."

"And?"

"And what?"

"You shot this guy in the leg as you escaped and he was so affronted that he came after the team, the mercenaries we used. And that's it?"

"They were ex-SAS soldiers undertaking unofficial work for their government," King said coldly. "They were good men. Not just *mercenaries*. You have since employed one of them."

Mereweather nodded. "Sorry, you're quite right," he replied. "But I still don't buy what you're saying about Cole. He killed Marnie to get to you. Then he goes off the grid and resurfaces with such ferocity to have vengeance on you, that he tries to kill Caroline, just to hurt you? And then there's this ridiculous hit he's put out on you... offering his services to your enemies that he even gets paid for the privilege of having his revenge!" He pushed the door closed and stared at King. "Right here, right now. You tell me everything."

"For what? For you to pull the plug, hand me over to the police and turn your back on me? Bullshit!" King snapped. "I've been stabbed in the back before!"

"Not by me!" Mereweather snapped. "I have covered for you time and time again!"

"Then what?"

"Because I want this finished and I will pull out the stops to make Cole go away." He stared at King intently, with more determination than he had seen in the man before. "But I want you to tell me everything."

King walked to the window, stared down on the world below. He could see Rashid standing beside the Range Rover, texting, or scrolling on his phone. But King was tuned into his environment and could see that Rashid was watching out for a threat and merely using the phone as a prop. The two, armed police officers were static. Like two toy soldiers placed outside a fort. If Cole tried again, the two men wouldn't stand a chance. The RAF St. Mawgan strategy was a stroke of genius and King was hopeful at last. "When I worked with MI6, I was once on a mission in Afghanistan."

"Charles Forrester sealed your files," said Mereweather. "But I knew you worked with those shits across the river…"

"To be honest, I never thought it through. Forrester found me because my wife…" He shook his head. There was never a good way to describe a lost one. Not an ex, but it was the survivor who got the title. Widow or widower. Nothing for the person who had passed. "Jane," he said eventually, "worked for Charles Forrester and we met a couple of times. The MI5 analyst who hooked up with the MI6 dark horse. One joint operation, and that was it…" He said reminiscently. He glanced at Caroline, for some reason feeling guilty at the fond memory in her presence. "When I left MI6, I headed for the remotest place I could, to live on my own. Paint, swim in the loch, shoot rabbits for supper. All that bollocks…" he scoffed. "Forrester found me though. Recruited me because MI5 were being laughed out of court and not playing rough enough. I was already on my second name, couldn't see a point of making up a third. But I didn't count on being around after I put down the threat. I was going to slope off into the shadows and disappear. But…" He looked at Caroline. "I fell in love. I remained with MI5 and all the while, under the same name that would get me killed if MI6, less than half a mile away from Thames House, came across it again."

"Well, they could try…" Mereweather said light heartedly. "The SIS have a good director and a solid team in the top tier. The past is the past, and I know from the whispers that the previous, I'll call it *administration*, had its problems. Corruption and treachery at the highest level. I imagine they would thank the person who *removed* them, if there ever was such a man..."

"If there ever was..." King mused, looking away from him. "Well, while on a mission to gather intelligence and *remove* a Taliban leader, Cole showed up in the back of a Taliwagon with five other prisoners. A downed pilot, a couple of French commandos, a US marine and a fellow US Navy SEAL."

"Instances like that were rare."

King shrugged. "It was a PR war, as they seem all too often to be." He paused. "Soldiers were taken and executed, but the allies often said they were killed in action. Can't give the impression of the enemy having any dominance. But you're right, it wasn't common. The French were on a watch list, had been snatched a month before. The other four went down in a chopper crash and the rest of the marine flight crew and two more SEALs were killed in the crash, supposedly. They were snatched before a rescue team could get there and whisked away through one of the high mountain passes." He paused. "We ditched the mission and attempted a rescue. Long and the short of it; we got two of them out. I guess we could have waited, but we'd have been looking at six dead soldiers instead of four."

"And the next time you saw Cole he was working with the NSA in that secret prison?"

"Yes. It's a small world, sometimes."

"So, you got in there, shot him in the leg and ruined his career, completed your objective and disappeared." Mereweather said ponderously.

"That's the short version, yes."

"Then, a certain politician who later become President uses Cole and his former NSA handler to get retribution and cut the loose ends, put an end to questions surrounding his fortune, but you sent him packing, so-to-speak." The MI5 deputy director paused. "And then there was Marnie…"

King nodded. "To rattle Cole, I had Marnie track down his family and send him the details we had on them." King hesitated, then said, "Ultimately, I put her at risk and took the fight to Cole a step too far. I think it tipped him over the edge."

"You figure?" Mereweather scoffed. "I have a psychology degree. I may have moved on with my career, but I recognise a combination of PTSD and psychosis manifesting in the belief that he must prove himself. To himself if nobody else." He paused. "It is my understanding that Cole is a fugitive, and the US Justice Department has placed his family in a protection programme. So, factor in losing his family, his emasculation on more than one occasion, his need for validation and ultimately what he sees as the regeneration of his entire being, you are the one obstacle that needs removing before he can achieve that."

"Well, I'm not going to be feeling sorry for him anytime soon." He looked at Caroline, a pang of frustration building within him as he looked at her helpless body lying still, the machines, air tubes and monitor the only indication that she was alive. "But I'll find him, and any pain he is living with day by day will soon be ending for him." He thought of that day in Afghanistan, pictured the soldier burning in the cage and the mercy shot he had delivered to the French. Nothing more than a humane dispatch. "I'll certainly see to that."

43

The investigation was in full swing and the property was cordoned off from the entrance to the lane and the entire perimeter. Within this cordon the scenes of crime officers worked to establish whether the evidence corroborated the version of events given by the deputy director of MI5. The bodies had been collected by the coroner and news had filtered back that the wounded Russian gangster had not made it, pronounced dead on arrival.

Cornwall's most senior police officer had spoken to the detectives and they were going to go along with the tall, enigmatic man in the expensive looking pinstripe suit. None of the officers would have suspected that the man's suit had cost more than a month of their salaries, but they recognised the clipped and polished manner of someone at the top of their game, and with the most senior officer in the county getting his orders directly from the chief constable at Middlemoor to offer every assistance, then the SOCO's work here was merely a formality. Terrorism acts were being quoted, as was the Official Secrets Act. Most of the police officers found the unusual event exciting and enjoyed the drama.

Four hundred metres away Newman handed Rachel Beam the binoculars he had purchased at an outdoor pursuits store in Exeter. He had no idea what had happened here, but he knew that once the police were involved, his contact in London would have access to the information he needed. He handed Beam one of two envelopes his CIA contact had given him on Lambeth Bridge. The padded envelope was in the boot of the hire car, nestled beside the spare wheel.

"What do you make of that?" he asked.

"Those guys are forensics officers, the British equivalent of CSI. The detectives are holding back, but the brass are calling the shots. That guy with the grey hair and peaked hat is senior for sure. He's dressed like commissioners do back home. The body language of the other officers around him is subservient. He's not just a department chief, he's in charge of the police department down here. Like state police back home."

"That's really astute."

"I used to profile crowds at events attended by POTUS. And I was exceptionally good at it." She paused, studying the scene further. "No bodies, but you can see where they've mapped them out. I can make out some bullet cases and markers their CSI guys have placed around the scene. I don't know, blood spots or perhaps empty shell cases."

"King's vehicle is out of commission, so my contact can't help out with the traffic cameras." Newman knew that the CIA had hacked into the Police National Computer, or PNC. The thousands of road cameras across the nation could automatically flag up number plates and in turn, Newman could be fed a coordinate of King's position. He felt like cursing, but it wasn't his style. He was becoming an enigma within the CIA as the most unflappable officer imaginable. He typed out a text and sent it. His CIA contact would respond with a lead soon.

"I want to thank you," said Beam.

"For what?"

"For the chance to get my career back on track. Capturing King will go a long way towards righting some wrongs."

"Capture or kill…" Newman shrugged. "He certainly won't be easy to take prisoner."

"I'm sure we can come up with a plan." She paused, taking her eyes away from the binoculars and looking at Newman intently. "With King in our custody, he can be interrogated about his involvement in the British operation on US soil. I'll clear my name and get my career back." She held his stare and said, "I need this." She reached out and placed her hand on his thigh and squeezed. "I *really* need this..."

44

Windsor

Bethany was a typical thirteen-year-old girl, but she attended an exclusive girls' school as a day pupil. For the daughter of such a valuable target, she had been sloppy, but she was only thirteen and nobody should have expected any different. No doubt, she would have been security briefed and advised on maintaining a low profile on social media, but girls were girls. Bethany didn't even know what her father did for a living, just that he worked in a government job. With *TikTok, Snapchat* and *Instagram* being the social media of choice with the under twenty-fives, it was obvious she wouldn't have a Facebook page, or even if she did, it would unlikely be used regularly. Even as the daughter of someone so important, it had only taken a few hours to find an account and regular posts and interaction between friends. Gennaro had his computer specialist in Milan trawl through the data and put a report together. As was the most common method, once friendships and connections had been established, information was reverse mined and gathered studying her friend's accounts. Bethany used simple and discreet account and usernames, and it had been easy to make the right connections. Everything else – school, clubs, sports teams and even her home address had been gleaned from three hours' work from a computer in another country.

"I've got her. I am certain of it…"

"Who the fuck is this?"

"Roberto. East side, one hundred metres south of the school gate."

"And you are certain?"

"Yes, boss… yes, I am certain, I am checking her against the photograph, she is talking to two other girls…"

"He's right, Gennaro. If it's not her, then it's her twin. I'm parked on the opposite side of the road," The other man paused. *"Looks like her lift is here. One vehicle. Range Rover, black,"* he said, his phone connected to the vehicle via Bluetooth. He read out the registration plate.

"Every other vehicle is a Range Rover…" Gennaro muttered. "Wealthy parents."

"And a few import ones…"

"Let us hope so." Gennaro paused. "Okay, I'm coming around to you. Everyone else stay in position until I confirm it."

There were muted responses on the conference call. They had hired two more vehicles and placed two men on foot. Vehicles were less conspicuous than pedestrians outside a school, but by placing two men on the two corners of the main entrance to the exclusive private school, they could cover every exit from the premises. Gennaro abandoned the hired Land Rover Discovery Sport and made his way to the east side on foot. The girls were in high spirits and there was a constant stream of vehicles pulling to the kerb and picking up, with teaching assistants standing beside the groups of younger girls and letting them go as their lifts arrived. The adults were familiar with the au pairs and nannies and parents and the operation was swift. However, it was still a public pavement and people who had misjudged the madness of the pickup had to negotiate their way past the school, which gave Gennaro all the cover he needed.

Gennaro stopped short of the loitering group of girls and said quietly. "Okay, that's her. Everybody to positions. The bodyguards are facing west. Get in front and behind, now!" He turned and walked back to the vehicle and got inside. "How many in the Range Rover?"

"Two men. Fifties and bald. Nothing special, just cops who have got used to a comfortable life." The man paused. *"They're chatting, occasionally looking at the girl. They are relaxed. They're acting like taxi drivers, rather than security specialists."*

"Good. Weapons?"

"They're wearing suits, so I guess they've got concealed pistols, considering they're police officers and who the girl's father is. They are too relaxed, though. Bad for them, good for us."

Gennaro followed the Range Rover as it roared past. Bethany would be traveling in the rear. The bodyguard always rode in the front passenger seat. That was standard operating procedure. Often, bodyguards would remove the headrest so they could get over the seat in an emergency. It was difficult to see inside because of the tinted side and rear windows, but not impossible as the vehicle had a discreet thirty percent tint on all the glass except for the windscreen, where in Britain it was illegal to tint. When the low autumn sun caught it right, the three figures could be made out until they drove back under trees or in the shadows of tall buildings.

"I don't want harm to come to her," said Gennaro. "Not until she has served her purpose, at least."

Gennaro followed the Range Rover leaving two vehicles between them. Behind him, Marco followed in a Mitsubishi Outlander. Neither the Discover Sport or the Outlander matched the Range Rover for size, power or mass, but the BMW X5 several cars in front of their target was a sizeable vehicle, and was equipped with a large towing hitch, upon which, they had fitted the base of a cycle rack, which looked like a wheelless trailer.

By the time they passed Eton College, heading north, the BMW had slowed enough to be directly in front of the target vehicle, and Gennaro was directly behind in the Land Rover. The Mitsubishi was bringing up the rear and all three drivers had said that they were in position.

Gennaro checked his mirrors and took a deep breath. It was time.

45

"What is this place?"

"It's a safehouse."

"Do you have many like this?"

"We have properties all over the country," replied Ramsay. "Some are just ex-council flats on deprived estates because that suits the brief. If you want to hide someone, then don't make it too comfortable for the person hunting them. Likewise, if an asset has come over, then we don't want to give the impression Britain is paved with gold, that way the intelligence you get is clean and true. Given from the heart, rather than the promise of riches. We have apartments and townhouses, remote cottages, too." He paused, looking at the façade of the building, the fields and woodland beyond. "This is a bit different. We use it for VIPs, as an operation centre and for training. Those woods are ours, too." He pointed at the stark, autumnal belt of trees on the edge of the field. "The property is over forty acres all told, and the previous director had it stocked with pheasants and held a few weekend shoots here."

"Rather unpleasant for the pheasants," Thorpe interrupted.

"Just a ruse. Now when we train operatives here on a Saturday nobody in the area bats an eyelid when there's a couple hours of gunfire. Small arms, pistols and the like." He paused. "I don't know much about it, but I trained with a pistol last year, just in case."

"I didn't think it was within MI5's remit to carry firearms."

"It's not. Technically. But we train agents and operatives for their use on overseas assignments, where it is both legal and prudent to carry a weapon. We have been able to call on the SAS in the past, and they're quite willing to be attributed to the death of an ISIS terrorist if it takes the heat off us. It's called a Soldier B scenario if it ever gets to court, with *Solider B* giving evidence via video link from Hereford."

Thorpe shook her head and scoffed. "I can see working for you is going to have me walking a tightrope. Between the legal, and the downright criminal."

Ramsay shrugged. "We have adopted a few questionable methods," he said dryly. "But as you get to know more, you'll see what occasionally has to be done." He opened his door and got out of the car. Thorpe followed. "But as I said to you earlier, I see your involvement as a point of balance."

"Right," she said unenthusiastically. She looked up as Big Dave strolled down the front steps with a pump-action shotgun resting casually over his shoulder. "I can see that this job isn't going to be easy."

"Oi, oi, saveloy..." Big Dave shouted to Ramsay. He beamed a brilliant white smile at Thorpe. "You're the copper. Alright luv?"

Thorpe looked at the man mountain in front of her and said, "Are you on guard duty?"

Big Dave glanced at the shotgun and smiled. "Nah, just going to get a couple of rabbits for dinner. There's bugger-all been left for us in the freezer."

"No shops nearby?"

"Yeah, a bloody big pantry out there." Big Dave swept his hand towards the woods and laughed as he walked away from them.

"Oh, dear god..." she muttered and followed Ramsay inside.

Ramsay led the way through the wood-panelled hall, ignored the central staircase and showed her through to what would once have been a substantially sized dining room, but was now an office with several tables with telephones, monitors and keyboards on them. There was an area with a photocopier, printers, and a fax machine that looked like it was gathering dust, and an interactive smartboard and a whiteboard fixed to the wall. To Thorpe it looked like any other incident room in any other CID suite around the country. Ramsay seemed to realise what she was thinking. "Not so dissimilar to what you're used to," he said. "We have full access to the PNC, naturally." He handed her a card with her log-in details. "That is for the traceability, by the book, transparent stuff." He paused. "When there's a conviction in the running, then you use the PNC, and you use the log-in and user scripts." He switched on a monitor and took a card out from his pocket. When it had run through its bootup, he clicked on an icon on the screen and touched the hologram on the card against it. "This is Athena," he said. "There wasn't really a Greek god of spies, but Athena valued knowing her enemy's secrets. That information was worth more to her than warriors and armies." He paused. "We contemplated calling the software and database Hermes, as he was the god of thieves, and when you think about it our job is merely stealing information, but Athena seemed to have a better ring to it. And the women in Greek mythology are far more cunning than the men."

"And in life, too." Thorpe stepped closer and stared at the screen. "What does it do?"

Ramsay smiled. "What doesn't it do? Should be the question. This is our best weapon against terrorism, foreign government interference and organised crime. We have patches, a bit like pixels, on the databases of the FBI, the CIA, the NSA, Mossad, Interpol and about a dozen friendly nations' police networks." He paused. "We also have access to a dozen more hostile governments' intelligence services. GCHQ developed Athena over the past ten years and hauled it out earlier this year. We have no idea how long it will be before those patches are found, but within the program is a patch, or more accurately, the virus will repatch itself using transgenerational coding..."

"You're losing me now, Brains."

"If someone discovers the patch, the act of discovery itself as well as the malware and firewalls in place simply allow the program, or virus, to reattach. They think they got rid of it, but they haven't. Like I said, ten years in the making with the highest qualified computer and software experts in the country."

"But illegal," Thorpe stated flatly.

Ramsay said nothing as he slipped the card back in his pocket. He looked at her watching him and said, "We'll let you settle in before I get you a card for Athena."

"Naturally." She frowned as a vibrating sound filled the room. She recognised it as a helicopter and walked to the window.

"Ah, they're here," said Ramsay and walked out the way they'd entered. Thorpe shrugged and followed.

The dark blue AgustaWestland AW 109 banked hard and came in low, its wheels dropping down from within the undercarriage as it was still in the turn. There was a gracefulness about the manoeuvre, nothing erratic, merely a concise and direct turn with limited showmanship, but maximum effectiveness. The craft put down in the neighbouring field some fifty metres from the house. The rotors slowed, along with the engine pitch as the machine powered down, but the pilot kept on the controls to stop the helicopter lifting and wanting to flip. The door opened and King stepped out onto the short grass. Rashid followed carrying his M4 in a rifle case. Both men ducked their heads a touch as they ran clear of the aircraft towards Ramsay. The helicopter was winding down when the pilot stepped out from the offside front door and tossed his headphones onto the seat. He walked clear of the rotors without dipping his head, confident his five-feet-ten inches would remain, even with three inches of afro crowning his head.

King nodded to Ramsay and looked at Thorpe. "You're the copper?"

"Not anymore," she replied confidently. "We'll see the lay of the land, and whether I can bring anything to the party."

"Well, make up your mind and get off the fence before you work with me." King turned and walked towards the house carrying his scuffed leather kit bag.

"I'm Rashid. *I* don't have a problem with the law." He smiled. "But King spent his youth running from it and doesn't know which side of it he'll be on when he wakes up in the morning, so he errs his bets on the side of crossing the line as a matter of course." He winked and said, "Don't worry, soon enough and he'll probably bring you down, too…" He turned and patted the pilot on the shoulder as he reached them. "This is Leroy, aka Flymo. He's our own three-star Uber on this one. Would have got a five star, but his last job for us got a bit bumpy…"

"Let me guess, Flymo because you hover so low?"

"Smart girl, this one," Flymo grinned. "Now, who's for a cup of tea?"

The nodding drove the consensus, and they headed inside.

Thorpe hung back and looked at Ramsay. "So, a tough-looking man who looks like he's ready for a fight and from his stare, hasn't decided whether he's going to kill me yet, or just view me with contempt. A chatty and flirty Pakistani with what I'm guessing is an illegal weapon, and a pilot who by the very nature of his moniker is both reckless and has an ego bigger than the cockpit." She paused. "Oh yeah, and a giant of a man who thinks that because the fridge is short on protein he'll wander off across the fields and blow the hell out of some bunnies with a shotgun." She shook her head with the timing, as two shots rang out and echoed across the valley. "And this is your team?"

"You forgot the white, middleclass analyst who everyone is convinced is riding high on the autistic spectrum, and the sporty ex-private school debutante who worked in military intelligence, and is as we speak, fighting for her life in a coma…"

"It's not sounding great so far."

"I wouldn't want to mess with them." He paused. "Nobody who has come up against them has succeeded. And the only person who has come close will soon be a footnote in our service's secret history."

Thorpe shrugged. "I'm just saying…"

Ramsay stopped walking and cut her off. "It's a hell of a team," he said. "And let's not forget the newest recruit. The successful detective suspended from her work pending a tribunal, who got herself into a messy affair with her married commanding officer. That same senior police officer who saw the situation unfolding and realised an opportunity to be rid of some baggage. Who gave her no support whatsoever, and is recommending that she be fired, demoted or transferred at the very least?" He paused. "Welcome to the club, you should have no trouble fitting right in…"

46

Windsor

Roberto pushed the thumb safety forward on the sawn-off shotgun, keeping the barrels pointed towards the floor. He dropped the window, and the wind buffeted the cabin. Gennaro was at the wheel. He watched the BMW X5 ahead. It didn't get any better than this. The pavement narrowed considerably on the left, and they were still two-hundred metres short of the petrol station on the other side of the road.

"Go! Go! Go!" he shouted and pulled out across the crown of the road and floored the accelerator.

The driver of the BMW slammed on the brakes and Gennaro drew alongside the Range Rover as it slowed. Roberto fired at the rear tyre, and then immediately at the front and both tyres tore apart and flattened. Roberto dropped the shotgun in the footwell and picked up the pistol. The Range Rover slowed further, but the BMW was in reverse now and slewing backwards until the rear cycle carrier and towing bar slammed into the front grille and the big SUV rocked on its springs before resting still. Both airbags had inflated, and chalky resin filled the cabin. The Mitsubishi slammed into the rear and Antonio got out, ran around to the passenger side, and fired his pistol at the window. The dazed bodyguard flinched, but the 9mm bullet ricocheted close to Antonio and he dodged to one side. He regained his composure and aimed at an angle. The bodyguard was reaching for his Glock 19 and the two men were locked in a battle to get on target first. Antonio fired three shots and the bullet resistant glass held. Roberto fired the .38 revolver he had drawn, and the driver's window held. The driver was struggling to restart the stalled vehicle, but he was panicking. Behind him, Bethany was screaming and reaching for her door handle to escape.

Gino got out of the BMW and jacked a round into the chamber of the pump-action shotgun. All around them, concerned citizens had started to gather at the scene of what they thought was a regular road traffic collision, but were now scattering as the gunshots rang out. Gennaro opened his door and walked calmly around the bonnet of the Land Rover, the AK47 held loosely in his hands. Gino fired the shotgun and was immediately peppered in the face with the rebounding lead shot. He screamed and fell to his knees, Gennaro flinched, catching some of the lead shot in his shoulder. He cursed loudly. The shot had pierced his clothing and broken the skin. Gino had suffered far worse and it was clear that he had taken damage to one or both of his eyes. Gennaro ignored him, raised the AK47 and made eye contact with the two bodyguards. He motioned for them to get out of the car. He did not want to hit the girl and knew the high velocity bullets would cut through the windscreen and both men like a hot knife through butter. Neither man liked his options, and the driver was talking, and it took Gennaro a few seconds to realise that the man was calling for support in either a radio mic or on his phone. Gennaro aimed the rifle, but he could see Bethany cowering in the rear behind the man's seat. Roberto fired twice at the driver's window, but the glass held. The driver slammed on the accelerator and the Range Rover lurched forwards, pushing the BMW forwards, but steam was wafting out of the grille and from under the front wheel arches. Gennaro looked at Gino, but the man was oblivious to what was happening. Somebody needed to get into the BMW and reverse it into the Range Rover before the vehicle broke loose from their box. Gennaro aimed at the side window and fired three shots. The glass spiderwebbed and the driver ducked his head. Gennaro turned and ran around the BMW and down the narrow pavement. The Range Rover was still moving slowly forward, the BMW sliding on its tyres, its brakes locked. There were sirens in the distance and Gennaro knew they did not have much time. From this angle, he could avoid hitting the girl and he fired three more shots, then flicked the select up into fully automatic and fired at the window, keeping his finger tightly on the trigger. The men returned fire and the glass gave way with the men inside taking a dozen or so bullets in the melee. Gennaro changed over the magazines then reached over the body in the passenger seat and unlocked the vehicle's central locking. The girl was screaming and as soon as he unlocked the vehicle, Antonio opened the rear door and dragged the girl out by her flailing ankles. She struggled valiantly, but the large Italian chopped the side of her neck with the edge of his hand and she went limp. He carried her around the wreckage and put her in the rear of the BMW. Gennaro fired a few shots towards the growing number of curious onlookers, forcing them to scatter once more. Gino was still cupping both eyes and wailing and Gennaro fired a single shot into the man's head as he got into the BMW and Roberto got behind the wheel of the Land Rover.

"Get us the fuck out of here, Antonio…" Antonio made his way around to the driver's seat, his eyes transfixed on his friend lying beside the steaming Range Rover. "I had no choice," said Gennaro, knowing exactly what the man was thinking. "He would have been a liability. He needed medical attention and the police would have made him talk…"

"Right…" Antonio commented as he tore away, the two vehicles separating and ripping off most of the Range Rover's front bumper and grille.

"You of all people understand that."

"Yes, boss." Antonio had barely pulled away, before he stopped just past the filling station. Roberto pulled in behind them and Nico hopped out of the vehicle and walked around to the boot. He pulled a milk crate out and placed it on the floor. The sirens were close, now. Back at the scene people were gathering around the Range Rover. Many were filming the scene with their phones. Antonio joined Nico and they took the bottles out of the crate one by one. They had been packed with cloth around them to stop them rattling or breaking if the vehicle had been hit. Each one-pint glass bottle contained half a pint of petrol and two-hundred grams of sugar and a piece of cloth had been rolled up and pressed inside with six inches or so poking out. The cloth had acted like a wick and soaked up the petrol. Each man picked up a bottle and lit the cloth with a disposable lighter and it ignited fiercely before they threw them into the forecourt. The petrol ignited with enough force to feel the disruption in the air and the heat on their faces. A vehicle burst into flames and a moped bore the full force of one of the bombs, and by the time each man threw their third bottle, the forecourt was ablaze, and the petrol pumps were burning fiercely. The sugar melted and the petrol had turned it into a burning sludge.

The two men got back inside both vehicles and sped away from the pandemonium with vehicles sounding their horns and people filming the incident rather than lending assistance. The inferno ablaze in their rear-view mirrors lit the sky like a clear summer dawn. Antonio led the way in the BMW while Roberto followed his lead. Gennaro finished taping the girl's wrists together and put the hood over her head. She protested that she could not breath and that she needed air, but he ignored her pleas and looked out of the back window, checking that Roberto was keeping up with the more dynamic BMW.

Less than a mile from the scene Antonio pulled into the residential street and took the next right. He parked against the kerb and got out of the vehicle, leaving the engine running. Roberto parked behind and both Antonio and Nico got out and removed the number plates. Each plate had been held on with an adhesive strip to reveal another false plate underneath. Antonio got back in and tossed the number plates into the passenger footwell. The two vehicles took off at a more sedate pace, re-joining the main road after a devious and elaborate route through two residential estates. After ten minutes, they parked up in another residential road, this time a more affluent area lined with trees. The leaves fell like gentle flakes of snow, the sky grey and cold. Again, the plates were removed to reveal the genuine articles underneath. The three vehicles they had used had all been hired under cloned credit cards and a counterfeit Spanish passport. Enough of a red herring to confuse the Italian accent in the subsequent investigation.

Antonio drove on northwards until they reached the river and a large multi-storey carpark and shopping centre. The structure was at odds with the old-world feel of the town, but it had a good access and with the CCTV cameras focusing more towards the other streets and the castle, their research had showed it to be the least surveyed. Antonio swung the big car around the ramp and pulled up close to a Mercedes GLK. A small and sleek SUV. He reversed close to the rear of the vehicle and opened the BMW's automatic rear door and with the other key fob he did the same with the Mercedes. Roberto drove past and climbed to the next level, where another hire car, a Volkswagen Tiguan SUV had been left for him.

Gennaro pulled the girl over the seats and she fell into the boot, where Antonio dragged her across into the Mercedes and shut the boot lid. Gennaro opened the rear door, hauled her over the rear seats and fastened her into her seat. He removed her hood and she sucked in the air gratefully.

"Stay quiet," he said to her with little emotion.

"Please…" she managed between breaths.

"If you make a sound, I will put the hood back on." He took the stiletto out of his pocket and whipped open the blade. "And if you make trouble for me, I will ruin that pretty little face of yours…"

Within five minutes, Antonio was behind the wheel of the Mercedes and Roberto followed in the Volkswagen. Fifteen minutes later, in another quiet residential street, the stolen number plates were removed, and they were heading northwards to the perfect property they had found using *Google Earth* and the poor unsuspecting souls within.

47

St. Petersburg, Russia

Romanovitch stared at the text message and put the phone silently down on the table. The computer screen in front of him showed his bank balance with Credit Suisse. For all his nephews' greed, they had not been prudent with the brotherhood's money, nor cunning with its investments. He pressed the button on the transfer and sent the entire balance of just over eleven-million two-hundred thousand Swiss francs. A pittance in the grand scheme of things, and with what they should have had. The brotherhood also held stock holdings of ten-million euros, savings accounts of twenty-million and properties valued at more than a hundred million, but time was a factor. The wolves were howling and starting to circle the wounded elk. Cautious advances, testing a powerful yet wounded beast's resolve. Dangerous, but weakening. The old Russian knew how it would be done. A nip here, a bite there, until the pack came in as one, teeth bared and claws tearing at the flesh. He was damned if he would give them the satisfaction.

Romanovitch's SVR contact had given him the news, the text outlining the details of his mens' deaths. Uri and the others slaughtered in a gun battle and who would soon be tarred not as organised criminals but as terrorists with deadly intent. With these men gone, the lifting of an informer who had operated within his inner circle, and the losses they had suffered both in St. Petersburg and Albania this past summer, there would not be enough men to guard their interests and raise funds through their usual means. Romanovitch was left unprotected and the opposition, the rival brotherhoods knew what was at stake. The wolves had smelled the blood and fear and vulnerability.

Romanovitch still had the quiet farmhouse in the south of France. It had been bought with money siphoned from the brotherhood years ago. He would live out his days there, on a pittance of eleven-million Swiss francs and forever knowing he had run like a coward and given his family's fortune away. His nephews' widows would have their assets and money and whether they lived or died or fled or lay down with the new heads of the brotherhood would depend on them, but he would not be offering assistance and certainly not give away his position by letting them know the score. It was tradition for the new leaders to lay claim to such women as their mistresses. A reminder of their power and position and the spoils of war. And a reminder to the women that there was a new alpha male in the pack.

Romanovitch was under no illusion that he only had hours to make his move. With the transferable assets taken care of, he would head for the dacha in the forest to the north and make further arrangements. The forest was slightly smaller than the United Kingdom and the dacha was on the shore of a lake. He had spent the summers there with his father and uncle and cousins, fishing for trout and hunting wild boar and brown bears, and in the winters, they would travel up at the weekends to hunt elk and wolves and reindeer. He still used the dacha as a hunting lodge and there were shotguns and rifles stored there, and enough supplies for him to hunker down for a month or two while the letting agents in Marseille made the farmhouse available for him and stocked it with food and the essentials. Then he would learn how to survive retirement and keep his resentment in uneasy company with drink.

The old man used a computer enough to email and check his money. He would throw the laptop on the fire after he sent one last email, and then he would never sit in front of one again. His mobile phone would join the device. He would buy a no frills pay as you go mobile phone later. Something to call the letting agent with or order groceries. He typed the single email to two recipients, opened his phone to relay the body of the text from his SVR contact. He had no idea if the recipient would open it, whether it would be of use to him, but it would go a long way towards avenging Uri and his men. The final act of a man feared by many, but suddenly not enough, so it would seem. He looked up at the sound of a gunshot. And then another. He hastily signed off the email and sent it. He took the CZ75 9mm pistol out of the desk drawer and walked to the window.

The wolves were here…

Romanovitch grabbed the laptop and tossed it onto the roaring log fire. He was about to toss the phone on too, but he wondered whether it was too soon, if there was someone that he could call for help. But who was he kidding? There were ten men in the courtyard and the only man available to stand guard was lying prone on the cobblestones and bleeding out. The laptop started to burn, then flashed white and melted, acrid smoke filling the air along with any secrets that had been held.

Footsteps grew closer. Hard boots on the polished wooden floors. The stairs taken two at a time. Romanovitch thought of how they had taken control in those early days. The men cut loose from the KGB carving out a future for themselves after the wall had fallen brick by brick and the iron curtain had gone down in metaphorical flames. They had been ruthless and cruel and had built a reputation which had lasted right up until this past summer when the brotherhood had taken a hit and lost face in the eyes of their competitors. And now Uri and his mean were dead, and the wolves had gathered, and the days of power were no more. How he regretted the things he had done to those men, in order to assert his dominance and reputation. The cruelty. The cutting, the gouging, the breaking of bones, the severing of digits and the humiliation of removing appendages. To make the men less of a man. To the victor, goes the spoils. And now, as those footsteps grew ever closer, the voices more confident, he knew what they would do to him. How they would kill the reputation long before the man.

Romanovitch sat down heavily in his chair. The footsteps were close, now. He thought briefly of killing the first few men through the door but knew enough of such things that such thoughts seldom went to plan. He could be shot and wounded, disarmed, and then it would be down to the wolves and whatever they felt needed to be done. He shook his head. They wouldn't get to have their way, and a part of him felt a pang of cowardice that he would have done dreadful things to them, had the tables been turned. Romanovitch took a deep breath, tucked the muzzle of the pistol under his chin and closed his eyes. They were at the door now. Unsure how to make their way in, who should go first. He imagined them readying themselves, weapons aiming tentatively as they hashed together their plan. Romanovitch pulled the trigger, the top of his head erupting, the pistol clattering to the floor. He slumped in the chair, legs twitching as the men from the rival brotherhood entered and surveyed both a defeated enemy and their brand-new empire.

48

Simon Mereweather stared at the text message, his heart racing, and a feeling of dread mounting in his stomach. His vehicle was rocking as the traffic roared past at seventy miles per hour, often more, and he knew he needed to find a safer place to park. He had seen part of the text on the screen of his phone in the recess of the dashboard and hammered on the brakes. The Jaguar was straddling the hard shoulder of the duel carriageway, hazard lights flashing and the wing mirror just a foot or two from the vehicles that were buffeting him relentlessly. He turned the wheel and crept forwards and further into the hedge giving him another foot of space, but it didn't seem to make any difference. He dialled anyway.

"Simon?" Director General Amherst answered on the second ring.

"Yes, Sir…"

"My god, man! Someone has taken my daughter!"

"Bethany? Where… how?"

"From outside her school! Or as near as damn it. Both protection officers have been killed and the

police have lost the trail. Traffic cameras have drawn a blank around a mile north of Eton College. The bastards bombed a filling station to tie the area up with emergency services…"

Mereweather closed his eyes. They had taken the tit for tat with Russia more seriously in recent months. Could there be a Russian element to this? It certainly had their heavy-handed approach written all over it. "Any demands yet?"

"Nothing. Counterterrorism are on it, Scotland Yard are with me now. I'm putting a team on this immediately."

Mereweather knew that SO15, the Met's anti-terror unit would be running the show regardless, but a support team from MI5 would leave no stone unturned and would already be working with GCHQ to pull footage from every CCTV camera and database in the area. "The team have got their hands pretty full on this," he said. "But in light of the threat, the fact that it's a personal issue, do you want me to redeploy the team to this and have King lay low?"

"I'm not sure. This whole vendetta thing with the Americans must stop. See how far they can get. I want you back in London now, working on this."

"Naturally. I'm on my way..." Mereweather hung up. He was near to the safehouse now, but he would text Ramsay and continue through Hampshire on the A303 and go straight to London. He had a feeling it was going to be a long night.

49

The farm was shrouded in darkness, a few warm lights glowed from within. The clocks had recently gone back with daylight saving time and the darkness of the season forced upon the countryside without the lights of the towns or cities to draw out the day. The air was colder than the night before and the men used to the pleasant Tuscan autumn had tucked their collars up against the cold.

"We must be careful. Most farmers usually own a shotgun at least," Antonio said. "To put something on the table, scare off vermin or put down an injured animal."

"There are four of us," Gennaro said without taking his eyes off the farmhouse. Nobody had mentioned Gino left at the scene. Nobody dared. But they all got to see how they would be treated if they succumbed to an injury, and it had been a morbid reminder of the deadly game they played. "And we are all armed."

"Looks like the farmer is heading inside," said Roberto, pointing to the right of the farmhouse, where an outside light had switched on, illuminating a yard area where a tractor was parked. A tall, lithe-looking man was walking across the yard. He seemed tired and laboured his way up the steps to the farmhouse. "He must have finished for the day."

Gennaro nodded. "Then we go now. Catch him unaware." He got back inside the Mercedes and waited for Antonio to take the wheel. He checked the AK47 and flicked the selector down two clicks to semi-automatic.

Antonio checked the Browning 9mm pistol and tucked it into his jacket pocket before starting the engine. He glanced at his boss, but Gennaro was staring straight ahead at the farmhouse. He had a strange, unnerving look in his eye. Antonio had seen the look before, and he knew things were going to end badly for the family inside the farmhouse. They had inadvertently crossed paths with Gennaro Fortez, for no other reason than the farmer had maintained an access route across his land that was well-used and straight, level, and wide enough to land a small aircraft. Fate was so often a cruel and terrible entity.

50

King looked at the printout in his left hand, took a sip from the mug of tea in the right. He nodded at Thorpe as he sat down beside the fireplace, a log fire roaring and suddenly making him feel tired. Big Dave had cooked curried rabbit, and it had been a good meal. As usual, Ramsay had picked at the vegetables and some rice, more so when he was warned to watch out for lead shot. He was a fussy eater and had some unusual eating habits, relying on texture and smell more than taste. Caroline had always said it was because of his autism, while Rashid maintained he was just a bit weird. King ate without question and Rashid joked whether the rabbits were Halal, but in truth he was a relaxed Muslim and never seemed to care much about anything. Thorpe conceded that the rabbit was good, and that had led Big Dave to wax lyrical on food shortages, production ethics and sustainability. She had asked if many other Londoners hunted for their own food and was duly informed that he had left his native Fiji when a British Army recruitment ship sailed up to his island and sold him and many other young and impressionable lads on improbable dreams and ideals, and until then if he wanted to eat, it either came from the sea or needed its neck wringing and feathers plucking. Either way, it needed killing and they only took what they needed. When he threw back at her if she'd ever thrown food out from her fridge, she relented. By the end of the meal, she had bonded a little, discovered more than she'd anticipated and decided that she would be able to work within the team, but noted that each member had their specialities and only time would show her what these really were.

Ramsay had taken the call from Simon Mereweather towards the end of their dinner. He had informed them but was unable to field their questions. Flymo suggested they take the helicopter to London and both Rashid and Big Dave had volunteered to standby on location, but Ramsay had stood the team down. The police and SO15 were pulling out the stops, and a small team from MI5 were liaising with them with direct contact with GCHQ who were ploughing through traffic camera footage and local council CCTV. It was highly likely Bethany Amherst had been taken in retribution for the assassination of a SVR officer who had instigated the killing of the former police Commander's wife and the Home Secretary's husband last summer in a blatant attack in response to the hard line the government had taken on Russian organised crime.

"I'm sorry about your… wife?" she said, looking up from the iPad she had synced with her computer terminal.

"Partner, girlfriend, fiancée," he replied. "All of those titles will do. But there's no reason to be sorry. You don't know her, or me for that matter. And she's tough. She'll pull through," he added, although he didn't entirely believe it himself.

Thorpe nodded. "Is it me? Or is it just me being a copper?" she asked, thinking of how he had addressed her earlier.

King sipped some of his tea. "I wasn't aware I had a problem with you, Thorpe."

"Tell your face that." She paused. "And it's Sally-Anne."

King shrugged, looked back at the printout. Ramsay had managed to lift the numberplate from Cole's hire car. He had the fake ID and cloned credit card details and he had a partial route from King and Caroline's cottage on the Lizard in Cornwall all the way to

Launceston, where he left the A30, was monitored again near Bude and not been picked up since. The moment the PNC picked him up again, they would be ready to move with the chopper and intercept him. Only, as far as King was concerned, too much time had passed without the numberplate being flagged on one of the hundreds of traffic cameras leading out of the county.

"You do though, don't you," she stated flatly.

King took a sip of his tea, then placed it on the table in front of him. The fire beside him was warm on his face and the meal had left him satisfied and relaxed. It was easy to forget what had transpired, forget that Caroline was hospitalised on a military base and that she wouldn't be walking airily into the room any minute. "I came to MI5 because the previous deputy director, who directed all field operations, could see that the service was operating with one hand tied behind its back. People were dying and the public were in fear, and barristers and lawyers were enabling known terrorists to walk free from court because of technicalities…"

"Technicalities that happen to be the law," she interjected.

King shrugged. "Clever lawyers get guilty people off. Fact." He paused. "Charles Forrester was killed by the same people he fought so tirelessly against. But before he died, he could see that there was a difference between the greater good and the legal technicalities that saw guilty people walk."

"It's the thin end of the wedge."

"Perhaps."

"Always."

"There is always the exception, and that is what we increasingly come up against," said King irritably.

She shook her head. "The law is the law and when we break it, we become criminals."

"Okay, I can see your position. But let me ask you this. Say a group of terrorists got hold of a nuclear device and planted it strategically so that dozens of military bases, an intelligence gathering agency, and millions of civilians are killed in its blast. Fresh water sources for half the country, agricultural land for over a third of the nation, commerce and at least one third of the country's land mass will be rendered radioactive for as many lifetimes as you care to count."

"Hypothetically?"

"The law is the law in your eyes. Hypothetically got in the ship and sailed long ago for you."

"So, what's your point?"

"The clock is ticking, the odds are stacked against you, but it's down to you, nonetheless. Millions will die. That's a fact. The ramifications beyond don't bear thinking about. The economy, the country's ability to function, trade, defend itself… all on your shoulders."

"Can I get some popcorn? This has the makings of a Hollywood blockbuster. I should have brought along a date…"

"I doubt it's ever that easy."

She frowned. "What the hell do you mean by that?"

"You're prickly. It's not appealing."

"Coming from you?"

"I'm not looking for a date."

She tutted and regarded him with contempt. "Carry on with your doomsday scenario, I have work to do."

"You get the picture. Would you torture someone to get the location?"

"No!"

"The clock is ticking…"

"There would have to be a better way."

"You've got two hours, tops. He's an old guy, a committed enemy of your country. He's killed one of your colleagues, wounded another."

"The end should not justify the means."

"The end should *always* justify the means." King leaned forwards and stared at her, his eyes cold and blue-grey like glacier water. There was little emotion there, with what they had seen over the years the warmth had been eroded and hadn't been allowed to return. "What about all those people? Millions. Mothers, fathers, wives, husbands, children…"

Thorpe looked at him incredulously. "That happened?" King looked back at her but said nothing. "I suppose…" She shrugged. "Okay, I suppose I would turn a blind eye at slapping him about a bit. But I sense that it has gone a lot further than that with you…"

"If you come on board and police us, our enemies will win," said King, standing up. He picked up his cup. "But everything starts with the thin end of the wedge. And you conceded, a little. Perhaps that's enough for us to keep winning…"

"Great tactic, by the way," Thorpe said, chuckling to herself. King turned and frowned at her as he reached the door. "Having your say, then leaving the room. Like most of the men I've dated."

King shrugged. "What, they didn't like being in the same room as you? I can't imagine why…"

She smiled thinly. "There's a great quote for men like you," she said. "I heard it on a course once. You know how the people hosting courses always like to leave you with something? Well, this was by Frederick Nietzsche, the German philosopher. It related to a trait in police work because, unlike what you said earlier, the ends should never justify the means. It went like this; Beware that, when fighting monsters, you yourself do not become a monster… for when you gaze long into the abyss. The abyss gazes also into you."

"Did your department get a refund on the course?"

Thorpe smiled. "There are monsters out there, King. I suspect you have encountered scarier beasts than I. But don't become one to fight one. Save a little of yourself before it's too late."

51

"Do you have a partner?"

"No. How about you?"

Newman thought about the opportunities he'd had, the career sacrifices he had made. There were a couple of women he hooked up with from time to time, but nothing with the potential to become serious. Maybe he'd subconsciously engineered it that way. Married women had financial commitments, emotional baggage. They couldn't be driven by love in the same way a single woman could, they needed to line up all the ducks in a row, make the right choice. Newman was not a choice any sensible woman would make. Late twenties, working overseas, never one to call back. But he always got in touch when he was in town. "No, nothing serious," he said. He reached around and cupped her naked breast, fingered the nipple tenderly. "That was... unexpected," he whispered into her ear.

Rachel Beam rolled onto her back, then turned and looked at him. She cupped his hand, holding it firmly to her, but making it clear she could do without the attention to her nipple. The moment had passed, she was sensitive, and it was now merely an irritation. "Really?" she smiled. "Inevitable, I thought."

Newman didn't have a clue what to say. He hadn't picked up on any vibe, was sure he hadn't sent anything her way. "Had to be done," he lied. "To get past the tension..."

She smiled and rolled over, straddling him. Newman feigned mock surprise as she rubbed herself on him. "You've given me a lifeline," she said. "I was washed up, my career parked up against a brick wall. I was even drinking too much, miserable and didn't even have the energy or will to socialise. And with whom? My work colleagues had turned their backs on me." She took hold of him as he responded to her movements, guided him gently into her. "Thank you..."

Newman glanced at his mobile phone as it vibrated on the bedside table. The urge to reach for it was almost too much, but Beam seemed to realise he had thought about it. She frowned at him, then looked at the phone as it vibrated and span through a slow circle on the polished wood as the series of text messages came in. Her expression seemed to dare him, but she could feel he had been distracted and rolled off him, taking the sheet with her, which she wrapped around herself as she headed into the bathroom.

Newman cursed and rolled for the phone. People had warned him about mixing business with pleasure. Now he had a complication he did not need.

There was no number displayed. Merely texts from an unknown sender. He knew that it was the CIA officer who may or may not have been called Callum on Lambeth Bridge. Either way, his contact had news. He read the messages one by one. He was naked and Beam had taken the top sheet with her to the bathroom, the duvet had earlier been ripped off and cast aside on the floor.

Beam opened the bathroom door and stepped into the room. She had showered and was wrapped in a towel. She started to get dressed, but with her back to him. "Important call?" she asked offhandedly.

"Just some texts. But we may have a location to go on," he replied.

"Where?"

"The police national computer picked up a licence plate that MI5 are watching for."

"King's plate?"

"No. Somebody else who is after King. He was identified at King's property and the CCTV caught enough of the plate to get the number after the footage had been enhanced at GCHQ."

"Which agency?" She pulled on her bra and turned to face him as she stepped into her trousers.

"Not an agency, a contract."

"So, we piggyback and hope they get close to their target and intercept?" Newman didn't reply as he bundled his clothes into a pile and walked past her into the bathroom. "I guess we don't need both these rooms now," she commented as he closed the door. "I may be the one signing the chits, but it's a good job you're the one picking up the tab," she called through the door after him.

52

Roberto knocked on the farmhouse door and waited. He could hear voices within, unaccustomed to visitors. Guessing and questioning as to who it would be, the most obvious solution of opening the door, several rungs down on the ladder in their reasoning. The door unlatched and opened inwards hesitantly. Roberto was greeted first by the aroma of grilled meat and boiling potatoes and then by the face of a woman of around sixty. She wore her greying hair tied back in a short ponytail and was drying her hands with a tea towel. The door opened wider and he could see that she wore a skirt and thin sweater and looked accustomed to hard work and sacrifice. Roberto thought she reminded him of his own mother, a life tending the land and at nature's mercy for their bounty. It had been a hard life for them in the hills of Umbria. Milking goats and wringing the neck of whichever unfortunate chicken he could catch for their dinner and harvesting the olives for their oil press to sell at the markets. He had shied away from the work in his teens and left for an easier life in the city. He had turned to a life of crime in Rome, then a chance meeting had landed him in the Fortez family and those days on the farm now seemed a world away and a lifetime ago. He looked at the woman and for a moment he seemed to hesitate before speaking.

"We are having vehicle trouble and would like to use your phone..." he said apologetically.

The woman frowned, looked past him at the two new SUVs. "There's a service station two miles down the road," she said. "They have a phone there, as well as toilets and a food counter. You may be better off waiting there for a breakdown vehicle to arrive."

"Yes, thank you. But perhaps I could use your phone quickly first?"

"What's all this!" a tall, wiry man in his sixties pulled the door wide open and stood behind the woman, a good foot taller than her. "Whatever you're selling, we don't bloody well want it!"

Gennaro walked up the slate steps behind Roberto and brought the AK47 around from where he had been shielding it from view behind his right leg. "You are so right on that count," he said.

The farmer tried to push the door closed, but his wife was in the way and all he succeeded in doing was barging her forwards into Gennaro's path. The Italian mafia boss pushed her back inside using the muzzle of the rifle and she screamed in pain as he winded her and she fell backwards onto a cold, slate floor. The farmer balled his fist and swung a right hook into Gennaro's face, and he went down hard, cracking his head on the door jamb. Roberto charged inside, but the farmer kicked out and caught him in the groin. As he went down, cupping his appendage with both hands, Antonio charged up the steps into the melee, but he stopped the farmer in his tracks as he pushed the sawn-off shotgun close enough to him to get the message, but far enough away to be able to fire both barrels if he needed to. The farmer raised his hands and stood back, but a glance to his right told Antonio there was another person in the room. He stepped inside, just in time to see a young woman pull back behind the doorframe and leave nothing more than the sound of her racing upstairs.

Roberto was getting back to his feet and grimaced as he helped Gennaro get up. The man looked incensed with rage and he stepped back as the man picked up the AK47 and walked over to the farmer.

"Call her down, now," he said coldly. "If she makes a call to the police, I will kill you all…" The farmer bellowed and there was a creek of floorboards above them. The farmer reiterated that she should come down, and the footsteps became more prominent, although they hesitated at the top of the stairs. "I mean it," said Gennaro. "I will slaughter you all…" The farmer shouted for them to come down, and after thirteen tentative footsteps down the wooden staircase, a woman of about twenty skulked into the doorway. Gennaro pointed towards the kitchen table. "Sit down," he said to the woman. He nodded to Roberto and said, "Tie them all up. Tightly."

53

He was in agony. Despite his best efforts to keep the wound clean and change the dressing, the bullet wound to his hand was becoming infected. He could feel the irritation and throb within, the sign of infection. He had cleaned the wound thoroughly again, but still it throbbed. The bullet must have chipped some bone on its passage through his hand, either that or fragments of the handle of the knife he was holding had splintered off like shrapnel and been left inside. The injury required medical attention, but with that would come questions he could not answer and that would raise some red flags in the system. He needed an extensive trauma kit and the time and will to operate on his own hand. The liquid morphine would go a long way towards alleviating the pain, but too much would render him unable to drive and operate, and the over-the-counter painkillers were proving ineffective. It was affecting his judgement, but he knew he was close to his objective.

The email from Mikhail Romanovitch had shortly been followed by two more. The SVR officer in the Russian mafia boss' pocket, and the spy's inside man in MI5. It had been Cole's game changer, because in killing the Russians at his home in Cornwall, King had left Mikhail Romanovitch with no room to manoeuvre and therefore sealed his own fate. The brotherhood factions had seen weakness and an organisation difficult to defend, and they had made their move. Romanovitch had paid it forwards and paved the way for Cole to avenge him. But now, not only did Cole now have an inside track, but he also now had a contact that would continue to provide him with information until he got the job done. All he needed to do now was lay the trail of breadcrumbs for MI5 to follow.

54

"We've got a location on Cole!" Rashid shouted round the door.

King woke with a start. He hadn't planned on sleeping, but the warmth of the fire and the large dinner had tipped the scales in the favour of rest. He was tired to his bones and for the first time in two days, he had forgotten the horrors of Caroline's ordeal and that there were people out there actively hunting him. A pang of guilt rushed through him, knowing he had been comfortable and rested after so much had happened. The thought of Caroline alone in a ward on a military base, broken and unaware of the world outside made him feel sick to his stomach.

"Are you okay?" Rashid frowned at him.

"Out of sorts, that's all," he said, his mouth thick with the discomfort of a short and unplanned sleep. He got up, rubbing some feeling into his face. "Where is he?"

"The PNC picked him up near Salisbury." Rashid swung the rifle slip over his shoulder. "Come on!"

King could see that his friend wanted Cole as much as he did. There would be wrongs righted tonight, blood spilled, and people avenged. King thought about Caroline as he followed Rashid down the corridor and checked the Walther PPK in his hand. This wasn't just his hunt. And that thought made him feel that he should have been with Caroline, rather than running around looking for a fight. But he knew to move forward with his life, he had to stop the threat. Besides, he couldn't leave Rashid to go up against the man alone. What if Cole got the upper hand? No, he was in it now. There was no changing the rules as he went along. King paused at the front door, put on his jacket, and checked the .38 in the pocket. He had thirteen rounds between the two weapons. Thirteen. Unlucky for some. Hopefully, it would be unlucky for Cole. King had never been superstitious.

Outside, Flymo was readying the helicopter for take-off. The rotors were spinning and both men adopted the classic helicopter run as they approached and boarded the craft. Belted up and with headsets on to shut out the noise and communicate with each other, the helicopter

took off and banked hard to port as it headed
west.

55

Cole had stolen two sets of plates from cars in a service station carpark on the M5 motorway near Taunton. He had chosen newer models, because he could not fathom the numberplate system and the significance of the numbers and letters in ageing the vehicles. He did not want to put older plates on a newer car, something the police might notice, so he chose two cars of similar shape and design, although he was unfamiliar with the makes and models. Most of the cars in England seemed so much smaller than those in the US.

He had bought some first aid items in the travel shop and used the privacy of the disabled toilet cubicle to redress the wound. It had been agony to clean, and he could tell all was not well because of the spikiness of whatever shrapnel was inside. He dowsed the wound with antiseptic, applied gauze both sides and padded plasters, before rebandaging. After tossing the bloody dressings in the sanitary bin, he washed his face and stared at his reflection in the mirror. He barely recognised himself. He wondered whether his wife and son would walk past him in the street. He was a shadow of his former self, hollowed out and gaunt. His eyes were barely recognisable, and he knew he was unwell. He was under no illusion that he was suffering from PTSD and depression, but all he knew was when he focused on King, the man who had cost him his career, his honour, he felt alive. Without the hate and sense of retribution driving him, he had no purpose in this life.

Cole bought some water and a coffee in a go-cup and a takeaway cheeseburger and made his way back out to the car. He re-joined the busy motorway and took the next junction, following the main road that would eventually lead to the A303, the alternative route to London. He drove steadily under the gantry cameras and after leaving it as long as he dared, he left the main road and took a series of small B roads to Salisbury. He then skirted the town and headed back into the countryside. He found a road with little traffic, then pulled into a lane to change the number plates over. He took more painkillers, especially as the simple task of unscrewing the plates and attaching new ones was both awkward and painful with his injured hand. He bit the bullet and took some of the liquid morphine and got back behind the wheel and headed cross country back to the A303. He was close now, closing in on his target.

56

Flymo banked hard and followed the road below them, while Rashid read out the coordinates. King used a passive infrared monocular to survey the ground below, while Flymo wore a set of PNGs turning the world below into a sea of green. He dropped lower, just fifty feet above the ground, mindful of the electric wires running parallel with the road and read the car number plate back to Rashid before lifting higher.

"Negative," said Rashid. "The bastard's disappeared into thin air." He checked the text he had just received and said, "The PNC has him near Ilminster, then nothing until Salisbury. Then he seems to drive a circular route and goes under the radar again."

"He's fucking with us," said King. "The bastard must be changing his plates or something."

"Why the hell would he do that?" asked Flymo.

"Maybe he's trying to unsettle us. Or King, at least."

"I'm not unsettled, just pissed off I haven't killed him yet."

"Me too…" said Rashid. "But I don't get why he's playing with us. What could he gain from flagging up on the PNC and then disappearing?"

"Shit…" King tapped Flymo on the shoulder and said, "Get in contact with the safehouse, now!"

"What's wrong?" Rashid asked as Flymo tapped into the phone on the dash. Their mobiles would never cope with the noise of the rotors overhead.

"Cole has an in. He found out where Caroline and I live. That wouldn't have been easy. But if he was given that information, then what other information could he have been given? It's not out of the question for him to know where I have gone. MI5 has safehouses around the country. What if he has been fed intel by someone with the Security Service?"

"Who?"

King shook his head. "Bugger, it makes sense. If he was doing a job for the Russians, then they could have fed him intel through their sources. We all know the Russian mafia and the FSB and the SVR have connections. We killed the Russian mob down at my place…"

"Hey, I only offed one when he was about to kill you," Rashid corrected him. "Jesus, I don't want to be lumped in with you when the report gets filed."

"Whatever, but if those Russian mobsters had enough intel to find me, and they have shared intel with Cole, then anything is possible."

"But more than that," Rashid said tentatively. "If the SVR or FSB can come up with that, then they *must* have a backdoor into MI5."

The phone rang in their headsets and Ramsay answered. "Neil, it's King. Listen carefully: get Big Dave and Thorpe, you are about to be contacted."

"Contacted?"

"Attacked, Neil! Fucking well attacked! Cole has led us here. He must know where the safe house is. He's been pinging on and off the traffic database on the PNC. Trust me, I know how this man operates. You are about to be attacked…"

57

"Put that down!" Big Dave pointed at the phone in Thorpe's hand. "Get yourself out the back and check the door to the kitchen is locked and turn off all the lights as you go!"

Thorpe hesitated, looking at the Remington pump-action shotgun in the man's hand. She looked about to protest but thought better of it and sprinted out of the hall and towards the kitchen. She headed into the dining room and through to the kitchen and put the catch down on the door. She thought about the lights, didn't feel she knew the layout of the building well enough to get by without them, but knew it was more about whoever was outside not seeing the people on the inside, like a theatre audience sees the players on a stage. She made her way back out through the dining room, flicking off the light switch for good measure. She looked at the phone in her hand and hesitated over the digit nine. Three taps and she could get help. She looked up as Ramsay walked into the hall. He was looking worried, but when he saw the phone in her hand, he shook his head.

"Put that away," he said, echoing Big Dave's take on it. "They're on the way back in the helicopter, ETA fifteen minutes."

"But we need to call the police," she said, but the realisation that she was no longer a police officer seemed to dawn on her and she shrugged. "We *do* need armed police here if there is a threat to life."

"There'll be a threat to life alright, when King and Rashid get here…" He paused. "Right, let's get upstairs."

"Upstairs?"

"We need to take advantage of the high ground," he replied, starting up the stairs. "Have you had weapon's training? No, of course not. I've read your file. Here, take this." He handed her a Glock 26 9mm pistol. It was short and stubby and a shrunken version of the police-issue Glock 17 and was marketed as the 'Baby Glock'. "You have ten rounds, but because it's so small it has a bit of recoil. It's ready to fire and there's no hammer to cock or safety to worry about. Keep your finger off the trigger unless you need to fire." Thorpe took the pistol and looked at it curiously. Ramsay pointed at a little spring-loaded flap on the trigger. "That's the only safety. It won't fire unless that is pushed flush with the trigger with your trigger finger. The sights are painted with illuminous white paint. You simply line up the foresight and the rear notch until they align perfectly, then squeeze... don't pull... squeeze the trigger. Failing that, just point-shoot if you're close enough to see the whites of their eyes."

"Jesus Christ! You make it sound like *Zulu*!" She held the weapon like it would burn her and said, "It's all right for you, you're an expert at this. I've never held a gun in my life!"

Ramsay shrugged. "Well, I've only had a morning's training on a range. I don't really like guns."

"Shit, we're dead..." Thorpe shook her head. "Where's Goliath? He's a soldier type, isn't he?"

"Ex-SAS and as tough as they come."

"Well, that's a relief."

"He's outside."

"He's what?"

"Outside."

"What the hell is he doing outside?" Thorpe switched off the hall light from the top of the stairs."

"No," said Ramsay and switched it back

on. "That's the only way he's coming upstairs, so we leave that light on and switch the upstairs lights off to illuminate him if he makes it inside."

Thorpe was visibly shaking and still holding the tiny pistol like it was hot. Which, in a sense it was. "But what's he doing outside?" she repeated herself as she crouched down beside a solid mahogany sideboard and aimed at the stairs.

"He said he was going hunting," Ramsay said quietly and laid down prone. He aimed his Glock 26 through the spindles of the banisters at the foot of the stairs, with just the muzzle poking through.

"What now?" asked Thorpe nervously.

"Now?" Ramsay asked tersely. "Now, we wait."

58

His intention was to probe at King's defences. Unsettle him further and slip away. He had operated in a similar manner in Afghanistan. Hit the enemy and slip away. Let them send hundreds of men into the Hindu Kush and tie them up with IEDs and airstrikes, while Cole and his team hit the next compound, the next cave, then next caravan of fighters laden with supplies heading through the mountains from the training camps in Pakistan. Hit and run.

He knew that there was a good chance they would head towards the last place he had ensured his vehicle would flag up on the police national computer via the traffic cameras. If he could hit whoever remained in the safehouse, he could shake King to the core. He had seen the lights go off, just one remaining downstairs. Possibly someone working late. But he knew that there would be a good chance of CCTV in the grounds, so he moved in the undergrowth and foliage of the garden – set back sixty metres from the house – and watched the windows of the property intently. He had concluded it was a soft target. If he could get across the open ground without detection, then he would be able to use the 3D printed .12 gauge pistol on the hinges of the door, and that left him with thirty rounds of 9mm in the MP5 he had taken from the police officer at the hospital.

Cole decided his best bet was to make his way around to the corner of the building, sprint the shortest distance of open ground, then make his way across the width of the façade right up against the building. Any arcs of fire from above would be too acute and leave the shooter exposed, and he would be in the best position to return fire at the ground floor windows as he kept moving. As he reached the edge of the lawn, covered by a large rhododendron bush, he made sure he could reach the 3D printed pistol in his pocket and shouldered the MP5, before taking a tentative step onto the gravel. Movement was critical. People noticed speed, like a scurrying rat in a chicken pen, or that house spider racing the length of the skirting board, peoples' eyes were drawn to anomalies. As a soldier operating in hostile territory, Cole had lived by the mantra of the seven S's. Silhouette, shadow, shine, shape, speed, shade, and sound. He would be breaking cover, but if he did it slowly the dark backdrop behind him should still mask his presence, and careful foot placement across the gravel would keep the sound level down.

Cole was five paces out when the gunshot rang out. He knew he'd been hit, but he chose to run onwards towards the house. Attack, attack, attack… The second shot floored him, and he sprawled across the gravel. He returned a short burst of fire, but even he was unsure of the direction and knew he was up against someone who would certainly not hang around in the same position they had fired from. Cole scrambled up, hearing the ratchet of the pump-action shotgun in the night-time silence. He slipped and sprawled on the gravel, hearing another shot but feeling nothing. The gravel ahead of him dispersed in a spray of chippings and earth and confirmed the gunman had a shotgun. Cole reached the grass and tore through the undergrowth, zigzagging to throw any pursuer off the pace and lessen the chances of taking a shot to the back. He could hear the whump-whump-whump of a helicopter above and risked a look into the night sky. It was banking hard and heading towards the rear of the house. Cole veered into the wooded area he had stalked in on, and raced on, his legs stinging from the first spread of lead shot. He was breathing hard, his ribs aching, and he knew he had taken some shot to his side, but just hoped his thick jacket had slowed it down enough to embed in his considerable muscle mass. He hadn't imagined King would have a helicopter at his disposal, so had not allowed enough time. He had been compromised, but undoubtedly saved from being overwhelmed by his enemy once he was inside the house. He would have been fighting on all fronts. He just hoped he could get back to his car in time, and that his wounds were not life-threatening.

He could only hope.

59

Big Dave broke cover once he had reloaded the shotgun. He had seen Cole reach the undergrowth but had chosen to remain near the house. It would be easy to follow the man, chase him down in a hot-blooded pursuit only to find he had taken up a prone position under a bush and prepared an ambush. Big Dave had learned enough in his career as a soldier that he should always live to fight another day.

He could hear the helicopter's twin turboshaft engines winding down and the rotors slowing. He cursed loudly. If he had been able to contact Flymo from his position, then he would have been able to have them guide him to Cole's position using their night vision goggles. He set off around the rear of the house to intercept them and avoid walking into a trap should Cole be lying in wait, either intentionally or wounded and unable to make it any further. He knew from fighting in the Tora Bora that a wounded fighter making what they knew to be their last stand was the worst enemy of all.

King had alighted the craft and was heading towards the house. Rashid was putting the rifle back inside the gun slip and detaching his headset. King looked up as Big Dave approached.

"He's here," said Big Dave. "I just shot him a couple of times with this…" He raised the shotgun. "Just number six bird and rabbit shot, and at sixty metres, so he's wounded, but he will keep going."

"Christ!" King glanced at the helicopter and caught Flymo's eye in the darkness. The moon just giving enough light to make out the man's eyes against his black face. King made a rotation signal with his index finger, and the man got back inside the helicopter and started up the controls. "Did you go after him?"

"Bugger that, man. He's more dangerous wounded. You take one side, and I'll take the other and we'll pincer him."

King nodded, looked up as Rashid jogged over to them. "Cole's here. Lomu nailed him with the shotgun. He can't have gone far. Do you want him?" he asked.

Rashid looked at him. "And you don't?" He had to raise his voice above the rising din of the twin engines and rotors. "I thought you wouldn't rest until he's dead."

King shrugged. "The more I chase

around, the more I wish I was at Caroline's bedside. Dead is dead, I don't care who does it. But he *must* go down…"

"Well don't let the detective hear you say that," Big Dave quipped. "Listen, I'll go check on Ramsay and the copper, you ladies decide who's going to slot the bastard and get back to me," he said, then turned and ran back towards the house.

"Well, that told us," Rashid grinned. He nodded at King and said, "I've got a night sight on this, you get me close enough and I'll take him down."

King patted him on the shoulder but said nothing. He jogged back to the helicopter and it lifted the moment he sat back in the seat. After he put the headset on, he picked up the monocular and held it to his right eye. "Cole's here," he said. "He's wounded; Lomu got him with a shotgun. He was last seen heading through the undergrowth to the south-east of the property."

"On it." Flymo banked hard and straightened up on a south-westerly heading so that he could come around on a hard banked-turn to give King maximum field of view with the monocular. "What's he armed with? It effects the height we fly at."

"Not sure." He pressed the telephone link and got through to Big Dave. "What is Cole armed with?"

"Something short and light. Nine-millimetre maybe, machine pistol by the profile."

"Okay, that fits the weapon he took from the armed police officer." He paused and said to Flymo, "He's got a nine-millimetre MP5." Flymo nodded and took the aircraft down to three-hundred feet. He was making seventy miles-per-hour, which would make Cole one hell of a shot. King went back to the call. "Are you with Rashid now?"

"One hundred metres apart, I'm on the left heading away..."

"Yeah, I think I'll spot the difference between you two. Stay put and we'll fly by and let you know if Cole is lying up someplace. Get Rashid on a three-way."

"Not to my taste, mate."

"Three-way conference call, dickhead."

"Well, hang up and get it done yourself. I'm in the dark down here and hunting some bastard with a machine gun."

King ended the call and tapped on the telephone display. Big Dave had a point. Flymo started the banked turn and King watched the ground below them. The monocular displayed everything in shades of green. When they finished the turn, Flymo banked to starboard and prepared to approach from the north-west, performing a perfect figure of 8. This time King could make out both Lomu and Rashid. There was no sign of Cole between them. Flymo pulled up another thousand feet and banked to port. He flew straight over the area with the nose tilted forward, forcing King to grip tightly to the door loop and press back in his seat as there appeared to be nothing between them and the ground. The manoeuvre and approach gave them a terrific field of view and King could see the area was clear.

"Fly a few more passes," he said to Flymo, then spoke into the telephone for the first time in their three-way conference call. "Boys, it looks like the bastard has disappeared. Unless he's dug in someplace, he must have reached his vehicle and taken off. We'll go over the area a couple more times then follow the road for a few miles and see if he got to the main road."

60

"He can't have just vanished into thin air!" Thorpe exclaimed.

"Well, he has," King replied.

"We need to call the police. He's out there with a weapon and intent on murder. "Who knows what he's willing to do…"

They had secured all the exits and Flymo was monitoring the CCTV around the property. Big Dave had insisted on performing a roving patrol around the grounds, and was now wearing Rashid's pair of PNGs, or primary night-vision goggles. He carried the pump-action shotgun and the Glock 26 Ramsay had previously lent to Thorpe. King, Rashid, and Thorpe had gathered in the dining room, primarily because it was an internal room with no windows and the most secure place to be.

King didn't reply to Thorpe, but he looked at Ramsay and said, "How the hell did he find us here?" He paused. "We have to have a leak somewhere."

"Agreed," said Ramsay. "Sally-Anne and I are returning to London in the morning where she will assist me in a matter of great concern. I am also meeting with Simon Mereweather to discuss the abduction of Director Amherst's daughter. But I want you to look at this first." He turned his laptop around and played the video. "That's Cole at Taunton Dean services on the M5 motorway. Note the bandaged hand. That ties in with Rashid's report on shooting him. Here he is buying first aid supplies from the travel shop, and then you can see him going into the lavatory." Ramsay paused. "Now, this video…" He clicked on a file and continued, "…is of Cole's vehicle in the carpark." Ramsay paused the footage. "The PNC flagged up the numberplate and police were dispatched, but he had already left when they got there and subsequent patrols didn't find him, and shortly afterwards he went dark. He must have taken the next exit and switched plates, then switched them back again to get the vehicle flagged up in Salisbury."

"So, he wanted to be caught?" asked Thorpe.

"No, he wanted to be discovered. Briefly. To divide our defences," said King. "He made sure he was pinged on the traffic cameras and then changed plates and headed here. He didn't bank on us having a helicopter at our disposal, so it cut his attack short."

Rashid smiled. "That and Big Dave with a shotgun in the bushes."

Ramsay nodded. "But look at this footage…" He played the clip, and a man could be seen walking past Cole's hire car. The man stooped and reached under the vehicle for a moment, then stood up and continued on his way. "I've rooted through the CCTV time frames that the police have requisitioned from the services and the traffic cameras on the database and have found this." He clicked again and the man could be seen getting into a car. At no time did his face come into view. However, as Cole left the services, the other vehicle followed two minutes later. Ramsay flicked to another link and the vehicle was picked up on the traffic camera. A woman was clearly visible behind the wheel, but still the man's face was out of view. "I don't know who these two people are, but I'm convinced they put a tracker on Cole's car."

"And how did they find him in the first place?" asked Rashid.

"It's obvious," said King. "There's a back door into MI5 and it's been left swinging on its hinges." He paused, looking at the footage, then paused it on the woman's face. The image was clear, and King spread his thumb and forefinger on the touch screen to enlarge it further. "We don't allow foreign intelligence services access to the PNC, do we?"

Ramsay nodded. "No. Not on your life. But we will obviously help them with their investigations." He paused. "Why do you ask?"

"I know that woman," King replied, staring at the image on the screen. "Her name is Rachel Beam, and she's an agent with the United States Secret Service."

61

It was a small railway viaduct across an even smaller country road, but it provided Cole with shelter from the searching helicopter above. He had pulled under its cover, switched off the vehicle's lights and waited. No other vehicles had passed him on the quiet minor road, but he could see distant headlights in his rear-view mirror. He would wait until the vehicle drew near, apply his hazard warning lights, and then take it from there. The likeliest outcome would be for the vehicle to simply drive past. If a concerned motorist asked if he needed assistance, then he would thank them and tell them a breakdown vehicle was already on the way. The third scenario would be a team from the safehouse, in which case he still had more than twenty-five rounds of 9mm in the MP5 as well as two .12-gauge shells for the 3D printed gun. He wouldn't be going down without a fight.

He had taken lead shot to his legs, and they hurt like a hundred bee stings. He knew it wouldn't be pretty, but he had already assessed that he was not bleeding dangerously, and morphine, tweezers and dressings would be sufficient once he found somewhere to rest up. The wound to his side would be nigh-on impossible to effectively treat himself, as several pellets had hit above his kidney and he would not be able to reach them. He could feel them under the skin but reflected that he had been lucky. When up against a shotgun, distance was your friend. Sometimes just a few paces meant all the difference and ten paces could be the difference between feeling the shot or just hearing it. There was no other weapon that could be as devastating at close range, but so ineffective after a fifteen second sprint from it.

Cole pressed some gauze down his side, sandwiching it between his skin and his shirt. His jacket was thick, and a snug fit and held the gauze firmly in place. The heavy-duty material had probably saved his life, too.

The vehicle drew closer, its lights illuminating the inside of the car and making Cole feel exposed. It pulled in behind him and the engine switched off, but the headlights remained on. Cole tightened his grip on the machine pistol and lowered his window all the way. He took a deep breath to steady his nerves and watched the man get out of the car through his rear-view mirror. He closed the door after him and as he approached, Cole could see he was of medium height and build and wore a light-coloured suit with no tie, and shirt open a couple of buttons at the neck. He did not look like King or the men he surrounded himself with, and Cole imagined this man was an office worker on his way home from a late shift or a meeting.

"Hi," the man said, his accent neutral but a fellow American. "Got some vehicle trouble, I see."

"The engine died," Cole shouted back through the open window. From his position he needed the man to take a couple more steps before he could get a shot off if required, but the man had stopped walking. "A tow truck is on the way, thanks." Cole added breathlessly, the liquid morphine starting to wear off.

"I'm referring to your run in with MI5," the man said. Cole opened the door and started to get out, but the pain to the shotgun wounds made him wince, and the pain to his hand was so acute, that he struggled with the door handle. "Relax, Cole. I'm with the CIA and I'm here to assist you, then get the show back on the road with the Brits." Cole continued to struggle his way out of the car, but when he finally got clear, he could see that the man was no longer a threat to him, and he had the advantage of the machine gun in his hand. "My name is Newman," he said, his accent a Virginian drawl.

"Who's in the car?"

"Rachel Beam," replied Newman. "She's with the Secret Service. King has a great deal to answer to. When he's down, the slate gets wiped clean and the Brits can become our buddies again. Only you're making a bit of a mess of it, getting all these Russian and Italian mobsters involved. I get it, you wanted to cash in as well, but the shit has well and truly splattered against the fan on this, and oh boy, is it going to be hard to clean up after you."

Cole looked at him, gave the machine pistol a little jab in the air. "Get her out of the car."

Newman turned and gestured Beam to come forward. She opened the door and stepped out into the road, then walked around the car and stepped onto the verge, then tentatively picked through the grass, and walked over to them.

"What's the Secret Service's angle on this?" asked Cole.

Beam shrugged. "King has ridden rough shod over the constitution, democracy and our liberty. He assassinated President Standing and just about every government agency has covered it up to save face. The bastard used me to get near to Standing, I want him to answer for what he's done."

Cole nodded. "He cost me my career, my health and my family. I want him dead. Is that going to be a problem with either of you?"

"Not with the CIA," Newman said quietly. "He looked at Beam and said, "Cole is going to want to disappear with his fortune. The CIA were never involved." He smirked. "You can take the credit and ride the bullshit wave all the way home to glory."

Beam looked at both men. It had gone too far, at too great a price. She nodded and said, "Sure, whatever works."

"Okay," said Newman. He looked at Cole and nodded to the weapon. "You can put the gun down now. You're obviously hurt, let's find someplace to hole up and look at your wounds. There's a *Travel Lodge* nearby. Rachel can go find a twenty-four-hour pharmacy and get what you need."

Cole visibly relaxed as he lowered the machine pistol. "Sounds great. I could do with some food, too. I've been running on empty since…"

Beam flinched at the gunshot as it echoed all around them, the noise hemmed in by the stone walls of the viaduct. Cole fell backwards into the road and Newman stepped forward and fired another shot into the man's forehead.

"What have you done?!" Rachel Beam screamed, her voice echoing almost as much as the gunshot. Newman bent down and retrieved the MP5, then turned around and faced her. "He was one of us!" she screamed at him. "Taking down King isn't a two-person job!"

Newman nodded. "I'm aware of that," he said. "But I'm not here for King. The man is a top agent with our greatest and longest standing ally. There has been a crossing of swords, some churlish tit for tat attacks on one another. The CIA are eager for it to come to an end."

"But why did you need me?"

Newman sighed. "You're the agent who almost got him. You're the agent who unwittingly led him to Standing. You're the agent who is confined to working in a boxroom office lamenting her career, with the stench of defeat on her. Nobody wants to be associated with you. I'm sorry, Rachel, but there it is."

"I don't get it. Why did I need to be here?" She looked down at Cole's body, then at Newman, the reason suddenly dawning on her.

Newman fired a short burst of the machine pistol and she fell backwards, her body on the grass verge and her feet in the road. Most of the bullets had hit her in the stomach, but two had struck below her heart, towards the centre of her sternum. She gasped for air, groaned, and kicked out her legs. "I'm sorry, Rachel." Newman bent down and caught hold of her right hand and pressed the small automatic pistol into her palm. She did not know what he was doing, but he positioned her fingers and fired a shot into the night. He then tossed the pistol into the road. "I'm sorry it wasn't clean," he said. "But it won't take long…" He stood up and returned to Cole, positioned the dead man's fingers around the grip and trigger of the MP5 and fired two rounds through the viaduct into the air. Both now had powder residue on their hands, and their fingerprints on the weapons. He dropped the weapon with a clatter into the road and walked back to check on Beam. She had died and was staring past him into the night sky. Newman walked back to the vehicle and closed the door. He took a breath to steady himself before starting the engine. What he had done would not sit easy with him. But there was always the bigger picture, and he had done his duty.

62

"And you are sure that's him?"

"Positive."

"And the woman is Rachel Beam, of the US Secret Service?"

King nodded. The police had pulled back behind the cordon and both King and Simon Mereweather had access to the crime scene. They were both kitted out in coveralls with hoods, face masks and over-socks covering their shoes. They had been instructed by SOCO not to touch anything. "No sign of the guy in the CCTV footage at the services," he said.

Mereweather shook his head. "Doesn't feel right, does it? Tell me, as a man of your experience and … er, expertise… what do you see?"

Simon Mereweather had called upon Flymo to come to London and taxi him down upon hearing of the discovery of Cole's body. The police were not aware of the man himself but had discovered the original number plates in the vehicle and they were flagged on the PNC. Ramsay and Thorpe were already on their way to London with Big Dave driving them. King had driven to the scene with Rashid and both men had felt numb at the idea the man had been killed by somebody else, and it had been difficult to accept that he really was dead, and that it wasn't some kind of elaborate ploy. But dead is dead, and they had confirmed it quickly and positively. Rashid had remained outside the cordon after Mereweather had arrived. He looked every bit as numb as King felt inside.

"What really happened? Or at least what we'll convince the police happened?" King replied.

"There are two outcomes? Which one is the truth?"

"There was a third person in this tidy scenario. He shot Cole first, because Cole was ex-special forces, and he was armed with the stolen MP5. Superior firepower…"

"Over that little pistol, yes," Mereweather concurred.

"Beam wasn't armed," said King. "She was shot by the same person who shot Cole, but she died unarmed and certainly confused at what was happening. I don't know who this other guy is, but I would bet everything that he's CIA. He came to shut Cole down, and Beam was a tidy end to it. The Secret Service agent who went to the UK to bring a criminal back to justice. Cole was a rogue agent mixed up in President Standing's criminal affairs. He killed a member of MI5 and went off the radar." King paused. "The poor woman was caught up in all of this, deceived by someone whom she clearly thought she was working with. This guy sold her something. Hell, she probably thought she was coming here after me. He played her like a fiddle, right up to the end."

Mereweather nodded. "The car was rented in her name, hotels booked in her name, also." He paused. "So, as far as the police are concerned, we sell her as the good guy and Cole as the bad guy, but the good guy was tragically killed along with her quarry in the shootout."

"That's about it."

Mereweather nodded. "Why would someone do this?"

King shrugged. "I imagine your doors to the CIA and the US State Department will open a little wider as the weeks and months pass. Someone has freed up the blockade." He paused. "We might all be friends again now."

Mereweather smiled. "That *is* insightful. Are you sure you don't want a comfortable desk job on my floor?"

"Thanks. But I'd rather die quickly in the field, than slowly behind a desk."

Mereweather looked at him, unsure whether he was joking or not, but decided he had been deadly serious. "Get back to Caroline," he said. "When she comes round, I have made arrangements for her to have a private room at The Duchy Hospital. It's a private hospital next to the main hospital in Truro. It will offer care second to none and she can stay as long as it takes."

"The service will pay for that?"

Mereweather did not reply, having covered it himself. His family were old money and he barely touched his own salary. "Go to her. This is over for you."

King nodded, but he thought about the text he had received earlier that morning asking him to travel directly and without delay to London. Director Amherst had reiterated that he should, *Tell no one...* And knowing the man's situation with his daughter, King didn't feel he could turn the man down.

As he walked back to the perimeter of the crime scene, he couldn't help wondering why he was putting off returning to Caroline's bedside and for the first time in years, he realised he was frightened. Frightened of what he would discover, and whether he would cope. Facing bullets and bombs was nothing compared to facing up to the reality of her condition.

63

London

King saw Amherst on the bench, his raincoat and briefcase beside him. The man looked hollowed out. His world had been turned upside down, and someone had reached into his inner sanctum and wrenched out the love. He knew the feeling.

There was no security detail in the vicinity, King was certain of that. He checked above the river, the road, and the buildings behind. He couldn't spot a drone, and he hadn't spotted a watcher unit. The man had been as good as his word. How he had escaped the security, now on heightened alert, he had no idea. But the man had said the window was small, so he walked over and sat down when Amherst removed the raincoat and briefcase.

"No news is good news," King said.

Amherst shrugged. "But I've had news," he said. "I've given SO15 and the watchers the slip. They'll be incandescent, but I can say the stress was simply too much. I just needed to breathe…"

"What do you mean you've *had* news?" King interrupted him.

"I don't know how, but they contacted my wife's mobile phone and made a demand. They must be well-connected and tech savvy. No police, nobody from MI5, no tricks. A simple exchange. It's not a ridiculous sum of money, either. Hardly a king's ransom."

"You're going to pay?"

Amherst shook his head dejectedly. "My head says that we should never bow to terror, but my heart says she's my little girl and I just want her back... need her back." He paused. "How can I look my wife in the eyes, knowing that I had a chance to get her back, but didn't take it because of the hard line we take on terrorism? I can't. Jesus Christ, our son thinks Bethany has gone to her friend's house for the weekend." He wiped an errant tear from his eye. "We just couldn't tell him."

King stared at the river, the brown, slow-moving waters of the Thames a constant in the busy world around them. He had come at Amherst's request. A simple text message telling him under no circumstances to let anybody know he had contacted him. He had added that it was vital he attend. King had been set to return to Cornwall and check on Caroline, but a call to Sinclair had confirmed that Caroline was still in a coma, and they would start to test her responses in a couple of days, and King had suddenly felt scared at the prospect of returning. Of feeling inadequate and useless, of what he would do if she could not go on without the life support system. He had pictured his wife Jane on the bed. Lifeless and imperceptibly still. All his life he had been surrounded by death, but he did not think he could deal with it on such a personal level again. He knew now, as he sat beside the intelligence chief and watched the muddy waters of the Thames, that he was running away from a fight he feared he could not win. And that was not something he was accustomed to. He had always genuinely believed that by meeting the battle head on, he had always improved his odds. Being the storm, rather than sheltering from it.

King looked back at Amherst. "So, you want me to get her out," he said flatly.

"God, no! I just want you to deliver the ransom. That's it. No guns, no heroics. Just a straight swap."

"You know it won't go down like that, right?"

Amherst shook his head. "No, it will. I have given my word." He handed King a piece of paper. "That's the place you wait. You text the number on there and wait for their reply. They will instruct you what to do next and where to make the drop." Amherst's lip started to quiver, and he looked away.

"We need to get snipers in place, electronic surveillance, a team of watchers…"

"No god dammit!" Amherst snapped and a woman jogging past swerved out from them a few feet, looking quizzically at them both. The director general leaned closer to King and said. "This is how it will happen. I'm not putting my daughter's life at risk and I can lose our life's savings if it gets it done simply, and safely." He reached under the seat and placed an airline pull along case at King's feet. "One hundred thousand pounds. If you think about it, it makes sense. I was never going to find a million and this way, they get all of a small amount rather than none of a larger, and unrealistic amount."

"This is crazy."

"Do this for me, King. Tell nobody, no guns, no heroics. I can trust you, can't I?"

King stood up and picked up the case and shrugged. "I think this is crazy, but yes. I will do it for you."

"And you won't try anything?" He looked up at him, his eyes glossy, desperation swimming in them. "Can I trust you?"

"Can I trust *you*?" King asked, staring at him.

"Of course, you can…"

"Then you can trust me to do the right thing," King replied. He looked Amherst in the eye, but the man had trouble holding his gaze. It had only been sixteen hours, but the man was a wreck. In King's opinion Amherst's judgement was affected, but that was only to be expected. King nodded at him and walked away, melting seamlessly into the crowd.

Amherst sighed. All he could do now, was wait. And hope that King wouldn't attempt anything more than he had tasked him to do.

64

The London underground system had bypassed this section of line and the track and station had been blocked off in the late seventies. Ramsay had seen the famed advertising poster of Twiggy promoting the Mini as he had walked across the platform, and he had to admit that it had felt a surreal experience. Prices of fares and concessions had remained the same and it was like walking into part of a museum feature or interactive experience.

This section had been used as a bunker during the Cold War and in a cover story involving sewers and drains and the removal of a giant fatberg in the early eighties, had been surrounded by lead, concrete and tonnes of metal to hold it all in place and became the centre of MI5 and MI6 operations in the event of a thermo-nuclear airstrike by the Soviet Union. Joined by similarly protected tunnels and stations, Downing Street and Whitehall operations were designed to continue in the same vein and connected by a train and carriages. Huge food and water stores and a fuel dump were secreted in the unused tunnels to keep the hub of the country running in a worse-case scenario. Churchill had deployed a similar system for the War Office during the Second World War.

Thorpe had been distracted, unable to take in either the concept or reality of the site. She had stared at the adverts for *Sugar Puffs* featuring the *Honey Monster* and was reminded of her childhood. Then she had stared aghast at a particular brand of cigarette featuring a man blowing smoke into a woman's face with the tagline, *"just blow smoke in her face and she'll follow you anywhere..."* She hesitated in front of a poster that had peeled and faded, but featured a semi-naked woman lying on the floor beside a pair of shoes and the tagline, *"keep her where she belongs..."*

"Jesus Christ. I mean, what's it even advertising?" she asked, then commented, "How we've moved on. Millennials need to see these."

"If you ever have a spare moment, look up seventies public information films," Ramsay suggested. "The dangers of diving into canals, the hazards of playing frisbee next to a power substation, rugs on polished wooden floors – the silent killer... they're priceless. People think health and safety has gone mad these days, but the seventies was on another level."

"Thanks, but I don't ever imagine being that bored," she smiled.

Ramsay shrugged and led the way, but he had only been down here once before. Ahead of them two separate lavatory blocks had been turned into interview rooms. Ramsay knew they had been used for far less amenable tasks during *the troubles* with the IRA and with more recently Al Qaeda and ISIS. There were stories of IRA terrorists having met a grisly end at the hands of interrogators and being bricked up in the recesses of tunnels. But as far as Ramsay knew, they were just stories.

Outside each door a uniformed security officer from the Security Service stood guard and both men straightened perceptibly as they walked towards them. Opposite them and leaning against the wall Big Dave was eating a large sub and holding a large soft drink in a cup with a straw.

"Who's in this one?" asked Ramsay.

"Hello to you, too." Big Dave looked at Thorpe and nodded. "Alright Sally-Anne? What do you think of this time capsule?"

"I would never have known," she said.

Big Dave looked down at Ramsay and said, "Door on the left is Richard Beckinsdale and door on the right is Stuart Baker."

"Did they resist much?"

"You're joking, aren't you? Like two little sheep."

Thorpe nodded. "Well, shall we see which one is a wolf underneath?"

"Do you have any suspicions?" Ramsay said to Big Dave.

"I'm the muscle," he replied. "I'm not paid to have suspicions. But if it helps, Stuart Baker is a monumental dickhead."

Thorpe laughed, saw that Ramsay didn't share her humour and became serious once more. "Well, that's not a crime. Otherwise half the senior coppers I've worked with would be in a cell."

Ramsay seemed to ignore her and said, "We'll take Baker first." He nodded to the guard nearest the door and he unlocked the door for them and stood to one side. "Leave the door open a touch," he said. "I don't like enclosed spaces." Ramsay walked through and ignored Baker as he took in the room. Cream staggered tiling, plain concrete floor, and a pitched ceiling with wooden rafters. A single lightbulb hung from a plain ceiling rose ten feet above their heads. There was a wooden table in the centre of the room and Baker was seated behind it on a plain wooden chair.

"What the hell am I doing here?" Baker protested. Ramsay ignored him as he pulled out one of the two remaining wooden chairs and sat down. He put a thick file on the table and sat back in his seat. "I want my bloody solicitor and a union representative!"

Ramsay nodded. "I think the FDA took up representation of the Security Service solely for pay grievances." He paused. "This is not a matter of pay and conditions."

"Then what on earth is it about?" Baker asked, red-faced and full of bluster. "You've never bloody well liked me, Neil. You've made that quite clear over the years."

"As have you."

"So, you're setting me up for a fall, is that it?"

"That's nonsense. We have a delicate situation and I wanted to see if you could shed any light on it."

Baker shrugged. "Well, go on, then…"

"Russian agents running around with guns, for one."

"That spook with the embassy? Alexander Putin. He was with the SVR."

"Do you know how he died?"

"Not officially. But the whispers are he was shot at some sort of exchange."

"With Russian mafia?"

"I wouldn't know about that."

"Why not? You run the Russia Desk, after all."

"I've put some feelers out, but nothing has come back yet. These things take time, and usually a payoff or two."

"One of our agents was attacked. By five Russians."

"Is the agent okay?"

"I can neither confirm or deny at this stage, but the Russians have either been killed or apprehended."

"Then if some have been apprehended, you should know more soon." Baker paused. "What else can I help you with?"

Ramsay stared at him, then touched the file. The manila folder was bursting with papers, dog-eared, and well handled. He glanced at Thorpe, who looked back at him impassively. Ramsay stared at Baker and said, "We've had a leak on the Russia Desk for some time now. I have copies of the financial records of personnel in the department. Is there anything you want to tell us?"

"No." Baker rubbed his brow. "Why would I want to tell you anything?"

"We've done a lot of digging."

"Good for you."

"And there's nothing you feel it would be beneficial to add?"

Baker shrugged. "I have a few credit card debts. It's nothing out of the ordinary. I book a family holiday and then pay it off throughout the year. Millions of people do the same."

"And Christmas and birthdays?"

"It's not bloody illegal. I have what, four, five thousand on card."

"Nine-thousand-seven-hundred and fifty-seven-pounds. And a few pence."

"Piss off!" Baker shook his head. "My wife goes a bit overboard sometimes."

"And that would be her car loan?"

"It all gets paid!"

"But debt is a service employment non-negotiable. Mortgages and manageable car finance excluded. Debt facilitates an opening and a reason to be bribed. Either by criminal elements or foreign organisations. The Russian

SVR for instance…"

"For god's sake!"

"Or women. I seem to remember you like women. Or womanising, at least."

"Now you're just being ridiculous!" He shook his head.

"Am I?" Ramsay peeled a few sheets off the top of the file. "You have made a few cash payments into your current account. The service pays your salary monthly into your account. So, how is it you have cash payments going in?"

Baker shook his head, then rested his face in his hands on the table. "I've sold off a few things to try and tackle the debt and spending. Some antique silver, a watch, some paintings, some jewellery my wife never wears and wouldn't notice missing. That and family heirlooms, mostly. Pawn shops and some social media selling sites. When it gets to five-hundred pounds or so, enough to make a dent in the debt, I pay it into the bank and then transfer it to where it's most needed."

"And as fast as you pay it off, the more she seems to ramp it up," Thorpe commented.

"I'm trying, truly I am."

"And when the SVR approached you, you had to accept," said Thorpe.

"No!" Baker stood up, slamming his chair back onto the floor, his fists hammering onto the table.

Thorpe stood up defensively, but Ramsay remained seated and didn't flinch. "Sit down, Stuart," he said calmly. He looked at Thorpe and said, "I think we'll leave it there." He stood up and gathered up the file.

"I want my lawyer," Baker said, watching them leave.

Ramsay did not look back, nor did he offer a reply and simply closed the solid metal door behind them. He nodded for the guard to open the door and stepped inside. Thorpe left the door open, but Ramsay nudged it closed and she frowned at him with confusion.

"I'm sorry about all this, Richard. I've asked one of the guards to fetch some tea, shouldn't be long now."

"That's alright, Neil. How can I be of assistance?"

"I'm sure you might have already heard." Ramsay paused. "This place echoes rather."

Beckinsdale shrugged. "I heard some shouting, but I couldn't make out anything other than that Stuart was angry about something."

Ramsay nodded. "Did you know your colleague had substantial mounting debts?"

"Stuart? No." He paused, looking shocked at the notion. "Not a clue."

"It's a delicate matter. Debt so often is." He paused. "We are certain Stuart Baker has been feeding the Russians information in return for cash payments."

"Oh, my lord…" Beckinsdale trailed off.

"We have a situation where hostile Russian forces tracked down and attacked an agent with the Security Service. We believe that Stuart Baker sold them the information they needed to get to him."

"I see. Do you want me to look into it?" He looked at them both with concern, then said, "You don't suspect me, do you?"

Ramsay shook his head and touched the thick file in front of him. "There's some conclusive evidence in there that would point to Baker. His log in number requesting information on the databases and the PNC. You worked alongside him, was there anything that aroused your suspicion?"

"No, sorry."

"Were you aware of Russians operating on UK soil?"

"Certainly not."

"We don't know how deep the SVR's infiltration goes, or what other channels they have access to, but we need to work backwards. Damage limitation and control."

"Of course."

Ramsay drummed his fingers on the cover of the file. "It's just not the Russian's MO, that's all."

"They're a ruthless bunch. Adaptable, too."

"Absolutely." Ramsay paused. "Interpol said as much. Informed us of an impending hit. How do you imagine it got this far?"

"With Stuart?"

"No, with the Russians."

"Tit-for-tat, I suppose. I know that we hit them at the end of the summer."

"In retaliation for the assassination of the husband and wife of two prominent figures."

"But before, with the operation last summer. A team hit them hard."

"Agreed," said Ramsay. "That's the problem with tit-for-tat."

"They wanted vengeance."

"I suppose it's to be expected."

"The Russian mafia don't let things go."

"And they're connected."

"Everybody is out there," agreed Beckinsdale.

"How do you think they would have done it? Border Force didn't flag anything suspicious, and Stuart Baker denies passing information, but he logged in and accessed the PNC. He can deny it as much as he likes, the evidence is damming."

"He will have used his SVR contact and in turn, they used the mafia to attempt the hit."

Ramsay nodded. "That's the second time you've mentioned the mafia. I don't recall saying it was anything other than Russian intelligence services involved." He paused. "And there is no record of us having a team hit the Russian mafia last summer. Only that a hit was sanctioned on the man behind the killings in London. To know that, you will have to have heard it from the Russians' end." Ramsay opened the file and said, "As you say, tit-for-tat. Again, even though you man the Russia Desk, the retaliation hit was a black bag operation. Until I was read in on it for this investigation, only two men knew about it."

Beckinsdale frowned. "Office gossip."

"One man above me, and the man who did the job. That was it."

Beckinsdale shifted in his seat and adjusted his tie as if it were hot, but the tiled room was cold, as was the rest of the forgotten station. "What are you saying, Neil?"

Ramsay remained silent, drumming his fingers once more. Thorpe smiled and said, "The PNC was accessed the day before yesterday with Stuart Baker's personal user ID. At the same time as he was logged in, we have footage of Baker leaving a meeting at Whitehall. Who else would have used his user ID to log onto the PNC? Someone who had something vital to find yet couldn't wait until the patsy was back in the building. Must have been important."

"I..." Beckinsdale shifted awkwardly. "I would like to see my lawyer now."

Ramsay chuckled. He was a mirthless man at best, so it sounded all the stranger that he should break his own perceived behaviour. "There are no cameras down here, Richard. But there *are* hidden cameras all around the Russia Desk. I had them installed over the bank holiday weekend in August. I wasn't happy with how close the Russians seemed able to get to us." He paused. "This file is three inches thick, and mostly comprising of reports of your indiscretions."

"I want my lawyer."

Ramsay smiled. "Have a look under the table, Richard." Beckinsdale leaned to the side and peeked under the table. The only thing he could see was a grate over a small drain, and a couple of narrow gullies feeding to it. "This used to be a public toilet block. The drains flow right down into the Thames. When this place was requisitioned, they made these rooms into interrogation blocks. IRA terrorists have bled out in this room, their blood sluiced down that drain, and their bodies bricked up into the myriad of unused tunnels. We're way past solicitors and the Crown Prosecution Service."

"You're threatening me?"

"Not personally. But that six-foot-four, eighteen stone man-mountain out there was looking particularly bored when we arrived. He's a loyal chap, too. Hates traitors and the unpatriotic. He used to be a mercenary but took a pay cut and far worse career prospects to fulfil his patriotic duty." Ramsay turned the file over and pulled out some loose sheets and slid them across the table.

Thorpe slid a pen across for him and said, "Start with who you've given information to, then who contacted you requesting information." She tapped the file on the table. "If it tallies with what we have, then you're in credit. If you leave out information we have, then you're in debt again."

Beckinsdale swallowed hard and loosened his tie. He started to scribble on the page and Ramsay stood up, picked up the file and nodded for Thorpe to join him. He looked down at Richard Beckinsdale and said, "Make no mistake, Richard. Your world will change from now on. You will work with us to feed your Russian contacts information we deem important for them to know. This will be *disinformation*. When we decide you have served your purpose, you will be quietly retired. Your pension stops from the moment you betrayed your country. And before you think about fudging the dates..." He patted the file in his hand. "We have been extremely thorough indeed."

Thorpe opened the door and looked back at him. "And try not to kill yourself with the pen while we're gone."

The guard closed the door and Ramsay looked at Stuart Baker who was drinking a cup of tea. "Thank you, Stuart."

"You got what you needed?"

"I think we will."

"I was worried I over-acted. Especially with the fist banging."

"No, it was convincing," Ramsay replied. "The fact he logged onto the PNC while you were in that Whitehall meeting was all we needed to pin the leak on him. And for him to either admit to it or at the very least, stop denying it."

"And what looks like War and Peace in your folder."

Ramsay nodded. "We've collated enough for a convincing case against him, but he will be more use to us feeding disinformation than he would in any courtroom." He paused and shook Baker's hand. "Thank you, Stuart. One of these chaps will see you out," he said, nodding towards the uniformed security guards. He watched Baker leave with the guard and when they had turned the corner onto the platform he looked back at Thorpe. "Well, this is what we do. Are you in?"

Thorpe smiled. "When did you collate all the evidence," she asked, looking at the file in his hand.

Ramsay flipped the file over and peeled off the first three sheets of type-written report. He flicked through the entire ream of blank pages. Five hundred in all. "Much of what we do is an illusion."

"The rest is downright blagging it," Big Dave chipped in.

"How long did you know about Beckinsdale?" Thorpe asked. "You had the cameras installed in August."

Ramsay shook his head. "No, there are no cameras. That's a potential security breach. If a computer screen is filmed and that footage gets into the wrong hands, then that is just as bad as somebody gaining access to that computer. Possibly more so. No, I had my suspicions but needed a catalyst. I did not mention Russian criminals, and in no report does it say so. The men killed at King and Caroline's property were always defined as terrorists. Simon Mereweather played that card to get some traction into silencing the local police. Only Richard Beckinsdale knew that they were criminal elements, namely, the Russian mafia."

"Like I said..." Big Dave grinned. "Downright blagging it."

"But we get the job done," Ramsay added. "Are you up for a challenge?"

Thorpe nodded. "Yeah," she said. "Too bloody right, I am."

65

Oxfordshire

King looked at the bag on the seat beside him. He had earlier pulled the car over and taken out the money, checked it over and then searched the empty carry-on for trackers, microphones or anything else that might cause him problems. He checked the pull-out handle and wheels, too. Satisfied it had remained unadulterated, he repacked the money with the neat bundles, each an inch thick and in denominations of five thousand pounds.

He could see the logic. One-hundred-thousand pounds was small change to many, but it was easily fundable by the hostage's family and did not take up much room. It was a sensible amount to ask for, and for terrorists it could keep them in operation for months.

King fastened the bag and checked on the Walther PPK in the lightweight plastic and Velcro ankle holster. He didn't enjoy the awkward feel of it, but he did enjoy the comfort a small automatic and eight rounds of ammunition brought. He had decided not to carry another weapon or spare ammunition, as he would undoubtedly be searched, but people often concentrated on patting down under the armpits or around the midriff and neglected to search further.

He pulled the Jaguar saloon out into the road and drove the mile or so to the layby, swept in and switched off the engine. He was to wait while he texted. He sent the text saying he was waiting, then looked around, but the road had high hedges and what little he could see through them was nothing but fields of head-high cob corn for animal feeds. If they had eyes on him, then it would be by drone or from a distant vantage point with binoculars. King tried to subtly look but could not see anything suspicious. No movement in the sky above, no glare from a binocular's lens in the sunlight. He looked down as his phone sounded the text alert. He read carefully and did as he was instructed, tossing his phone out of the window. Then he started his own plan and took out the burner phone, dialled the number from memory and when it connected, he left the line open and slipped the phone back into his pocket.

King drove onwards and after another mile he pulled into the entrance of a lane, drove on for fifty metres, then stopped and switched off the engine as he had been instructed. He waited ten whole minutes, counting them down on his watch, then restarted the car and continued down the lane. Presumably, they were watching him, or watching to see if he'd been tailed. King could see the farm nestled between two hillocks. The nearest had a stone ruin on top and the furthest one was four-hundred metres away and largely wooded with sparse trees that had shed most of their dry, autumnal leaves.

King was suddenly aware of movement behind him, and could see a small, sporty SUV in his rear-view mirror. He continued to drive steadily, and when he pulled into the yard, he noticed that another SUV was parked in front of the house. It looked to be a working farm, and the vehicle was a *lifestyle* SUV, rather than a practical model. There wasn't a trace of mud on it, either. King suspected that both these vehicles belonged to the kidnappers, and at once he worried about the amount of ransom that they had demanded. One-hundred thousand pounds changes a single person's life, but not a team. And any budding terrorist group who could have two new SUVs at their disposal were not going to find their money going far enough.

King watched as a man walked out with the girl. He held a sawn-off shotgun to the back of her neck. The girl was as white as a sheet, traumatised. Behind King, two men got out of the Mercedes and took up position. King reasoned whether he could take them with the tiny Walther but conceded he didn't have a chance. He would never bend and retrieve the pistol from the ankle holster fast enough. Bethany would be killed for certain, but his own odds wouldn't be great, either. He could see various weapons including an AK47 in the hands of another man who stepped out of the farmhouse and walked down the first three steps. No contest. And King did not yet know how many more men could be inside.

The man holding the AK47 nodded for King to get out. King obliged and stepped out onto the gravel, straightening up slowly. Another man stepped out of the farmhouse and spoke with the man with the AK47, whom King now assumed to be the leader. They seemed to work through a couple of things, and the new guy jogged down the steps and across the farmyard. King watched the man as he disappeared through a gate and into a field.

"I have your money," said King. "Let Bethany go." He had personalised her, used her name. It always paid to remind people that hostages were living, breathing souls and not just a commodity. "Bethany, come over here and get into the rear seat of the car. Your mummy and daddy are so excited to see you." Paint a picture of a family unit, draw from the kidnapper's happier memories. These were all psychological techniques King had picked up along the way. He kept hold of the bag but raised it for the leader to see.

The leader spoke quickly in Italian and the man with the shotgun rammed against Bethany's neck pulled her to one side and did not allow her to go. King knew the men looked European, but now he had heard the Italian, he couldn't help wondering what terrorist group the men represented, and what worried him more was if they were criminals, not terrorists as he had been led to believe. And besides, one-hundred thousand was not going to cut it for this bunch, so what else did they want?

"My brother was Luca Fortez..." And there it was. King knew the name, knew the man, and knew how he had died. So, the kidnapping was a ruse to get to him. "Sound familiar?"

King shook his head. "I only remember the important ones, the ones who put up a good fight." King studied the man's expression, but he didn't get anything back. He had hoped to rattle him. Now his overriding thoughts were how Amherst had been duped into sending King, but he kept coming back with the same answer. The man hadn't been duped, he'd been compliant. Amherst had wanted his daughter back, and these men had wanted King. So, was Amherst banking on King taking them on? He had expressed no heroics, pre-empting King's behaviour from his track record, but if it was a simple life for a life, what the hell was the exit strategy for Bethany? King could see the desperation and the flaw. If they killed King, they would take the money *and* the girl, and they'd have a cash cow with which they could financially milk a man dry. A man who had already crossed the line and would pay any price. "I'm guessing you're pissed off that he's dead," said King.

The man nodded to the two men behind King and they walked over. One handed his pistol to the other, then preceded to search King by patting him down like a beat cop would a suspect. He found the phone and tossed it over to Gennaro Fortez. King had read Luca's file and knew who the man was. He'd just needed prompting. The Italian looked at the phone and frowned. The phone was locked, but it was an open channel transmitting everything said thus far. King noticed that the man searching him had stopped at the discovery. He tensed as the man drew near, but it was only to take up position in front of him after he had retrieved his pistol from his colleague.

"You were told, no phones."

King shrugged. "I was concerned that after you let Bethany go, she may be left high and dry. The phone was for her to call for help with. After all, she needs a ride out of here." He turned as engines started up and the unmistakable sound of airplane propellers started spinning. "Is that your ride home?"

"For us, yes. But not for you." Gennaro dropped down the steps, agile and confidently. "Of course, Bethany *will* come with us. If your boss can come up with a hundred grand so quickly, then he can come up with ten times that given a month or two to re-mortgage and free up assets. Business is business."

"So, you want me," said King. "You'd terrorise a young girl for that?"

"I would do *so* much more for that." He paused, stepping nearer. He waved a hand around the yard. "The owners of this place were collateral damage. A means to an end."

"You killed them?"

"Yes. A couple of my men amused themselves with the daughter, but she was a screamer and…" He looked down at the rifle in his hands. "Well, even out here we couldn't risk someone hearing."

King looked at Bethany. The man holding the shotgun to her neck had lost concentration as he watched. The double barrels were not quite on her, but then they drifted back, as did King's attention on Fortez. "Leave the girl," he said. "Please."

"What do you care?"

"She's young. She has her whole life ahead of her. You really are playing with fire, because there are plenty of ways the director of the Security Service can get to a man. Leave Bethany here. Take the money. Do what you want with me, but don't harm the girl. With what you've agreed with Amherst, that will be an end to it."

"Like I said, what do you care? Your boss was all too willing to hand you over. He avoided going through the proper channels, kept this deal of ours quiet from the police, gave me his assurance that you would come alone. What is he to you?"

King shrugged. "He's nothing. But the girl has done nothing, either. She doesn't even know what her father does for a living. Be the bigger man."

"Like you, perhaps? *You* killed my brother..."

King looked again at the man holding the shotgun to Bethany's neck. Again, he had moved the barrels away. King calculated how long it would take for a soft-nosed Swedish match grade 5.56mm bullet to travel four hundred metres. Approximately nine-hundred and ninety metres a second. So, half a second, tops. Half a second more for the reaction time. He watched the shotgun barrels sway again, then touched his ear. A second later and the man's head disappeared in a puff of pink mist and his body started to drag Bethany down with it as it fell. The sound of the shot echoed across the flat ground a second later, but King had already swung a punch at the man to his right and knew that would clear the target for Rashid. Sure enough, the expert sniper hit the second man between his shoulder blades. No time to go for a headshot after the first. King punched again, and the man went down, but caught King around his waist and tried to tip him over. King lowered his centre of gravity to counter the man's efforts, then kneed him in his face. The man fell backwards and sprawled against the Jaguar. King turned to see Gennaro coming to his senses. He looked down at King but had the presence of mind to keep moving. A sniper had killed two of his men and that threat was still out there. Gennaro fired most of the AK47's magazine towards the distant trees, then turned and raced up the steps towards the house. He darted to his left and dragged Bethany off the slate step and bundled her over his shoulder as he ran towards the direction of the idling aircraft. King felt the man grab at him again, and he struggled to free his hands from his waist, the man bear hugging him as he pulled himself back up to his feet. He managed to get the Walther out of its holster and turned it on his opponent, but the man was strong and fought hard, gripping King's wrist and trying to pull his own weapon on target. King kicked and kneed him again, then drove a solid headbutt down onto the bridge of the man's nose. The man released his grip as he recoiled, and King tucked the muzzle of the pistol under the man's chin and fired. He stepped away as the body crumpled to the floor. Another closed casket at the Fortez family funeral.

King could see Gennaro Fortez disappear behind the hedge as he raced through the gateway. He looked towards the hillock to see the Agusta helicopter lowering to the ground. A figure broke from the trees to meet it. Rashid had tracked King's burner phone using a basic track-my-phone app and taken position in the treeline. Flymo had put down a mile away, kept the rotors turning and was in a call with Rashid, being kept in the loop. The moment Rashid squeezed the trigger, Flymo had taken off and by the time Rashid had fired the second shot, he was a thousand metres out and heading in fast.

King sprinted after Fortez, but he could already hear the change in engine pitch, and when he rounded the gateway, he could see the twin-engine Beechcraft bouncing over divots on a long, straight grass and earthen track worn into the edge of the field. It was the ideal runway, the far hedge of the field some thousand metres distant. Having got Bethany into the cabin, Gennaro was busy closing the door as the pilot headed for take-off. King was still sprinting when he realised there was no hope, but he heard the thunder of the helicopter behind him, and felt the storm of wind and debris as Flymo put the aircraft down, its tail rotor missing the ground by mere inches, the nose high in the air. He ducked his head and ran towards it. The nose came down hard and it bounced heavily on its three retractable wheels. Rashid had the rear door open and King hurled himself inside.

"Go! Go! Go!" he shouted, and Rashid handed him a headset as he got off the floor and onto a seat. "Get above it and stop it from taking off!"

"On it…" Flymo said.

The helicopter was driving forward as they climbed, and the ground raced underneath them, falling away as they gained height. Ahead of them, the Beechcraft started to lift. It would have the speed and ceiling advantage over them, but only if it could climb to a manoeuvrable height and reach enough revs.

Flymo climbed, moved to starboard and

banked. He immediately banked back to port, and when he straightened the helicopter was ahead of the airplane and twenty-feet higher. He looked behind him, then shouted, "Jesus! He's not backing off!" He kept on his course, but the Beechcraft was just mere feet from the tail of the helicopter and still climbing. Clearing the ground by just thirty feet, the pilot banked to port and broke away. Flymo mirrored the manoeuvre and when the airplane straightened and levelled, he was above and ahead once more. The pilot banked to starboard and climbed. Flymo changed their course. He knew he was out of options and asked, "What the hell do we do now?"

"Get above him and match his speed!" King shouted. He looked at Rashid and said, "Jettison the door…"

"Oh, hell no…" Rashid shook his head, but he pulled the safety bolt out and pulled down the lever and the door flew out into the air. "What are you planning?"

"Get right over him!" King shouted again. He looked at Rashid and said, "You've done a lot of jumps. Will I glide forward or fly backwards?"

"Wait, what?" He shook his head. "Er, forward momentum, at what? One-hundred and twenty miles per hour air speed? It's suicide, we're a hundred feet off the ground!"

"And gaining!" shouted Flymo.

"You'll match it." Rashid shook his head. "But only for a couple of seconds. Get closer, Leroy."

"You want *Flymo* today, mate," he replied.

Flymo took the helicopter to within ten feet of the plane and matched the airspeed. The pilot was easing upwards, but he was aware that any sudden movements like a dip and rise of wing would take them all down. It was a case of stubbornly eking out as much as he dare.

King eased out onto the edge of the cabin entrance, buffeted by the wind and rotor wash. He checked the Walther in his pocket and took off the headset, a hurricane of noise and wind in his ears.

"King, this is crazy," Rashid shouted. "But if you're going to do this, it's vitally important that you... Oh shit, he's gone!"

King hadn't waited for him to finish the sentence and had launched himself out and into the air. For a second or more, he matched the speed of both craft, arms and legs outstretched and gliding forwards like a flying squirrel at over a hundred miles per hour, but he was slowing rapidly and when he landed, it wasn't on the roof of the airplane, but along its tail. He gripped on like he was riding on a mechanical bull, ungraceful and desperate but not surrendering to overwhelming forces.

"Shit!" Rashid screamed. "Flymo, get closer and match the speed. If the pilot has room to move the plane, then King is dead!"

King managed to grip onto the communications antennae on the top of the fuselage, gripping with his legs and ankles. All the time, the helicopter was lowering and pressing the airplane into all it could safely do - fly straight and level. Even to fly lower would cut off the pilot's ability to manoeuvre because of the undulating terrain and trees.

King worked his way towards the wing, then dug his fingers into the starboard aileron, which gave him a handle. He pulled, but not only did it give him traction to move up the fuselage, it changed both the plane's attitude and altitude and it started to bank and dip in height. The pilot fought against it, and the aileron came back up, straightening the craft. But it had provided King with stability, and he took out the Walther and jammed it up against one of the windows and Gennaro Fortez, watching transfixed at King's efforts suddenly struggled to bring the Kalashnikov round on target in the confines of the rear cabin. King best guessed and fired, and the bullet tore through the Perspex window and out the other side. Gennaro, only two feet from King, almost had the rifle in position, but King fired twice more and Gennaro rocked in his seat. He dropped the AK47 and a single gunshot rang out and the pilot slumped in his seat. Bethany was screaming, but King could barely hear against the wind. The plane started to drift lazily to port and lose height. King put the Walther to another window and fired until the gun clicked in his hand. He smashed the butt against the window until the Perspex shattered and let go of the weapon, taking a grateful hold of the window frame.

"Bethany!" He shouted through the broken window. "We have seconds to do this!" He struggled for breath against the rushing air. "On the door is an emergency jettison lever. Pull it and the door will come off completely!" He looked at her earnestly. "Unbuckle your belt and do this now!" He watched as the child did as she was asked, but she was crying and did not want to get any closer to Fortez, who was still dying and bleeding from his neck and face. "Do it Bethany... You have to do it..."

Bethany Amherst steeled herself and crawled over the dying man, reached over the righthand seat, and studied the emergency door release. She removed the bolt but struggled to pull down the lever. She took several attempts, then finally managed it, but looked back at King, confused why it would remain in place.

"You have to push it! The wind is holding it in place!" King roared at her through the window.

Bethany pushed, but nothing happened. The ground was getting closer, the trees below just fifty feet from the undercarriage of the plane. She pushed harder, and it gave a little. Again, and a crack formed, and wind whistled into the cabin. And then she thrust both hands upon it and it blew out and spun off wildly at over a hundred miles per hour, narrowly missing King and the tail rotor of the helicopter flying just ten feet above them.

"Give me your hand!" he shouted.

"Aren't you flying it?" she asked, her face ashen and the wind blowing her hair wildly.

"I can't fly, and there's not enough time to learn..." King grabbed her by the wrist and heaved her out onto the wing, where she screamed, but still had the presence of mind – or instinct – to lay flat and hold onto the edge of the open doorway. They were both pressed closer to the wing by the downdraft of the helicopter, now flying offset to them and lowering by the second. The retractable wheels were up and tucked into the undercarriage, and Flymo put the entire belly of the craft an inch from the wing. The helicopter drifted to port, towards them.

Rashid reached out and shouted against the wind and engine and rotor noise, and King gripped the aileron tightly with his right hand, while tugging at Bethany with his left. She got the idea and crawled, pulled, and squirmed her way over King's back, to where Rashid could catch hold of her and pull her into the rear of the helicopter.

The undercarriage of the Beechcraft brushed against the treetops and the tail rotor of the Agusta tore through them like a garden strimmer. Rashid reached for King, but he shook his head. "No time, get out of here!"

Rashid looked at him, saw the seriousness in his eyes. He pulled back into the helicopter wrapped the loose seatbelt harness around his wrist, extended it fully, then lurched out and caught hold of King's belt and screamed at Flymo in his headset and mic. "Climb!"

The helicopter lifted as the airplane struck the trees and Flymo banked to starboard. King was prised away from the wing and Rashid screamed in pain as he took King's full fourteen stone in one hand, his other tethered to the helicopter. Flymo was already heading to a clearing and lowering the helicopter by the second, as Rashid strained and cried out in agony. Eight feet from the ground, he released his grip and King fell unceremoniously in a heap on the grass. Rashid pulled back inside the cabin, heaving for breath as he fought the pain, his right shoulder dislocated and useless. To their left, the plane had already crashed into the trees and was burning fiercely.

Flymo put the helicopter down twenty feet from King, who got up slowly and limped back to them. Rashid was cradling his arm and panting for breath. Huddled on the floor against the padded leather seat, Bethany Amherst was sobbing quietly.

"How heavy are you?" Rashid managed as King got inside and put on the headset. "Still eating steak for breakfast?"

"Only on Saturdays," King replied. "And you could do with bulking up a bit."

"You're welcome, by the way."

King nodded and patted him on the shoulder. Rashid screamed and King smiled. "I'll put that back in for you, if you like?"

Rashid shook his head. "No, I don't like. I want a professional to do it. Preferably a thirty-year-old nurse who's nice looking and open to the prospect of having a drink after their shift."

"They have a lot of male nurses these days."

"The second word's, *off...*"

King laughed as the helicopter lifted and Flymo banked it gently towards the farm. "I mean it, you'll go to hospital, wait for ages, meet a nice female nurse who'll sort out your shoulder with gas and air and a lot of manipulation. But she'll end up being a lesbian, or have a good looking boyfriend, or probably just have good taste in general for that matter and you'll get absolutely nowhere and wish you'd gritted your teeth for two seconds and had me take care of it."

"Thanks, but I'll take my chances with the lesbian with good taste."

King shrugged and sat down beside Bethany. He helped her into the seat and buckled her into the harness. "You did great," he said. "That took a lot of courage. You'll see your parents soon."

She reached out and hugged him. "Thank you," she said. "Thank you so much." She looked at him, her eyes glossy with tears. She hesitated for a moment, seeming uncertain before relenting. "Is what the man said about my daddy true?" she asked quietly.

King thought about Amherst, their meeting beside the river. The hollowed-out shell of a man, who had changed so much in just twenty-four hours. The desperation in his actions. Parenthood did not recognise boundaries. He had never experienced it from either end. He did not know what it was to hold his own child. But his own childhood had not shown him love, nor what the bonds of parenthood meant. He could only imagine and knowing that he and Caroline had been robbed of the experience gave him some empathy towards the man's plight, where until recently he would have looked on in judgement. He smiled at Bethany and said, "Of course it isn't true. You father is a good man." He paused. "And he can't wait to see you."

66

Thames House, London

Amherst's secretary brought in the tray and discreetly placed it on the low table in front of King. She poured the director general's coffee and added cream and sugar and placed the cup and saucer on the mahogany desk, leaving him to stir it himself. Amherst did not look up, still reading the report. She handed King the mug of tea, having already added the splash of milk and spoon of sugar. She smiled at King as she handed him the mug, and he smiled back. No frills, just a plain, white mug that would have been used by the staffers. King liked it that way. He got more tea, and the thick ceramic work mug kept the tea hotter for longer. Not that he would be here long.

"I can't thank you enough, you know?" Amherst put down the report and looked at him. "Bethany got quite a scare, understandably, but she's otherwise okay."

King nodded, took a sip from his cup. Stared back at him. "Your position is untenable," he said.

"What?"

"You heard me."

"How dare you."

"How dare you!" King roared, stopping the man in his tracks. "That wasn't an exchange, it was a meant to be an assassination!"

"I beg your pardon?"

"You just might. But not while you fill that chair."

"Now, King..."

"You did a deal with the Italians. That's why we met on the bank of the river and you made me promise that there would be no heroics. You sold me out. That was their price and you agreed to it." He paused, glaring at him. "Cole was paid to fulfil the Italians' contract on me. The head of the Fortez family, for whatever reason, maybe to hedge his bets, sent his own men to find me. That much was confirmed by Interpol. I was led to believe that terrorists unknown had taken your daughter. If I'd known there was an Italian connection, I would have known what I was walking into."

"But you had the ransom, it was just about money." Amherst stammered and reached for the phone on his desk.

"Really?" King opened his jacket and revealed the butt of the .45 pistol sticking out of the inside pocket. "It would pay you to hear me out…" Amherst brought his hand back from the phone, did his best to look relaxed, but failed. "They didn't care about the money. And their leader told me as much," said King. "In fact, the son-of-a-bitch told me everything. I just wanted to get the measure of you before I told you that."

"Please, King, I was desperate." Amherst looked at him pleadingly. "You don't have children, you wouldn't know…"

King thought about Caroline lying unconscious and broken, and how she had lost their baby at the hands of Cole. He clenched his fist, it was all he could do to remain seated and not pull the man across the desk and pummel him in his face. He took a breath, his glacier-blue eyes boring into him and for a second it was as if Amherst had seen into King's eyes and glimpsed the horrors he had witnessed over the years. The man visibly recoiled before trying to regain composure.

"You were a bloody fool. Fortez was taking Bethany to wring out your money. How the hell did you think you could trust a mafia boss?"

"I wasn't thinking straight. He named his price…" Amherst paused. "I'm sorry King, but I'd do anything to save my little girl."

"Well, you should have bet on me," King replied. "That's why it was just a hundred grand, it was never about the money to them, but they saw an opportunity in taking Bethany with them." King paused and stood up, Amherst pressed himself back in his chair like an extra inch of distance would make any difference. "People don't live after crossing me. But Bethany is a gutsy kid, and she doesn't deserve to lose her father. Not after what she went through. So, it would be understandable for you to want to reconsider your position, spend more time with your family. I expect to hear that you met with the Prime Minister and handed in your resignation. Naturally, Simon will take the helm for the foreseeable future, until it is made official, or someone else suitable is appointed."

"You can't be serious!"

King stared at him coldly. "All I know is that I've given you an out. I'll kill any man you send after me. And then I'll be back for you and all you hold dear." He walked to the door and paused with his hand on the door handle. "Believe me, in this life, there are worse things than dying. Whether you discover this will depend on what you do next."

Amherst watched him leave and sat for a moment in the silence of his office. He could hear his own heartbeat, feel it pulsing against his chest. He closed his eyes for a moment and pictured Bethany and his wife, the joy at being reunited and how complete he had felt and relieved that his gamble had paid off, despite how the scenario had played out. Amherst reached for the telephone, pressed the intercom, and said, "Marcia, please come in, I want you to dictate a letter."

67

Virginia, USA

The trees were still heavy with leaves, unlike the views he had seen back in England, where autumn was usually a short affair helped along by high winds and rain that stripped the trees of leaves quickly. Here, the colours were fading, the reds having turned to yellow and gold and now dry and curling, the leaves fell gently like the start of a flurry of snow.

It was cold, and Newman tucked the collar up on his jacket before sipping the coffee and staring silently at the view. The trout weren't jumping anymore. The sudden cold had either killed off or sent the mosquitoes and midges away and the lake was mirror calm and reflected the late afternoon sun like molten gold. After a few minutes, the sun dipped from view and the sky turned from orange to blue to black, with a million shades along the spectrum in between.

Lefkowitz sipped his coffee and said, "I like a man who can keep his mouth shut when there's a stunning sunset. Not everybody can. I took my first wife to the Grand Canyon and she yacked and chattered the whole time. One of the most awe-inspiring views you'll ever see. A place where you think about who we are, where we're from and the journey mankind has taken to get where we are. How much time has passed to erode something so spectacularly vast, bigger than some countries, even. Some people simply can't handle the silence, the apparent awkwardness between two people." He paused. "But you can handle such things. You, my friend, can handle anything placed in your way. You are a genuinely capable man. An asset to the agency. "

Newman nodded, sipped some more coffee, but it was already turning tepid in the evening chill. "Thank you, sir. I hope the mission has the desired effect."

"It will," replied Lefkowitz. "I intend to leave my tenure with the CIA in a better state than I found it, and with this current state of play, we can look forward to the British being our allies within the intelligence community once more. All that tit-for-tat garbage is done." He paused, and Newman thought he seemed a little breathless. He certainly looked less healthy than he had a week ago. "The USA and Britain are the greatest allies of all time. Controversial leaders, the rise of social media where everybody's damn opinion is out there without necessarily being factually correct, a media with its own political agenda and bias, and a general world-wide feeling of dissatisfaction in peoples' lives has created a gulf of resentment between us. This must change. Terrorism isn't going away. Russia and China are a constant economic and potential military threat, and North Korea is a wild card, so we need a strong ally. Britain can't find this in Europe post Brexit, so we must be there. What you have done has helped us a long way towards this."

Newman nodded. "Another unfortunate sacrifice, though."

Lefkowitz regarded him closely. "Cole was a lost cause. PTSD and manic depression in its worse manifestation. Sad, but true. The man went too far and needed putting down." He paused. "And Rachel Beam, well she was a loose end. Her career was over, and she was drinking herself into an early grave. She wasn't the sort of person you want knowing the things she did. She was a loose cannon."

"Two birds, one stone," Newman ruminated.

"That is always the best outcome in this game." Lefkowitz paused. "Minimum effort for maximum result. Forget about Rachel Beam. She's a footnote in history, and she has notoriety in her epitaph, heroism in the conversations that people have about her for ever more. Her parents will be proud of her. Rachel Beam had a full church and a Secret Service ceremonial rifle salute, and her parents have a neatly folded flag and a medal to place on their mantel, where they could quite possibly have had her drunken suicide and barely a handful of mourners at her funeral, who would only have been there because they felt a sense of duty and nothing more."

Newman nodded, but he knew he would see the shock and surprise on Rachel Beam's face forever more. The lake was almost black now, with a sliver of red on the surface as the sunset kissed the horizon. He watched in silence, but it had nothing to do with the view or Lefkowitz, and everything to do with the cold realisation in a woman's eyes that she had been used and set up to die. At that moment, he knew he had stared into the abyss and there was no going back.

68

RAF St. Mawgan, Cornwall

Sinclair looked at King, the bruises, and cuts to his face, and said, "Are you okay?"

King shrugged. "Tough week."

"You can say that again. This has all been highly irregular." The consultant paused. "Look, I don't know what you people do, perhaps it's better I don't know, but it certainly caught up with Caroline. She's lucky to be alive."

"We still don't know if she is," said King. "Technically, at least."

Sinclair nodded. "I've treated a lot of people in my time, seen a lot of terrible injuries. But there are some people who give you a little more hope than others. Caroline fits into that category. She's strong and fit physically, but I imagine she's mentally tough, too."

"You got that right."

"Okay," he said. "So, let's do this. The team are ready."

"Can I be there?"

Sinclair sighed. "You stand aside, and you keep quiet and out of the way until we know it's okay."

"I can do that." King looked through the window at Caroline. A nurse sat beside her and a woman in scrubs was reading her medical record from the clipboard normally kept at the bottom of the bed. "What if it doesn't work, if she can't breathe for herself?"

"Stay positive. The anaesthetist is in there with her now and we have a full crash team waiting. If it doesn't go as planned, we induce her into a coma again, and take it from there. But like I said, stay positive." Sinclair nodded decisively. "Right, let's get you into some scrubs and cleaned up. I don't want to take any chances."

King followed Sinclair into a room with windows looking out into an operating theatre. There were a dozen medical staff in scrubs wearing gloves, masks and blue plastic hair covers. King watched Caroline being wheeled in, the monitors, air, and intubation all on a separate trolley. The medical team started altering and adjusting the wires, tubes, and drips.

"She's in safe hands," said Sinclair, appearing to read his thoughts. "These doctors and nurses have done several tours in combat zones and disaster areas. As a crash team, they've seen some terrible things and had incredible success rates. Caroline was severely injured in that RTC, but she has been stable, and the brain function test went well."

King tore the PPE off and headed for the door. "Come and get me when she's conscious," he shouted over his shoulder and pushed his way out through the doors. He ran down the corridor and barged out of the door into the small, unmanned reception area, then headed out of the double doors outside. Two soldiers from the RAF regiment looked at each other, then stood to with their L85 A2 rifles in readiness. They looked confused. They had obviously had orders to guard the building from entry but hadn't expected a civilian to exit. King shook a hand in front of him, as if waving away any intent, and turned around to lean over the railing as he collected himself and tried to steady his breathing. He hadn't felt like this in over five years. Again, he pictured Jane, the clinical way in which she had taken her own life, sparing them both from the horrors and suffering of her cancer and the morbid prognosis, the spectre of death she lived under. He couldn't lose Caroline. He had gone to the ends of the earth and done unspeakable things to rescue her, and that couldn't have been in vain. They deserved more time together.

King hung onto the rail, leaning over as if he was about to be sick, but he just needed the support of the railing and the fresh air calmed him down. He had visited the worst places on earth, seen things nobody should and fought wars nobody had heard of. He had been outnumbered more times than he could remember, and he had prevailed. Always prevailed in the face of adversity. He closed his eyes and thought about his journey from petty criminal growing up in a council tower block and trying to feed his siblings from nothing while his mother got high and laid and paid for things he preferred not to think about, to the care homes, the bare knuckle fights, ripping off gangland bosses and being on the run, to prison, to a night he would never forget that had shaped his life and left two men dead and a life sentence hanging over his head. And then the lifeline, the training, the missions, and his mentor who had made it happen. Turned him from a thug into the man called upon when diplomacy fails. King had turned the tide on disaster, war, political unrest and allowed people to sleep safely in their beds at night. He had loved and lost, and now he wasn't sure whether it would happen again. Whether history would repeat itself and leave him a broken shell once more.

"Stop feeling sorry for yourself and grow a fucking pair..." The broad Scottish accent rasped.

King turned and looked at the two soldiers of the RAF Regiment. "What?" The soldiers looked at him, one frowned and the other hadn't seemed to have heard. "What did you say to me?"

"Nothing, mate," the young soldier replied in a distinct London accent. King reckoned on south – Lambeth or Peckham.

"Yeah, what's the problem?" the other soldier asked. Geordie accent, confidence bolstered by the rifle in his hands.

King knew the voice he had heard. He didn't believe in the paranormal, but it had been as clear as a summer's day. His Mentor Peter Stewart. The man who had recruited him, trained him, deceived, and betrayed him, and later made amends on a mission in the Arctic when he had sacrificed himself so that King could make the shot. King shook his head, perhaps he was simply so worn physically and mentally, so stressed and anxious, that he was imagining a dialogue in his subconscious. He pressed himself off the railing and pulled the door wide open. Whatever it was, the voice had been right. He wasn't beaten yet. Caroline wasn't beaten yet. King strode through the corridor and into the scrub room, where he could see Caroline blinking and in a fugue state between sleep and awake, where she looked like she was constantly nodding off and waking with a start. Sinclair looked up and saw King, raised his thumb, and nodded. King almost lost his footing, his legs feeling like they would give way as the relief surged through in waves. He struggled to put on the PPE, and then scrubbed his hands with the wash and hot water, then dried them and sanitised them as he followed the bed towards the ward.

Caroline was in and out and asking for water. A nurse promised her some as soon as they got her into the ward. King reached for her hand but was reminded of her injuries by the dressings and gently touched her knuckles with his fingertips as they wheeled her in place and set up the screen monitor. She looked up at him, her eyes locking with his own. She seemed relieved that he was there, managed a smile. The bed was wheeled into position and the wheels locked, but the sides remained in place. The air and drips had gone, but she was still hooked up with four function displays pulsing across the screen.

Sinclair rubbed King on his shoulder and said, "She'll take a while to come around, an hour before she's remotely *compos mentis*, at least. But she's breathing well unaided, and her brain function is excellent." He paused. "She's been under a while, so the effects of the anaesthetics will be with her for a week or two… tired and lethargic… but it does vary for different people. Plenty of bed rest and then we will have to look at physio, but that's a long way off with her injuries."

King nodded, struggling to take it all in. He'd had his share of anaesthetic and operations, knew what it could feel like. "What is the extent of her injuries?"

"We'll give her a scan and a series of x-rays and take it from there. We caught what we could in the early stages, pinned and bolted her bones together, but with the patient… sorry, Caroline… conscious, then we can certainly learn more and soon have an accurate prognosis and realistic rehabilitation mapped out for her."

King looked at her. She seemed peaceful. A nurse had fetched some water, but Caroline had drifted into sleep. She put the cup down and another nurse had taken up position on a seat in front of the monitor on Caroline's right side. She motioned for King to take the chair on the other side of the bed. King walked around the bed and kissed her gently on the forehead before sitting down. Caroline opened her eyes and briefly mumbled something incoherent, then drifted back to sleep once more. She woke after a minute or so and asked for a drink. The nurse allowed her a few sips and replaced the cup to the table, before carrying out her vigil and marking something down in her notes.

King touched her hand and she looked up at him, confused for a moment, then smiling and again drifting off to sleep. He looked at her and wondered when and how he would tell her she had lost their baby. She hadn't told him, but he knew her better than anybody, and she would have wanted to have accepted it, planned it all out in her head before telling him. She was a control freak, and she would have wanted to be in control and have all the answers ready for King's various questions.

"She'll do this for a while," the nurse said amiably. "She's had quite an ordeal. Coming back around is different for everybody."

King looked up, snapped out of his thoughts. He nodded, but he couldn't think of anything to say and for the first time in days he felt relieved, and it washed over him like a warm wave of emotion, and he struggled to fight off falling to sleep in the chair. He pulled his chair closer and rested his head against Caroline's thigh and stroked the back of her hand, as he drifted off to sleep beside her. For a briefest of moments, feeling safe and warm and complete once more, despite the pain and anguish and uncertainty which lay ahead. But for now, he was lost in the moment, enjoying the safety around them, knowing that once again, he had beaten the odds.

The storm had come for him in the guise of warriors. But he was the storm and had met them head on and beaten the odds. Once again, he was the last man standing.

Author's Note

Hi – thanks for reading and I'm so glad you made it this far. I couldn't do this without you, so I hope you enjoyed my story and look for my other books.

If you have the time to leave a short review on Amazon, I'd be extremely grateful. You can also sign up to my newsletter, find out a little bit about me and get those all-important links to my other books here:

www.apbateman.com

Thanks for reading, and I hope to entertain you again soon!

A P Bateman

The Alex King Series
The Contract Man
Lies and Retribution
Shadows of Good Friday
The Five
Reaper
Stormbound
Breakout
From the Shadows
Rogue
The Asset

The Rob Stone Series
The Ares Virus
The Town
The Island

Standalone Novels
Hell's Mouth
Unforgotten

Short Stories
A Single Nail
The Perfect Murder?
Atonement

Printed in Great Britain
by Amazon

20429667R00253